Blue Ruin

Blue Ruin

Hari Kunzru

 Alfred A. Knopf · New York · 2024

THIS IS A BORZOI BOOK
PUBLISHED BY ALFRED A. KNOPF

Copyright © 2024 by Hari Kunzru

All rights reserved. Published in the United States by Alfred A. Knopf,
a division of Penguin Random House LLC, New York, and distributed in Canada
by Penguin Random House Canada Limited, Toronto.

www.aaknopf.com

Knopf, Borzoi Books, and the colophon
are registered trademarks of Penguin Random House LLC.

Library of Congress Cataloging-in-Publication Data
Names: Kunzru, Hari, [date] author.
Title: Blue ruin / Hari Kunzru.
Description: First edition. | New York : Alfred A. Knopf, 2024.
Identifiers: LCCN 2023024641 | ISBN 9780593801376 (hardcover) |
ISBN 9780593801383 (ebook)
Subjects: LCSH: Artists—Fiction. | COVID-19 Pandemic, 2020—Fiction. | LCGFT: Novels.
Classification: LCC PR6111.U68 B58 2024 | DDC 823/.92—dc23/eng/20230628
LC record available at https://lccn.loc.gov/2023024641

Jacket art by Chad Wys
Jacket design by John Gall

Manufactured in the United States of America
First Edition

To my friends

Poverty Piece:
Remain poor until the war ends
—LEE LOZANO, April 1970

EVEN WITH THE MASK ON, I recognized her at once. She was standing on the porch of the house at the end of the drive, her weight on one foot, the other leg relaxed, her left hand gripping her right wrist so the fingers and thumb made a cuff, a distinctive gesture that I had sometimes teased her about, telling her she looked as if she were handing herself in to the authorities. Her hair was still long, pushed up into a messy bun. She wore flip-flops and cutoffs, a faded band tee shirt, a clear visor and a pair of blue surgical gloves. Her arms and legs were smooth and tan.

The house itself wasn't ostentatious, at least compared to some of the mansions visible from the road, but that very modesty was a sign of almost unimaginable luxury. From the gate, I'd driven almost a mile through woodland, along a driveway that led up a hill overlooking the glittering water of a lake. The scale of the property was completely unexpected, a world in miniature that seemed to extend away to the horizon in every direction. In the center stood, not a robber baron's castle or one of the hedge fund follies that littered that part of New York state, but a two-story craftsman cottage with sharp gables, clad in blackened cedar shakes. Trained over the door, a blue wisteria. Beneath it, Alice.

I hadn't seen Alice in twenty years. There had been no letter, no goodbye. One day we were together, living in her aunt's airless London flat, the next she was gone, leaving me to pick up the pieces. To come face-to-face with her after so much time was a physical shock, a sudden impact that I felt all over my body. I was already light-headed. Lifting the bags out of the trunk of my car was taking all my strength; when I realized who she was, I had to stop and steady myself. Twenty brown paper sacks were filled with groceries, each one printed with a code word so I would know which order it belonged to. The code words, randomly generated from a dictionary, were one of the few interesting aspects of the job. I always paid attention to them, sometimes even noted them down. Once I might have made a work out of them.

I expected Alice to go back inside. That's what most of the customers did. They didn't want to get too close. VECTOR was a code word one day. I couldn't really blame them. Nobody knew anything. We were ruled by fear and misinformation. I can't say it didn't get to me, all those quickly slammed doors, the nervous faces mouthing instructions through closed windows. It's hard to be seen as a threat all the time, it grinds you down. I found myself muttering at the customers under my breath, conducting one-sided arguments. *You think I want to be out here?* But Alice stayed. She stood on the porch, cuffing her wrist, watching me.

Part of the pact I'd made with myself, years previously, was that whatever I was doing to stay alive, I wouldn't accept humiliation. If people viewed me in a certain way because I was cleaning a toilet or picking up trash, that was on them, not me. But it was hard to see myself through Alice's eyes, a middle-aged man in a grubby surgical mask, stooping to lift her groceries out of the trunk of a beaten-up car, limping a little as he walked up the path towards her.

I dropped the first bags on the doorstep, trying not to meet her gaze. Without warning, I was being pulled back to a version of myself that I thought I'd left behind. If you'd asked me ten minutes earlier, I'd have said that I could barely remember my time with Alice, at least not in detail, how it actually felt to be with her, the various things we did. I'd have admitted that I wondered about her once in a while, but would have said—and it would have been true as I said it—that my memories were indistinct and had no particular emotional tone, unless you counted a vague sense of embarrassment. We'd been very young. Neither of us had behaved well. At the time, the breakup had felt as if it would leave a permanent scar, and maybe it had, certainly it deformed the months afterwards, even the years, but so many things happen in a life. There are so many losses. Alice barely registered anymore. That's what I would have told you.

I started back to the car, trying to absorb what was happening, this living woman who'd suddenly dropped down over my memories like a shutter. Twenty years of change, all at once, her evolution from skinny chain-smoker into the mistress of some kind of fairy-tale kingdom. My knees were throbbing. I was short of breath. I had one, maybe two more trips to make. Two more chances for her to recognize me. She'd ordered some crates of bottled water. They felt unusually heavy as I picked them up and as I carried them to the porch. I staggered, grimacing in pain, grateful that she couldn't see my face.

"Jay?"

All I wanted was to let the moment fall away, to drive off and put Alice from my mind. There are fleeting events that touch our lives so briefly that afterwards we wonder if they even happened. FIGMENT was a code word one day.

"Jay?"

Of course I've changed. I'm heavier than I was at twenty-five. My beard is turning white and my eyes are sinking into their sockets like pebbles slowly dropping down a well. For many years I've worked manual jobs, often in the sun, and if I catch sight of myself in a mirror, on a good day I'm reminded of a piece of driftwood. Knotted, ground down by sand and water, but at least smooth and clean. It's always been important to me to keep clean. Almost the worst part of meeting Alice again was knowing that I hadn't showered for several days. I was aware of my smell, offended on her behalf. The anxious sweat of precarity. The stink of ill health and gas station food.

"Jay, is that you?"

What choice did I have? It took an effort of will to turn and face her. I felt as if my spirit were being pulled from my body with tongs, stretched out on display. See me, Alice. Nothing but a ragged membrane. A dirty scrap of ectoplasm, separating nothing from nothing.

"Hello Alice."

Just like that. The two syllables of a name. Our friends used to run our names together. Jayanalice. Aliceanjay. At first I couldn't make eye contact, knowing that I was going to see pity, perhaps disgust. When I did, I felt an intensity for which I was completely unprepared. I wasn't just confronted with her as a judge of my failings, some problem from my past, but by *her*, another person who existed beyond me, beyond my understanding. Alice was suddenly present, fully present, then excessively present, breaking her banks, blazing forth, a torrent, a stream of stars. She said something else that I didn't catch because I was lying on the ground, gasping for breath, gravel pressed uncomfortably into my right cheek. I could feel it against the palms of my hands. My heart hammered in my chest and I surveyed a landscape that looked, from that angle, like the surface of Mars.

MY BODY WAS SOMETHING I rarely thought about when I was younger. It only came to my attention when it didn't do what I wanted. Usually it was an obedient vehicle, carrying me through crowds and parties, up hills and over fences, under water, into beds and beaches and tents and clubs and toilet stalls, into other bodies. Like most physically able young men, I lifted and carried without ever imagining what it might be like to find it hard to do those things, or slow to recover afterwards.

A partial list of my scars would include the ugly red welt on my calf, from when I slipped and cut myself on a sharp piece of metal as I was getting out of a truck, a flatbed with a sort of hand-welded frame bolted on the back. I have burns on my forearms from kitchen work, and the big toe on my left foot lost its nail when I dropped my end of a steel beam on a construction site. On the back of my right index finger is a fine white L-shape, relic of an accident with a glass jug, also in a restaurant kitchen. I've cracked my head a few times on boats, and I've cut up my hands in all sorts of ways on ropes and lines. I was once cleaning out the inside of an industrial storage tank when my mask got knocked off and I breathed in toxic fumes. No one could tell me exactly what had been in there, but I coughed blood and my lungs haven't been the same since. I am often in pain, but I've rarely been able to see a doctor, and, like a lot of people, I've gotten by. My knees are the one thing that trouble me. One winter I worked as a picker in a warehouse and they got sore and I couldn't afford to take time off to rest them. Each shift was worse than the last and I ended up getting fired anyway. I was too slow, hobbling from aisle to aisle, missing my targets.

Alice stared down at me as I lay on the ground. Over the pale blue band of her mask, her eyes were wide with concern. From my low angle she seemed both monumental and unreal. The sun was behind her, lending her a soft, golden aura, though that could also have been an artifact of my fever. She looked glossy to me, radiant with the kind of health that's made of yoga and massage and raw juices and money. Once upon a time our bodies had cleaved together. They had looked right, they had matched. If someone had been there to see us at that moment, to witness the sentimental tableau—the lady outside her little house with its white porch and tumble of blue flowers, bending down over a prostrate beggar man—our divergence would have been painfully obvious. A challenging workout is not the same, physically speaking, as trudging twelve miles a day over a hard floor carrying a barcode zapper.

She reached out instinctively to help me stand, then hesitated, unsure if it was safe. I made a clumsy effort to sit up unaided. She bent down to support me and for a moment our faces were within a few inches of each other. She recoiled in confusion, then stood up and took an embarrassed step back.

"Sorry," she said. "I mean, are you sick?"

"Not anymore."

"I really can't catch this thing."

"Don't worry. I'm not contagious."

"How do you know?"

"I tested negative. You don't have to be afraid."

Two months had passed since the morning I realized that I couldn't taste the empanada I'd just bought from a vendor on the subway platform. Some people barely felt the disease, but it had wrecked me. For ten days I'd barely left my bed, lying on my belly as I tried to drag air into my lungs. Some symptoms had persisted. My mind was foggy. It was hard to assemble my thoughts. I tended to embark on convoluted mental journeys, which made driving, for example, stressful and dangerous. Mainly I felt tired, bone-tired, like a puppet whose strings had been cut.

I sat down heavily on the porch step and waved her away. "I need to take off my mask. You better—"

She stepped back. I unhooked the strings and wiped my eyes and mouth with a handkerchief. Showing my face felt uncomfortably intimate, like being naked. She stared off into the distance, giving me a moment.

"It really is you, Jay. I didn't think I'd ever—I mean, I didn't even know if you . . ."

She trailed off.

When I'd known Alice, her French accent had been overlaid with a thin skim of East London. After we'd been together a year or so, she was dropping t's and calling people "fam." None of that was present anymore. I could still hear French, and maybe even the rise and fall of her mother's tonal Vietnamese, but the rest had all been smoothed away. She sounded placeless, international. The change was disorientating. For a moment, illogically, I wondered if I had made a mistake. Was it actually Alice? Or was this woman her double, an imposter? I tried to speak, but I was still having trouble catching my breath.

"Do you want a drink of water?"

I nodded.

"I'll get you one."

She went inside. I slumped back on the steps, wondering what was happening to me. I felt as if someone had crammed my chest full of wet sponges. The setting was suspiciously beautiful; the gingerbread house, the lake water glinting through the trees.

Where was I? Where was I really? I forced myself to think of practicalities. I badly needed to lie down, but I was only partway through my route. I had drops for several other addresses. Right then, I didn't see how I was going to be able to get up and walk to the car, let alone drive away.

I'd been in extreme states in the past, cold, hungry, wanting for whatever reason to give in, but sooner or later I'd always summoned some final reserve of strength. I tried to will myself upright, to leave that lulling place and go back to reality, my reality, my proper sphere. But I was tired. I could feel myself slipping, seduced by the thought of sitting on that step until the earth pulled me down and I could finally let go.

"Here you are."

I took a little blue glass bottle from her and cracked the seal on the cap. She hovered some distance away, watching me drink. The water filtered into my body like an elixir. Maybe, I thought, I'm dead, and Alice is here to take me over the water to the other side. I braced myself, ready to fight. I would not allow it, I would not let myself get lifted up into—whatever it was, that treacherous swirl of air and sunlight.

If I got an hour's rest, even half an hour lying down in the car, maybe I'd be able to finish my route. There was a Walmart a few miles away, with a huge lot and a line of dumpsters that obscured a section of it from the security cameras. I'd been parking there to sleep, but I didn't think I had the stamina to make it back. I was either going to have to ask Alice to call an ambulance or persuade her to let me park the car on her property, at least for a few hours. I did not want to call an ambulance. I would have to explain myself, throw myself on Alice's mercy, and I didn't really know how to begin. Too much had happened. It was too complicated. I was out of the habit of talking. I felt overwhelmed, flooded by inertia.

Make conversation. Say the things that people say.

When I asked if the house was where she always lived, she laughed. "God no. We borrowed it. We really needed to get out of the city."

I didn't have to ask who she meant by "we." She could read the question in my face.

"Rob. We're still together."

Alice carried on, explaining that another couple was staying there too and Rob had gone for a walk with them, but I wasn't listening. *So they lasted.* I'd always assumed that Alice's relationship with Robert was a rebound, a safe way for her to leave me. Ghosting me with my closest friend was, I'd convinced myself, a scorched-earth tactic, a sign, paradoxically, of how serious we'd been. It had made me very angry, but I always blamed him more than her. I'd trusted Rob. I thought he respected me. I'd thrown the two of them together—I understood all the ways in which I'd been at fault—and maybe I had been naïve for wanting them to like each other, but when something happened between them, he should have had the courage to tell me to my face.

Even in the weeks after they vanished, when I was more or less in a state of collapse, I understood that I hadn't been making Alice happy, and this had allowed me, gradually, to forgive her. I would have left me: I was no fun to be around. I'd always assumed that once she was clear of the strange web we'd spun together, Alice would have left Rob and gone on to someone else. It had pleased me to imagine her in a situation of abstract freedom, living some life that I knew nothing about. It allowed me to think of her as someone who had just faded away from me, got lost in the fog of time. Instead I found that she and Rob were still together, their lives connected directly back to the old days, to who we'd been and what we'd done with each other. It was a cruel relegation. I'd always complacently imagined that the story revolved around me, when actually I was a minor character in the story of Alice and Rob, someone who'd be mentioned, if at all, as a setup ("she had this terrible boyfriend") when other couples asked them how they met.

"So you got married."

"We did."

There was a long, difficult pause.

"Do you have children?"

"Just one. Sophie. She's fifteen. She's staying with her cousins in Paris."

"Fifteen. You had her quite soon after . . ."

"Yes."

"And your sister has children too."

"Four." She shrugged. "They like big families over there."

"It's hard to imagine . . ."

"Carine."

"That's it—Carine—as a mother."

"She's become very respectable. On the street, people congratulate her on doing her Catholic duty."

Alice's older sister had been working at an investment bank when we were together, and Alice had always painted her as driven and career-minded, working long hours, downing shots with the boys and pushing herself through various physical challenges, marathons and Iron Man competitions. It was odd to think of her shepherding her flock around the Faubourg Saint-Germain.

I felt exhausted by this conversation, the longest I'd conducted in weeks, but I knew I couldn't afford to fall back into silence.

"It must be hard to be apart from your daughter right now."

"It's not great. She's been there almost three months. We got caught out by the travel restrictions. Then, well, it just seemed safer for her to stay."

"That's a long time."

"The numbers are very low in France. And Rob and I have some things to sort out. In a way it's good that she's not around."

Though I couldn't see Alice's mouth behind the mask, I knew she was frowning. The situation was awkward, and when Rob came back, it would be much worse. The silence strung out, as I tried to get air into my lungs without making it look like a struggle.

"It's been so long," Alice said, redundantly.

I nodded, thinking about Rob. I wondered if he'd achieved all the grandiose ambitions he'd had for himself as a young painter. Judging by where we were, he had.

"How about you? Do you live near here?"

Her tone had turned bright, brittle. Cocktail party chat. I didn't know how to answer. "Not far."

"Do you have children?"

"No."

"You didn't want them?"

"It just never happened."

She said again, "Jay, it's been so long."

She was flailing, searching in vain for words. I felt sorry for her. I decided it was pointless to pretend that a connection could be salvaged from our wreckage. The past was both painful and dead. I tried to force my body to do what I wanted and stood up, swaying a little on my feet.

"Hey," said Alice. "You really don't seem OK."

"I'm fine."

"I wish I could let you into the house. But . . ." She made a defeated gesture with her hand.

I put my mask back on, wincing as I hooked the loops against the notches where my ears met my temples, which the elastic had rubbed raw. "I should go."

"Are you sure?"

"Yes, I think so, don't you?"

She didn't answer.

"It was good to see you, Alice." I began to walk away. One foot in front of the other. Left, right. My head was swimming. Near the car I stumbled again. She came running up behind me.

"This is crazy. You need a doctor."

"I'm fine," I said, coughing and tugging the mask down around my chin.

"I think I should call 911."

"Please don't do that."

"Why not?"

"Just don't."

She looked confused for a moment, until she worked it out. People in her world had insurance.

"Well, you can't drive."

At the same moment, our eyes were drawn to the open trunk. Beside the bags of undelivered groceries was a cardboard box full of clothes, a rolled sleeping mat poking out of the top. I saw her realize that I was living in my car, and a sort of cavity opened up inside me.

"Jay—"

"Just stop. You don't have to worry about me."

"What happened?"

"Nothing happened. I'm living the way I want to live."

"I never said—look, I heard you disappeared, left England, but I never had any news after that."

"It's all such a long time ago. Just give me a moment, then I'll be gone."

"Jay."

"Just give me a moment."

I slumped against the car. She stood there with her arms folded, rocking back and forth on the balls of her feet.

"Look Jay, I'm not judging you, and I'm really not trying to get in your business, but you don't seem like you're doing well. You're sick."

"I was sick. I'm not anymore."

"You just fainted."

I made an odd little noise in my throat, an attempt at a laugh. "I admit I want to lie down."

"I can't bring you in to the house. It—I mean, it's not possible. One of the people staying here, Marshal—he's Rob's gallerist. This is already hard for him. He's kind of a hypochondriac."

"I understand. I'm not asking for anything."

"Oh, this is so stupid. You promise me you're not infectious?"

"I caught it two months ago. I have antibodies. It's just—you know, the after-effects."

She thought for a moment. "Get in the car. I'll drive."

"Thanks, but I don't want to go to a hospital. I'll be fine if I lie down."

"I don't mean that. There's somewhere you can stay, at least for a night. It's on the other side of the lake."

I was going to explain that I had to finish the rest of my deliveries—I'd almost certainly lose the job if I didn't—but I was so tired that I couldn't find the strength. I got into the passenger seat of the car, ashamed again of my pungent, meaty smell.

Alice rolled down the windows. "I'm sorry. Could you put your mask back on?"

"Sure."

I pulled the mask over my face, breathing in its stink. I'd been wearing it for days, and it was loose and soggy. I pinched the little metal strip against my nose, trying to improve the fit.

Alice's competence had survived even the last year of our relationship, when we were actively trying to crash and burn, to let ourselves go to hell. It was a kind of weakness in her. If you're a problem-solver, sooner or later people learn that they can bring their problems to you, and after that you're never free. She started the engine, and I remembered how she could never focus on her work in the way that Rob and I did almost automatically. She always got tangled up in other people's projects, helping out, doing favors. So as I slumped into the passenger seat, it felt familiar. I'd come to her with a problem. She was putting aside her other tasks and sorting it out. We drove downhill towards the lake. Around the house, the grounds were landscaped with wide lawns and beds of meadow flowers. I glimpsed some outbuildings, a big red barn up on a rise, a boathouse.

"What is this place?"

Alice shrugged. "Greg, the guy who owns it, is Marshal's backer. He's not here. I think he has a ranch in New Zealand. He's staying in his bunker until the pandemic dies down."

"An actual bunker?"

"Some kind of shelter. A complex, Marshal called it. An underground complex. Marshal's desperate to see it, of course."

As Alice drove, I was acutely aware of our proximity. I tried not to stare at her, grabbed visual details when I could. The strands of hair falling over her face, the inoculation scar on her upper arm, familiar and yet utterly new. We drove beside the lake, following the shoreline round until we could see the little house across the water, set in an extraordinary frame of ancient trees. It looked like an old postcard, something that ought not to have existed in the present day. As I stared out of the window, we turned uphill into the woods.

"This is all one property?"

"Yes. Amazing, isn't it?"

She swung the car off the track and parked by a barn with a steep pitched roof and a set of double doors. Its blackened shingles gave it a superficially similar look to the house, but they were mossy and uneven. The place didn't look as if it were in regular use. Alice got out of the car and pushed at the doors, first one, then the other, sliding them aside. Then she ran the car forward into the barn and switched off the engine.

"Do you need help walking?"

"I'm OK."

I pushed open the door, and she helped me out of the car. The barn smelled of must and rotting wood. Motes of dust floated in the sunlight; indistinct shapes resolved themselves into gardening equipment and building supplies. A few rusty tools, some cans of paint, a pair of broken deckchairs with mildewed canvas. Lurking in one corner, wreathed in cobwebs, was a ride-on lawnmower. Alice led the way through the mess and up a flight of stairs into an unexpectedly clean and airy space, an attic with dormer windows on one side, looking down the path towards the lake. There was a bed, a rug on the floor, a little fridge, even a hot plate.

"I think it's for the gardeners. I'm not sure. In any case, you can hole up here. I don't think it's too dusty."

"Thank you."

"One thing, you can't go outside. I'm sorry, but we're not supposed to invite anyone else here. Marshal says there's some particularly advanced kind of security system. I don't fully understand what. Cameras. You mustn't let yourself be seen. Even in the forest."

"There are cameras in the forest?"

"So he says. I'll come back later and bring you something to eat. After that, I don't know. We'll work it out."

Obediently, I lay down, and almost at once I began to drift into an altered state, neither sleep nor waking. I saw Alice, disembodied, eyes and hair and patterned mask fabric floating over me like the Cheshire Cat. I thought about the deliveries I hadn't done. I should have told Alice that she didn't need to bring me food: there were a dozen bags of groceries spoiling in the trunk of the car. Maybe the company wouldn't treat it as theft. Accidents happen. I would message them that I was sick. I would promise to bring back what I could. Pay for the rest . . .

Then I was back in Queens, in the house in Jackson Heights. It was very confused, because Alice was there too, not at the house but waiting for me somewhere else. It was urgent to get to her, because she was about to leave, but I didn't have the strength. The place was a warren, even more than in real life. I was so weak that I had to prop myself against the wall as I staggered to the bathroom, though in the dream the bathroom didn't seem to be where it usually was, and I turned a corner into a corridor of half-open doors. Bunk beds and card players. Augusto, sitting like a toad against the giant gilt headboard of his bed.

That house had no business existing, in or out of a dream. Set back from a busy street of jewelers and sari stores, you got to it down a fetid little alleyway that ran between a laundromat and a bodega, ending in an irregularly shaped yard, an interstitial cavity traversed by rats and blasted with hot chemical air from the laundromat's noisy HVAC. A scuffed wood-veneer door that could have been salvaged from an office opened onto a bike-clogged stairwell that led through into a jumble of awkward spaces, rooms carved out of other rooms, wedges and slices, abject subdivisions. There were usually between ten and twelve of us living there, new arrivals taking over vacant beds as people moved on. The others were mostly in their twenties, delivery drivers, construction workers. I was the oldest by far, working nights for one of the ride-hail companies and sleeping during the day. Once a week, the landlord's agent, a sullen young Hasid, came by for the rent. We all paid cash. The same young man showed me around when I moved in, gesturing vaguely as he talked on his flip phone. He was in the dream too, sitting in his usual place in the kitchen, peering about with distaste as one of the Bangladeshis pleaded with him about the broken toilet. There was always something. Mold or roaches. We knew the place wasn't built to code, and the landlord, I think he was the kid's uncle, knew none of us would say a word. Any trouble you're out, you play music you're out, Augusto says do something you do it, otherwise Yoni hears about it and guess what you're out. Augusto was a short, stocky man who acted as a kind of trusty, making sure people kept the noise down and didn't use the place to drink or get high. That kind of behavior always led to trouble. A lot of us did shift work and people got angry if they couldn't sleep. I don't know if Augusto worked. His idleness seemed almost supernatural; as far as I could tell, he never even left the house. He had a big room at the back with its own bathroom and he sat up there listening to talk radio at low volume, his door either cracked open, if he was listening out for someone he needed to threaten, or else bolted with heavy locks.

I gave up and went back to my room, a narrow cubicle with pinkish tile on the floor and squares of mirror glued to the back of the door. My bed was as I left it, a tangle of damp sheets on a foam mattress, haloed by food packaging and water bottles. I lay down again, coughing and wheezing, and all of a sudden it was late at night and I had no voice. I couldn't make a sound, however hard I tried. I wanted to shout but all I could force out was a croak, a whisper for Bunchie, who was the only one who would help me. I'm thirsty Bunchie, Bunchie you there? Bunchie was Guyanese and when I got sick he took pity on me. I'd crawl to the door and slide money under it. Bunchie would take it and some time later he'd leave food outside. I was very grateful. I'd have starved otherwise. No one else wanted me anywhere near them. Now it was too late, Bunchie had gone. A baleful yellow light seeped in from the alleyway and someone on the street was shouting to a friend in Spanish, the trap beat from an idling car setting the bug screens buzzing.

You can't quarantine in a house like that. There's no way to keep your distance. Bunchie blamed me when he got sick, as if he'd caught it through the door or something, not from one of the guys he drank with after-hours at the salvage yard, and I guess he must have told Augusto, because one afternoon, he let himself in to my room. I was lying there, shivering and struggling to breathe, and I was so far into my own world that for a while I thought he was in costume, on his way to a party. That made no sense, of course. What party would Augusto go to? From somewhere he'd found an old army surplus gas mask, and he stood there filling the doorway, his enormous body grotesquely topped by a long rubber insect face with two glass disks for eyes. He was a figure from a nightmare, a bad place in my psyche, and because of the mask and the fever I couldn't understand what he was saying, I kept asking what are you supposed to be Augusto, and he got angry and came back with a car antenna and made like he was going to whip me with it. "I said you got to go pops why you don't listen?"

Then I was driving, in the time of no time, pandemic time, formless and without direction. As I weaved through the deserted streets, listening to the whine of the old car's engine, I looked back, lost in darkness. Augusto in the doorway. "You can't stay here no more, Tio Jay, you getting everyone sick." Bunchie was behind him, Iqbal too. Either Iqbal or Hamid, a plaid scarf pulled up over his face. Vigilantes, running me off. I told Augusto I'd stay in my room, not come out at all, shit in a bucket, whatever it took. "No dice. Yoni heard you got the 'rona so he don't want you here no more." And I landed on the sidewalk, weak as a newborn, with a backpack and two cardboard boxes of possessions. That was one time I could have given up. And for a while I did. I just sat there, passively waiting for something to happen.

Sitting on the sidewalk, dream-driving through pandemic Manhattan, along the broad empty avenues. The last man on earth, waiting without hope for the app to ping, to give me a sign that there was at least one other survivor, a passenger to sit in my back seat. I glanced in the mirror and saw I'd already picked her up. She was vaping and looking at her phone.

Hello Alice.

You should have gone to the hospital.

I know, but it's complicated.

Sitting on the sidewalk, looking up at the sky. Sooner or later the cops would roll by. The old junkies outside the bodega were pretending to ignore me, but their energy was secretly snaking out in my direction. They looked chaotic—crutches and cigarettes and masks round their chins, squabbling, showing each other whatever on their phones, all their busy bullshit—but those guys worked the angles all day all night. *What's in the boxes? He looks sick. He couldn't do nothing.* So, although my legs felt like water, I picked up my possessions and walked.

It took all my strength to get to the car. I reclined the driver's seat and lay there, my heart racing. Some time later, when I felt a little stronger, I drove out of the city. I didn't know where I was headed. I felt like a cat slinking off to a private place to die. I had a vague image in my head of trees. Cool air, a green canopy, the rustling of leaves. I didn't want to end my life in Queens. Somewhere in the suburbs, after drifting into my thoughts and nearly sideswiping a truck, I parked behind a strip mall and fell into an exhausted sleep.

In the dream I tried to talk to Alice but she couldn't hear me. She was absorbed in some video on her phone, and often when I looked back, it wasn't her at all but one of the hundreds of other people I'd driven in that car. The streets were an empty gameworld, generated on the fly as I drove Alice to wherever she was going. It looked like we were on our way to the airport, but somehow we came off the BQE into an unfamiliar tangle of streets lined with body shops and discount furniture stores, and all of a sudden we were passing people I knew, Patrice and Oleg on their way to work in the bakery, Olu standing outside the tax preparer, dressed as the Statue of Liberty, twirling his cardboard sign. I said to Alice, *I know those guys,* but she didn't look up. I said to Alice, *I think this must be the end of the world.*

In the way you think you remember the thing that gave you food poisoning, the bad shrimp, the odd taste of the chicken, I think I know who gave me the virus. In the middle of March, just before the city closed down, some people were taking it seriously, but most were just carrying on as normal. I needed money, so I didn't really have a choice about working, but I'd found a little bottle of hand sanitizer, the last one in the store, and though it was bitterly cold, I was keeping my window cracked open, which some passengers didn't appreciate. Outside a club I picked up a trio of young women who wanted to go to Inwood. Hair and heels and bronzer, spilling out of wrap dresses. They were deep in their Saturday night, screaming with laughter and hassling me to put the heater on, change the music, drive faster. One of them was coughing as she blew out vape smoke. I remember—though how could I remember, really, it's just an artifact, an image my mind has found for the anxiety I felt—a spray of tiny droplets arcing out of her mouth.

There are people, new people, living in big houses, on high floors, and for them the end of the world didn't matter, because disaster had already been priced in. Safely hedged, they could dream their timeless dreams. For the rest of us there was no choice. History did not stop for us. It came howling on.

I woke up and didn't know where I was. I was frozen and the car windows were streaming with condensation. I woke up in my bed, tangled between damp sheets in the pink-tiled room, coughing and calling out for Bunchie. I woke up in a hundred other places, all the other beds I'd ever slept in, all the different qualities of morning and evening light. Finally I woke up into a dead silence, and I knew I wasn't in a city, because the room smelled of damp wood, and I could hear birdsong. From my bed I could see tall trees, and I wondered if at last it was all over.

·   ·   ·

I SWUNG MY LEGS OUT of bed and stood up carefully. I felt light-headed and hungry, though better than before. I decided to go and scavenge through the bags of groceries in the car, but when I got to the bottom of the stairs, I found a tote bag filled with supplies and a note from Alice saying I'd been asleep when she came and she hadn't wanted to wake me. There were some cut sandwiches wrapped in aluminum foil, bottled water, painkillers, toilet paper, a toothbrush, hand sanitizer, fresh masks. I held the bag as if it were a bomb. It had been a long time since anyone had made me a care package.

One corner of the barn had been partitioned with plasterboard, and I opened a door to find a basic but functional bathroom with a shower stall wedged next to the toilet. I went to the car to see if I had any fresh clothes. An hour later I was washed, dressed and shaved, feeling cleaner than I had in days, but so tired that I had to go back upstairs to lie down. Almost at once I fell asleep, and when I opened my eyes, the light was failing and the trees were vague black shapes outside the window. I shut them again and woke into another bluish-white morning that smelled of earth and leaf mulch and wood exhaling the moisture of the night.

I sat upright. I felt shaky, empty and insubstantial, but my head wasn't throbbing and my vision was clear. The little cot above the barn was the first proper bed I'd had since the day Augusto drove me out of the house in Jackson Heights. Sleeping in a car, you're always anxious about a tap on the windscreen, a flashlight, a hand trying the door handle. Though I'd been trav-eling for years, and I'd often slept in strange or unfriendly places, I'd been feeling very vulnerable. With a good night's sleep came a flood of emotions that I found hard to master. I breathed deeply, fighting back tears.

In the car, tucked into the glove box, was a skinny roll of twenty-dollar bills. I'd calculated that I would need to work for another six weeks before I had enough saved for a security deposit. I was thinking about trying Long Island, maybe getting summer work in one of the tourist towns. I was too weak to work construction or landscaping, or any of the other heavy jobs I'd done in the past, and my recurrent bouts of fever and faintness were forcing me towards a question that I'd always known I'd have to answer sooner or later, about what I'd do when I could no longer physically sustain my way of living.

First I needed to get a room, somewhere to stay, then I could think about the rest. Experimentally, I stood up and made my way gingerly downstairs, two feet on each step like a little child. I took another shower, giving thanks for each second of hot water. Since I wasn't sure when I'd next be able to do better than a public bathroom, I wanted to remember the sensation, the jet hitting my neck and shoulders, sluicing the back of my head. I opened the trunk of the car and dressed, wishing I'd thought to wash some clothes; they could have dried overnight. I rummaged in the bags of groceries for breakfast. Some of the food would have to be thrown away. There was a whole chicken, pieces of salmon, milk, all of it slightly warm. I tore chunks off a loaf of bread and smeared it with runny butter, using a plastic knife from a stash of cutlery and paper plates that I'd swiped from a supermarket salad bar. I wondered what I should do with the rest of it. Most was usable, but company policy was to throw away anything that was returned to the store, regardless of the reason. There were giant dumpsters full of perfectly good groceries, padlocked so that no one would take anything. Maybe if I texted the help desk and volunteered to pay for the losses out of my wages, I'd be able to keep the job.

When I went to make the call, I found my battery was dead. I hunted for the charger and took it upstairs to an outlet, knowing that when I switched it on, I'd probably find it full of angry messages. So I left it and went downstairs and very cautiously opened the barn door, just a crack, staying behind it so I was out of sight. I sat with my shoulder against the door, breathing in the air and listening to the woods, increasingly aware of what wasn't there, the absence of the high white sound of the city, the screaming at the margins of perception composed of air conditioners and power cables and buzzing fluorescents and the stress of too many people packed into a tight space.

I could see a meandering path leading off up into the trees. There was something perfect about the solitude, the greenish light filtering through the canopy of leaves. A held breath. I imagined walking uphill, subsiding into moss and forgetfulness. Instead, I closed the barn door and prepared to go back out on the road. I cleared out the trash that had accumulated in the car footwells. The interior smelled of sweat and snack foods, poorly masked by a pine tree air freshener. Even if it were vacuumed and steam cleaned, I'd never again be able to use it to pick up passengers; the grime of weeks of occupation would always lurk around the edges, in the window seals and the seat pockets, saturating the upholstery. Though the car was twenty years old, it was mechanically sound, worth the money I'd paid for it. I'd looked after it meticulously, so that even though it barely met the standards of the ride-hail companies, passengers didn't complain. My star rating had been good.

It's a fiction we seem to demand, that a person be substantially the same throughout their lives—human ships of Theseus, each part replaced, but in some essential way unchanging. We are less continuous than we pretend. There are jumps, punctuations, sudden reorganizations of selfhood. I'd always had goals, even if they weren't ones that other people could understand, but at some point I'd lost touch with the person who'd set them. If you had asked me what I was doing, delivering groceries in upstate New York, I would only have been able to give you a superficial answer.

Clearing out the car was tiring, and I went upstairs to rest. I drifted off to sleep and woke again to find that it was dark and a voice was calling my name.

"Jay? Are you OK?"

I sat up groggily and fished around for a mask.

"Yeah. I'm fine."

"Can I come up?"

"Just a moment."

She climbed the stairs. She was dressed in athletic gear, leggings and a long-sleeved top, her hair tied back in a ponytail under a cap. Her mask was the same dusty orange as her shoes. Looking at this precisely matched outfit, I wondered again who this woman was, who she had become. When we were together, her primary form of exercise had been walking to the shop.

For a while we exchanged awkward small talk, like people who'd met at a boring party and were making the best of it. I told her I was getting ready to leave, that I needed to get back to my job. She said I didn't seem healthy enough to work.

"This can't be the first time this has happened to a driver. Call them up, sort it out with them."

"It's an automated system."

"So? There must be people."

It was hard to explain to her. She was a rich person, used to interactions in which she was respected, even courted. On the rare occasion when her status wasn't recognized—by some official or service provider—it was, I imagined, a memorable outrage. She'd find it hard to understand that I had no relationship with the company outside terms set by the app. It was designed that way. Even if you stayed on the phone for hours and finally got to speak to someone in a far-away call center, they had no agency. You could never appeal to anyone's humanity.

"Is someone waiting for you?"

I hesitated, confused by the change in direction. "No."

"Well then."

"It's not that simple."

"I just don't see why you're leaving. If you're anxious about money, we can work something out." She stood up. She seemed irritated.

When I first met Alice, I wanted to devour her. I wanted to exhaust her and exhaust myself, wear us both out until there was nothing left. I understood, in a confused way, that what you can see of other people, what they let you see, is only the part of the iceberg that's visible above the water. When I was young I thought of that as a challenge, a mystery to be explored. I would reflexively try to "get to know" everyone I met. Gradually, the purpose of this deep-sea diving began to seem less obvious. What is the point of knowing people, really? What does it achieve? We try and touch each other, but it is impossible.

Alice started down the stairs, then turned.

"If you're leaving in the morning, you're going to need me to open the gate. There's a code. I'll come by, I don't know, around 9:30, OK?"

"Sure."

She hesitated.

"So where did you go? Where have you been for all these years?"

I shrugged. "Traveling."

"Have you been making art?"

"I don't really make anything."

"Nor do I."

I stared at her, trying to gauge what she meant. The mask made it impossible.

"What do you do, Alice? I always assumed you'd be writing books, running a museum."

She laughed, a clipped little percussive sound. "I clean up Rob's messes."

She broke eye contact. She cuffed her wrist with the fingers of her other hand, rotated it a couple of times, then let it drop. The familiar sequence complete, she looked back up at me. "How about you?"

"I just do whatever the app tells me to."

It was meant to be a joke. The pause that followed was broken by the sound of her phone.

"Hello?"

I noted a slight tension in her voice. As she answered, she instinctively took a few paces down the stairs.

"Hey you. Oh, I'm just out for a run." She went a little further down. "I know it's dark. I just wanted to be out of the house."

So I was still a secret from Rob. I tried to ignore the little hit of satisfaction this gave me. I wanted to feel nothing, to remain unmoved. Instead, rusty emotional gears were beginning to turn, and I found myself setting out on a familiar elliptical orbit.

Alice's voice rose sharply in response to some question.

"My God, whatever you want there to be! Just look in the fridge, use your imagination."

ROB WAS IN MY FIRST CRIT at art school in London. He showed his work directly before mine. As he prepared, pinning some small watercolors to the wall, I didn't take much notice of him. I was nervous about my own presentation, for which I had high hopes. The previous night, lying awake in bed, I'd imagined a flattering scenario—I would be taken aside by the tutor, told confidentially that I had a big future, and so on. I was impatient to begin my brilliant career and Rob didn't seem like a promising vehicle for the delivery of Great Art, so I pretended to be looking at something in my portfolio. Surrounded by students signaling distressed bohemia, all patches and thrift store irony, he stood out for his neatness. He was dressed in baggy corduroys, so new they had a slight shine, a track suit top that he'd zipped defiantly up to his chin, and a pair of bright white tennis shoes with fat laces. You could barely see his eyes below a white bucket hat.

Where I came from we called them "casuals," young men who bought expensive clothes, followed football and went out on Saturday night to chase the Goths down the High Street with bats and knives. Essex casuals didn't dress like Rob, that was a Manchester look, but he had that casual thing, that slightly fussy precision that made it easy to tell him apart from the middle-class children in the room, with their torn jeans and uncombed hair. Keep yourself nice, we used to say. It meant don't let yourself slip, don't wear anything old, anything with holes in it. But also, don't lose your pride. I thought to myself *I know you. I know the kind of place you come from.*

The work Rob presented that day would surprise people who only know the big flashy canvases he showed later on, the drips, the flourishing impasto. It would be hard to connect the painter he became with the boy who pinned those torn-out sketchbook pages to the studio wall. They were still lifes, done with incredible modesty and economy. I remember one of some pocket litter scattered on a table—a pack of cigarettes, a tube ticket, coins— executed with a few washes of watercolor that gave each object real volume and presence.

"Are they studies for larger works?" asked the tutor.

"No," said Rob. "I think they're done."

I barely remember any of Rob's pictures from the period, later on, when we became friends. We argued theatrically in front of them, waving bottles and cigarettes, drunkenly performing our painterliness for whoever else was in the studio, but they're gone, lost through some grate in my memory. Yet somehow the little watercolors from the first crit are still around. I can call each one to mind. It's possible that if I saw them now, I wouldn't think they were any good, but back then, in that room of hypervigilant students, they sent me into a panic. Newly arrived at art school, my own painting was cramped and self-conscious. I was trying to train myself to loosen up, but it wasn't going well. A week or so earlier, at one of those terrible first-year parties where everyone sits on a bedroom floor and passes around a single soggy joint, some boarding school girl had told me, speaking in a sort of drawl that didn't require her to move her mouth, that I was too into being cool, and I'd actually be much cooler if I stopped trying. Easy for her to say. Maybe she could live the unexamined life. Mine presented itself as an endless decision tree, a constant steeplechase of exhausting and difficult choices. I tended to be obsessive, and because of that it was best if certain things were squared away, removed from my list of worries. I had to look right, to be showered and have fresh breath, to know my art books were alphabetized on my shelf. Then I could begin. I wasn't a casual, I didn't spend my money on polo shirts and cashmere sweaters, in fact rather the opposite, I wanted my clothes to say nothing, to mean nothing, but I did want to keep myself nice, according to my own personal definitions. If I didn't have to fixate on a missing button or a shirt that was too loose or too tight or too short or long, I was free to make conversation, to sit on the floor without stimming and behave more or less like someone who belonged in the world.

I had learned to live according to the rules my brain imposed, but for my work it was a problem. Everything I made was neat and perfect, totally planned out before the brush hit the canvas. My paintings and drawings were airless and dead and I was sick of making them, which meant I was essentially sick of myself, so a few days before my first crit I'd hit on the idea of getting stoned and doing drawings that were just supposed to feel good, mark-making that didn't detour via my head at all. Now, years later, I have the words to express what I wanted—for the line to go straight to the hand, to be like a Zen monk drawing a circle, becoming perfectly empty as the brush moves. If I'd known about the Zen monks and their circles in those first weeks at art school, I might have saved myself some humiliation, because I'd gone badly off track. I'd got caught up in the experience of making the marks, trying to be as present and expressive as I could, because wasn't that supposed to be the point—self-expression? The result was a forest of incoherent pencil lines, some so forceful that they'd gone right through the paper, which I thought was excellent, evidence that I was feeling something, probably something grand and beautiful, treading the royal road to *Kunst*.

I thought I'd had a breakthrough. Then Rob got up and showed his work and I realized I was a fool. My drawings were histrionic. While I was floundering in narcissism, he'd found a simple creative language to express his experience of the world. I looked around the room, expecting to see faces suffused by a glow of awe. One or two people said uncertainly that they liked it. Others said they "weren't moved" or "didn't really get what he was doing." The tutor, on whose opinion we all relied, seemed bored.

Rob thanked people for their comments and put the drawings away in a portfolio. He didn't show any particular emotion, though later I found out that he'd been so angry he'd almost given up and gone back home to Manchester. As I hung up my enormous scribbles, I felt so embarrassed that I could barely open my mouth to introduce them. "I did these," I said. "They're an experiment. I don't think they're really working." It took an effort of will not to walk straight out of the room. Eventually the tutor, whose pedagogy usually consisted of gnomic remarks and long periods of awkward silence, came to my rescue, guiding the conversation along until it was respectable to move to the next student.

I didn't see Rob again for a while. He wasn't in any of my classes, and for a time, he became a sort of symbol in my mind, the true artist, who existed on a higher plane than all the callow exhibitionists jostling for attention around me. We met again when someone took me to a party in an old factory in Hackney Wick. This was some years before gentrification crept out that far, and a feral ecosystem was thriving just beyond the grasp of the developers who were beginning to line the canals with glass boxes and plastic-clad towers. The place was like an ant colony, and I think the owner must have got some kind of tax break for renting to artists because whole floors of the building were subdivided into cheap firetrap studios. Somehow I ended up breaking away from the main party, where there was a dance floor, and going over to another unit to smoke hash. I remember a wall covered in silver foil and an enormous potted plant, some kind of massive palm, like a specimen in a Victorian greenhouse. As I sprawled on a saggy sectional sofa, ignoring the guy trying to talk to me about dub reggae, I looked at the host, who was skinning up a joint on an album cover. It took me a moment before I was sure it was the same person. In a few months Rob had shucked off his Manchester skin and emerged as a perfect art school bohemian. The designer sportswear was gone, replaced by a sort of beatnik look, a Breton shirt and black jeans. Later I would discover Rob's sponge-like quality, his ability to metabolize culture, efficiently and rapidly, to break down its sugars and use them to grow. He had none of the defiant outsider energy he'd radiated in the crit, but though he chatted easily with the people there, he still seemed tightly wound, impatient.

I was starstruck and more than a little jealous. This was my platonic ideal of an artist's life, the world I wanted to inhabit. Like most students I was making do with a partitioned studio space provided by the art school, and I was living on the other side of the river in a rotten little flat with four housemates, breathing in mold from damp woodchip wallpaper and banging on the bathroom door when I was late for class in the morning. Somehow Rob had transcended all that. Once again, he was effortlessly ahead of me. I told the reggae guy I'd mostly grown up listening to New Wave and while he tried to process that, Rob leaned over and passed the joint to me.

We fell into conversation. I told him I liked his studio and he offered to give me "the tour." Though it was against the terms of the lease, Rob was living there full-time. In a little cubicle there was a showerhead rigged up to a length of hose. One corner had been partitioned into a sarcophagus-like box that enclosed a double mattress, discreetly curtained at the foot. There was a long worktable stacked with books and papers and a paint-spattered swivel chair in front of an easel. A stack of canvases had been turned to face the wall.

Later I found out that below the serene surface of the pond,

Rob was kicking his legs as hard as the rest of us, financing his life through a complicated carousel of favors, loans and credit cards. It was a rickety system that was always in danger of collapse. Within a year he would fall behind on his rent and lose that beautiful studio; I would have been distraught, but he barely seemed to notice. He was always more resilient than me, and he never minded leaving a little wreckage in his wake.

I can't remember exactly why we decided to be friends, but soon we were spending all our spare time together, cooking up a sort of double act that lasted, on and off, until well after graduation, essentially until Alice and I locked ourselves away. My relationship with Rob was always tempestuous, balanced on a knife edge of competition. There were times when we couldn't be around each other, but we always gravitated back again, falling drunkenly into each other's arms in some bar or gallery, long-lost brothers, comrades, drug buddies. We both had stamina, him more than me. I liked to get high and stay up all night, but sooner or later I'd need to sleep. Rob could start on Friday and still be going on Sunday afternoon, bug-eyed and grinding his teeth.

The thing that united us, running deeper than our taste for pranks or our compulsive need to close out every party, was painting. Though the art school we attended was famous for disdaining traditional ideas about medium and craft, we both wanted to be painters. Not artists, painters. We were in love with painting's mess and machismo, and we were young enough not to know what a cliché it all was. In the year or so after our first crit, Rob's work transformed. When he showed it to me, soon after the studio party, I had to hide a pang of disappointment. The delicate watercolorist had left the scene, to be replaced by a roistering New York School action painter, more or less preserved in amber from 1955. Rob thought of his pictures as records of his vital energies, something of that sort. He was using house paint, making big marks that he interspersed with passages of fiddly dabs and hatchings. His great goal in life was to be able to fire at his paintings with a shotgun. For a while, this was the kind of thing I was excited by too. We put canvases on the floor and rolled around. We squeezed paint out of rags and punched holes in cans and squirted it out of water pistols. At some point on every big night out, we would put our faces close together and yell wordlessly at each other, as if to confirm that we were generating energy, living in the middle of the action.

DAYS PASSED. I allowed myself to lose track of time. I would drift in and out of sleep, and when I was awake, I lay in bed, listening to the small sounds of the world; the wind in the trees, birdcalls, the various rustlings and creakings of the barn, all seemed miraculous to me, as perfect and fleeting as ripples on a pond. I ate a little. My phone was charged, but I didn't switch it on. Sometimes I would go downstairs to find a wicker basket of useful things and a note from Alice, written on a little hand-laid paper card slipped inside a matching envelope. These notes never said much. She hoped I was regaining my strength. She'd come again the next day. Once she wrote "Don't disappear!," underlining it twice. In the dusty sunlight of the attic, her fear didn't seem unreasonable. The world was soft around the edges, a reproduction of itself, yellowed and vignetted. Wherever I was, I was far away.

At night I would dream about driving through the pandemic city, but I never mistook the darkened shopfronts and deserted bridges for reality. In a depopulated Times Square, giant signs beamed unreadable messages into the silence, but I didn't slow down to read them, because I knew they weren't for me.

By the third or fourth day, I began to feel stronger. I found a plastic bucket and washed my clothes, hanging them to dry on a line I strung between the car and a nail on the barn wall. In the shower, as the thin trickle of water played over my neck and back, I felt present in my body, in that way you only ever notice when you're recovering from an illness. I wished it were possible to go for a walk. Were there really cameras in the trees? I was beginning to feel a little trapped, oppressed by the damp of the barn, the aura of neglect. I would sit near the door, looking longingly at the path leading up into the woods. I was doing this one morning, leaning against a wall, and I suppose I must have dozed off. I was woken with a start by the creaking of the door.

"What are you doing?"

Alice stood in the doorway, dressed in her running clothes, the dusty orange mask that matched the stripes on her shoes. Immediately I began to fumble in my pockets for my own mask. She waited for me to pull it on, before coming inside.

A silence began to form or congeal, thickening the air between us. There was a sadness about her, a weariness that wasn't physical.

"I brought you some things." She swung a little daypack from her back. "I feel like a spy. I've been hiding the stuff under a tree a little way from the house, so nobody sees me leaving with a bag."

"I'm sorry."

"I wasn't trying to get you to apologize. It's funny. I find it funny."

Just then we heard the sound of feet on gravel. Someone was running up the path from the lake. Alice swore and tugged at the barn door, trying to pull it closed.

"Hide," she hissed.

We both moved out of sight. The running footsteps got louder, then fainter again.

"What's she doing? I didn't know she ran this trail."

"Who?"

"Marshal's trophy girlfriend."

She peered cautiously out. "She might come back down this way, but I don't think so. There's a loop you can do round the lake."

She took a few agitated paces, and checked something on her smartwatch. I asked her if she wanted me to go. I said I was feeling better. I didn't want to cause trouble.

"Do you want to leave?"

"I can't hide in here forever."

She sighed. "There are only four of us. Rob is usually asleep on the couch in his studio. Nicole—that's the girlfriend—and I both go running, though never together, and Marshal takes walks to do his calls. That's it, in all these hundreds of acres. It seems ridiculous that you can't go outside. But Marshal says Greg has a thing about people on the property."

"Maybe he already knows I'm here."

"Marshal says he can see everything."

"Why would you stay here? How can you stand it?"

"I remember now. You never did like the idea of being watched." She shrugged. "It's so Rob can paint. Also he was scared of getting sick. I didn't want to be in the city either. All the China virus stuff. Women getting acid thrown in their faces. I didn't feel safe walking on the street."

I saw she was about to confide in me, and I wasn't sure I wanted that. Sharing intimacies with Alice felt risky, like stepping out onto an icy lake.

"So maybe Rob's in the studio making the paintings that Marshal already paid for, or maybe he and Marshal are doing coke and beating their chests. Who knows?"

Unable to find a good response, I let another pause unfurl. She sighed.

"So what I'm saying is—stay. Just fucking stay. Rob doesn't know you're here, and yes he'd have a problem with it, but right now I don't care."

"You mean it?"

"Of course I do. I lie awake thinking that I will never forgive myself if I let you leave without—I mean, you just arriving here? Out of the blue? What are the odds?"

"It doesn't seem possible."

For a moment, I saw her eyes narrow as she processed the truth of that thought. What were the odds? How unlikely was it, the three of us finding each other again? She fixed me with an appraising look. Do I really know this man? No, I wanted to say. No you don't. She smirked ruefully, and I saw what she wanted— to take a risk, to do something that had a chance of burning the house down. "OK," she said. "That's settled then." I listened to the sound of her feet as she crunched away over the gravel.

SHE DIDN'T COME BACK UNTIL the next day. Though it was already lunchtime, I'd just woken up. I'd been getting dressed, but I'd stalled, as I often did, lost in my post-Covid fog. She found me sitting on the bed in my undershorts, staring blankly out of the window.

"Oh, I'm sorry."

She must have come upstairs very quietly, or more likely I'd gone so deeply into my own thoughts that I was unaware of my surroundings. She was standing there, looking at me, her eyes narrow, as if I were a difficult passage in a book. She half-turned away, pantomiming her willingness to go back down if I needed her to.

"It's OK," I said, reaching for my mask.

"Don't put it on."

I was surprised. Masking had given her visits a sort of propriety. We remained masked and socially distant. It was a way to off-set the dreamlike strangeness of what was going on between us.

"What time is it?"

She looked at her phone. "Just after one. How are you feeling?"

"OK, I think. Better."

I couldn't meet her eye. I knew she was examining my body, its knots and scars. I felt like an epileptic triggered by a strobing light. New Alice / Old Alice, New Jay / Old Jay. Her familiarity was a small miracle. It changed time's straight line into a plane, a landscape across which, for a while, I could move in any direction. The only way to diffuse the tension was to focus on her voice, her flat international voice saying just after one how are you feeling, because if I did that I could think of her as someone I'd never met before.

"Can I take mine off?"

"I'm sorry?"

She laughed and pointed to her mask. "It seems unfair otherwise."

"Oh, sure," I said, trying to cover my confusion.

"Don't look horrified when you see my face."

I stood up. Somehow, the mood had turned formal, ceremonial. She unhooked the loops of the mask. I felt like a bridegroom.

Twenty-five-year-old Alice had chain-smoked and didn't eat or wash her hair. She would snort ketamine in the afternoons and sit on the couch in graying underwear and a tee shirt spattered with soy sauce, watching game shows on TV. Twenty-five-year-old Alice had looked pallid and soft, a nocturnal creature caught in the wildlife photographer's flash. Now the years had carved scoops into her cheeks and drawn fine lines around her mouth. There was something stern about her, something final, achieved, as if a process that had barely begun when we'd first known each other was now complete. She watched me, dryly awaiting my assessment.

"You haven't changed at all," I said.

ROB ONCE JOKED UNKINDLY THAT the song was about her, the indie pop hit about the art school girl who wants to do whatever common people do. That wasn't fair to Alice, but it was true enough for us to find it funny. Sooner or later, rich kids always told on themselves. It could be heroin, piercings, shoplifting, sex—whatever would most efficiently scandalize their parents. They were desperate to dirty themselves up, and the really rich ones always took it too far, because that's what they were in it for. Not the fun, which was easy to come by. The scars. Alice's family was wealthy and unhappy and she seemed to be studying in London to get away from her mother, who considered it acceptable for a girl to be artistic, but only in an ornamental way.

Alice should have channeled her interests into her art history course. That would have been respectable. She should have got a little job at an auction house. Instead she was lost in the East End, trying to get scars. Back then, East London was cheap. A combination of Victorian industry and the Luftwaffe had created a streetscape full of weird gaps and hidden places, alleys and railway arches, yards and courts and terraces. I remember a room at the back of a kebab shop where you could drink room-temperature beer out of cans at four in the morning, and no one batted an eyelid if you chopped out lines on the table. You might go out for the evening and end up on the wind-scoured roof of a tower block, or getting knocked off your bike into the canal by the London Fields Crew. There were pubs with lunchtime strippers, who writhed on the beer-soaked carpet, then went round with empty pint glasses to collect money. There was the junk market where, if you got up early, you could buy back the bike that had been stolen from you the night before. There was a bar in someone's front room, and a bar where you could buy drugs through a metal hatch by the cigarette machine, and a Jamaican bar with a glitterball turning over a little dance floor, where I once drunkenly allowed myself to be felt up by a pair of mature ladies who wanted to take me back to Tottenham for a coconut oil rubdown. Messy was a word we used. How was last night? Messy.

Rob and I met Alice together, at a lock-in at a Shoreditch pub. It was a ratty little mock-Tudor dive on one of the back streets, a sliver of nineteen-twenties bad taste surrounded by postwar low-rise council blocks. The landlord already knew he'd lost his lease, so he was trying to go out with a bang before the pub was converted into flats. It looked like a disreputable hobbit tavern and was usually busier after-hours than when it was legally open, which must have been hard on the neighbors.

Rob and I were trying to patch things up. We'd fallen out at the time of our degree show, and in the year since graduation, we'd seen little of each other, nodding in passing as we shouldered our way through opening crowds. When we ran into each other at a house party, we avoided talking about our careers and made each other laugh. I was reminded of why I liked him so much. Getting wasted and having an adventure was how we'd always bonded, so we agreed to meet up.

We'd spent the evening with a group of friends, I don't remember exactly who. It was a fairly typical night out, starting with a round of gallery openings and then going downhill. For some reason all the galleries had the same alcohol sponsor. Outside each one, assistants would fill enormous buckets with ice and water and bottles of the same brand of beer, and we'd drink until the buckets were empty and then move on, usually to eat cheap Vietnamese food, or to one of the bars that were beginning to open up around Hoxton Square. That night, we'd ended up at someone's place in Dalston. Rob and I weren't tired, probably because we'd been working our way through a wrap of something that had been sold to me as MDMA. It probably wasn't, but it was doing something, so when the others turned in, we mounted our bikes and wove our way through the darkened Victorian streets, in the direction of The Conqueror.

As we cycled unsteadily down the Kingsland Road, I felt my throat tighten, and the streetlights began to dazzle me. At first the landlord wouldn't let us into the pub, but then some other people left and we squeezed into a packed room of drinkers, yelling in a haze of sweat and cigarette smoke. There were one or two art kids in there, but that place didn't belong to us, or less to us than the other subcultures that coexisted with ours, the older white men with tattoos and football shirts, the bedraggled-looking girls drinking with their so-called boyfriends before they were sent back out to the railway arches behind Brick Lane. The atmosphere was volatile. Everyone was riled up on cheap triples and terrible London cocaine, snorted off keys or chopped out in the doorless cubicle of the pub's rank-smelling gents. I felt off-kilter, floaty and loved-up, not at all in the right state of mind for that pub. I was about to suggest to Rob that we leave, but I had a sort of sixth sense that something was going to happen, so I stood there, holding an untouched pint, swaying woozily in the middle of the crowd with Rob swaying woozily next to me, until we were sucked into the orbit of an argument that suddenly turned into a physical fight. A young woman was accusing a man of putting his hands on her in the crush. He told her to shut up and called her a slut, so she threw a drink at him, some of which splashed on me. Before I knew it, she was calling him a pervert in a strong French accent and he was swearing back at her in what I think was Polish, trying to throw a punch at her over my shoulder as I blocked his way. It wasn't the sort of venue that had security, but some of the regulars waded in, and about thirty seconds later Rob and I were out on the pavement, being called cunts by a man holding a length of pipe, as two of his friends chased the Pole down the street. I was high enough to have experienced the whole thing in a sort of blurry freeze frame, and I remember mumbling apologies and making pacific hand gestures until the man got bored of issuing threats.

"And take that little tart with you and all."

"Fuck off!" chirped a voice from near my feet.

"Fuck off?" growled the man with the pipe, taking a step forward. The girl stood up. Her face was hidden under a curtain of black hair and she was balancing unsteadily on a pair of white high-heeled ankle boots.

"Come on," said Rob, grabbing her wrist and trying to pull her away.

"Get your hands off me."

He didn't let go until he'd pulled her round the corner, and even then she made a lunge in the direction of the pub, as if she wanted to charge back and start throwing punches.

"Christ, just leave it."

She shouted down the street about how she'd kill him, and I looked around nervously. Soon enough some sleep-deprived neighbor was going to call the police.

"Are you OK?" I asked.

"Go to hell. I know what you two want. So go to hell, OK?"

She pulled her hair back from her face and I saw that her cheeks were flushed and she'd smeared mascara in a diagonal across her forehead. She looked like a Franz Kline. The adrenaline was making me rush on whatever I'd taken, and I peered around into the Dickensian darkness, wondering who was watching, feeling like my legs had turned to jelly. I asked if her friends were still in the pub. She was having trouble focusing. So was I.

"They left."

"I wonder why?" muttered Rob.

"Fuck you."

"How are you going to get home?"

She began to sob. "None of your business."

She turned on her heel and tottered off down the street. Instinctively I started after her, but Rob stopped me.

"Leave her. She'll be fine."

"No she won't. Look at her."

"She doesn't want your help."

"Just a minute."

I jogged after her and told her she was going the wrong way. I offered to put her in a taxi.

"I don't want to go home with you. Or your ugly friend."

"I don't mean that. There's a cab office just up there."

"I just want to go to sleep."

"Whatever. Just don't do it here."

I looked round for Rob. He was walking some way behind us, his hands shoved into his pockets. I jogged back and told him I'd walk her to a cab office. He shrugged and did a sort of pedaling mime, then turned back towards where we'd parked our bikes. I thought he was going to meet us, but he never showed up. It was the last I saw of him that night.

The cab office was on the main road, positioned between a strip club and a takeaway. Outside, drivers were leaning on their cars, cracking pistachios and throwing the shells into the gutter. They looked us up and down as we went in. The office was tiny and bare, just room enough for me to stand in front of a counter and talk to the dispatcher through a scuffed plastic screen. The girl leaned drowsily against my shoulder.

"Where are you going?" I asked her.

"Knightsbridge."

"Really?" I'd always thought of Knightsbridge as more of a store of capital than a neighborhood; I'd never actually met anyone who lived there. It was on the other side of London, an expensive ride. The dispatcher quoted a figure.

"Have you got enough money?"

She said something indistinct that I took as a yes, and I gave the dispatcher the thumbs-up through the milky plastic. He called out a name, and a driver came out of a back room. He was maybe in his fifties, a portly Bangladeshi with a ginger beard and trousers hitched up piously over his ankles. He looked at the girl skeptically.

"She sick in my car you got to pay fifty quid to clean, mate."

Sure, I said. It wasn't my problem. I'd done my duty. I was going to throw her in the back seat, find Rob and then maybe go back to his and drink or smoke my way down off whatever it was we'd taken.

"You coming with her?"

"No."

"Sorry mate. I can't take her on my own. Look at her."

I looked at her. The cab driver looked at her. It was hard to disagree. She was sagging against me, nearly unconscious. I swore under my breath.

"Can't you drive her?"

"No way, mate."

"OK," I said. "Whatever."

I pushed her into the car and went round to the other side. The driver scrutinized her, slumped in the footwell.

"I got a plastic bag in the seat pocket there."

"OK."

"You see it?"

"Yeah, I see it."

"Fifty quid."

"I heard the first time."

"You shouldn't let her get like that. It's not healthy."

"Nothing to do with me, bruv."

We headed off into the night. I looked blearily out of the window, my high beginning to fracture into tiredness. The girl seemed to be asleep. Her hair had fallen away from her face, and now that she wasn't snarling, she looked almost beautiful. I stared at her halfway across London, the drugs sending shivers through my body. I had a powerful desire to stroke her, to touch her face. Somewhere near Holborn she woke up and asked where we were going. Knightsbridge, I told her.

"Why?"

"What do you mean, why?"

"I don't want to go there."

"That's where you told me you lived."

"It's a secret," she said, and went to sleep again.

I woke her up as we rounded Hyde Park corner, and after a minute or two of grumbling, she gave an address to the driver.

A little later we pulled up outside a smart red-brick mansion block, the kind of place with topiarized shrubs flanking the front entrance. With surprising speed, she opened the car door and stumbled off. I called after her that she needed to pay, but she let herself into the building without speaking or even looking back. One minute she was sleeping beside me in the car, the next she'd gone. There was a long and significant silence. The driver examined me in the rearview mirror, one hand on his door handle.

"Don't worry, I won't do a runner."

He relaxed slightly.

"But I haven't got enough on me."

After some negotiation, he took me to a bank near Marble Arch. When I'd got some cash from the machine, he drove away, leaving me to wait in the cold for a night bus. I got home at dawn, exhausted and bitter, but still unable to fall asleep.

I DIDN'T THINK I'D SEE the drunk girl again, and I didn't really want to. She hadn't said a friendly word to me, and she'd cost me thirty quid that I couldn't afford. When I told Rob what had happened, he treated it as a huge joke. I knew she was trouble, he said. You wouldn't listen.

About a month later I was at a film screening at a venue on Hoxton Square. It was a rainy night, and I was settling into my seat, taking off my hat and jacket, trying not to drip water onto the person next to me, when a girl leaned forward from the row behind. It was a stranger, a snub-nosed blonde in a biker jacket.

"Excuse me," she said, in a thoroughbred Home Counties accent. "I know this might be a bit odd, but were you at a lock-in at The Conqueror a few weeks ago?"

"Maybe."

"My friend wants to know if you were the one who took her home."

I looked at the friend, and I saw the girl from the lock-in, or rather someone who could have been her sister or cousin. The person I'd scraped up outside the pub had been an incontinent, angry mess. This one was poised and icily beautiful, occupying her seat with a sort of infinite slouch, a posture that made her look somehow broken.

"How did you recognize me?" I asked. I was surprised she could remember anything at all.

She looked mortified. "I'd seen you before. Someone brought me to your opening at Jago Purvis."

"They did?"

"You do have a distinctive look." She made a gesture near her head. I'd started to wear my hair long, tying it up with a scarf. I'd always found it hard to allow even a touch of wildness into my appearance, but growing it out had been a relief, an end to years of hostile white barbers shaving it off because they didn't know what to do with it.

The show, which had been up at a gallery in Hoxton, was an installation, a sort of stage set made out of salvaged junk. There was a timber frame holding up a set of French doors, a couple of concrete urns. It added up to a sort of three-dimensional sketch of a patio or terrace. Behind the door was a cramped space in which, at the opening, I had stood with my back to the room, staring into a corner at a little postcard of the Thames Estuary that I'd pinned to the wall. There was a speaker hidden in one of the urns. Every so often, a female voice would echo round the gallery, saying, "It's OK, he's gone out now."

I was amazed. "Are you an artist?"

"I'm—that is, I want to be a curator."

"I'm in arts marketing," said her friend, who obviously didn't want to be outshone.

The girl took a deep breath. "I'm sorry," she said, wincing, as if the apology was costing her a lot. "I wasn't at my best."

"I hope not."

She gave me a sharp look, gauging the extent of my sarcasm. "I don't usually drink."

"I'm not judging you."

She smiled and held out a hand. "I'm Alice."

"Jay."

Jay and Alice. Alice and Jay. Alice's friend Charlotte ("call me Charlie") looked excited to be playing a supporting role in our little drama. Just then, the lights were dimmed for the start of the screening. "I'll talk to you afterwards," Alice whispered, squeezing my shoulder.

I tried to concentrate on the program, an hour of artist's video from the nineteen-eighties, smeary tapes of experimental work that required a kind of attention I wasn't able to give it. All I could think of was the pressure of Alice's hand on my shoulder, the slightly feral way she'd appraised me as we talked to each other, as if deciding whether or not to bite.

After the screening, Alice and Charlie invited me to dinner. We went to a restaurant that had opened nearby, not one of the cheap Vietnamese or Turkish places that I usually ate at, but a fancy supper club, with a DJ and a late license, a trap for the new money that had begun to flow into that part of London. We walked in past a doorman onto what looked like a set for a French house video, with underfloor checkerboard lighting, space age retro furniture and a massive chandelier hung dramatically from the ceiling. The clientele was older than us and flashily dressed, city boys stepping out of the comfort zone of the square mile, creative economy types. I felt instantly awkward, knowing that I was going to have trouble paying my way. My unease must have shown, because Alice tapped my arm.

"It's OK Jay. I invite you. I owe you for the taxi."

Charlie ordered a sickly-looking pink Cosmo. I had a gin and tonic, which came in a tall blue glass, like a cocktail in *Star Trek*. Alice pointedly drank mineral water. We talked about the films we'd just seen. It quickly became apparent that Alice knew a great deal more than I did. Almost all the artists had been new to me; she'd seen other work by several of them, and spoke about subjectivity and "the male gaze" in ways that made me feel I'd missed a lot of nuance. As she talked, Charlie nodded in an authoritative way, though she never offered any opinions of her own, and I suspected that she understood less than me.

I found Alice intimidating, and the effect was heightened by the luxuriousness of our surroundings. Though I'd walked past the restaurant many times, it belonged to a part of the urban landscape that did not figure in my geography, a zone or dimension that, being not for me, I'd subconsciously edited out. I began to fixate on my appearance. I was wearing jeans, a waterproof jacket and a dirty old pair of tennis shoes, clothes for biking to a screening on a rainy October night, and somehow my shoes became the focus for my anxiety. I tucked my feet under my chair and tried to emulate Charlie and Alice, who seemed supremely comfortable. Their ease was an aura, a diffuse light that blessed the table. As my second and third drinks worked their way through my system, I listened to Alice talk about Lacan and thought I'd never been in the presence of such perfection, the way she turned up her jacket collar, the movement of her fingers as she rolled up bread into pellets, laying out a kind of diagram on the table to illustrate her point.

After a while, she got bored of talking theory, and started a kind of flirtatious interrogation. I answered her questions as best I could, but I felt slow and clumsy, a rude peasant, lost in the enchanted wood. As I realized that she was attracted to me, and that something might even happen between us, I had a feeling like a trapdoor opening in my chest; an interior collapse, a rush of endorphins. I kept catching her eye, then having to look away.

Though I'd always looked older than my age, and my first sexual experiences had taken place when I was not quite into my teens, in most respects I was a rank outsider, and had an outsider's insecurities. I was suspicious that my faults were obvious to others, always afraid of being laughed at. In the same way that I fussed over my clothes, so as to remove a source of anxiety and distraction, I would chase after very beautiful girls, even if I didn't like them very much, even if on some deep level I didn't actually desire them, because they were the ones other people seemed to want. If they were boring or stupid, I would find a way to think of them as smart and interesting, charming them to the point where they'd sometimes give in and sleep with me. I wasn't cynical, or perhaps it would be more accurate to say that I didn't find myself cynical. I thought I was an idealist, looking for "the one." Unfortunately for my love objects, my forced interest would only take me so far. Sooner or later I'd run out of fuel, and the blimp of my romantic persona, which had been held aloft by sheer willpower, would come crashing to earth. I'd feel disgusted by myself, stop calling and eventually fade away. I'd been told on more than one occasion that I was full of shit, a user, a liar. I found these accusations very wounding. So of course Alice was one of these girls, a goddess, a moonshot, and my interest in her that night was no less shallow than my interest in a dozen other pretty art girls. I had no idea how deeply she would mark me.

Years later, long after the time when I knew Alice, when I was closer to the man delivering her groceries than the self-conscious boy at the restaurant table, I began to understand that we slip from one life to another without even realizing. There are breaks, moments of transition when we leave behind not just places or times, but whole forms of existence, worlds to which we can never return. It's hard to picture myself in that restaurant, with its slick nineties interior, raising my voice to be heard over the music. I remember drinking quickly, cracking jokes to hide my nerves. I experienced a strange teetering feeling, a sudden need to assert myself. When the first dishes arrived, I greeted them with an exaggerated yokel's delight. Alice was smiling, so I played it up, addressing each plate with a visceral growl of approval. Other diners were looking over, and I growled at them too, wafting a little menace at the well-dressed people who were cutting their eyes at me. Alice and Charlie laughed, enjoying my rude boy act, and Alice moved her chair closer to mine. She became conspiratorial, touching my arm and speaking with her mouth close to my ear, as if the music were louder than it actually was. Afterwards she paid for our meal, slipping a sleek-looking black card to the waiter. Charlie ignored the transaction, texting on her phone. It was clear that there was never any question of splitting the bill. Abruptly she announced that she had to go and meet someone. She kissed Alice on both cheeks.

"You two be good," she smirked, directing her gaze at me. Alice and I sat at the table, occupying the silence.

"You want another drink?"

"I should stop."

"So what do you want to do now?"

"Would you like to go on somewhere?"

"Not really. You?"

"No. Not really."

"Well, I don't want to go home."

So she came back to mine. My housemates were out and we had the flat to ourselves. She sat on the kitchen counter, watching as I made tea. When I brought her a cup, she put it aside and gave me a straight look. Suddenly my mouth went dry and I wanted her with a hot sick longing, wanted to inhale her, gulp her down. I battled to keep myself in check, as I always did back then, when I was young and afraid of my feelings. That's what I thought I had to do, what good men did, and I had no idea how deep they went, or where they would take me. I could feel myself tensing up, to the point where I knew I'd need to make some excuse, the bathroom, anything just to pause what was happening, and I began to dissociate into an assessment or inventory of my room, which was not tidy, not at all prepared for a woman, certainly not a woman like her, surely accustomed to luxury, to big windows and views of city lights. Nevertheless, there she was in my kitchen, among the crumbs on the counter and the dirty coffee cups, raising her face to mine, and it was now or never and I began to kiss her and she kissed me back, pushing her tongue hard into my mouth and molding herself against my chest. Wait a moment, she said, slipping off the kitchen counter. She pulled off her shirt and started to take off her jeans, an awkward maneuver that involved tugging at her boots, hopping up and down on one leg. I knelt in front of her to help, pulling the waistband over her thighs. She laced her fingers into my hair and pulled me into her until her knees began to sag and we ended up in a kind of urgent heap on the floor. Together we tumbled into the bedroom, and after that there were fits and starts and when I was inside her she made weird moans and yelping noises that seemed somehow fake, until I began to suspect that she was copying something, some porn thing she thought I wanted, and oddly that made it all better, to know that she wasn't a paragon of sophistication, that what we were doing was strange for her too, and then we were finished, a pair of young animals who by some miracle hadn't freaked each other out, panting and grinning in the dark.

We smoked a joint, lying tangled together in the sunken hollow in my ancient mattress. Gradually I heard her breathing grow deep and regular, and though my arm was trapped, I wanted to stay in the moment, in the space that had suddenly opened up, so I lay there, unable to sleep, with my arm growing numb, listening to her breathing and watching a patch of watery gray dawn light spread slowly across the wall.

How much of that came back to me as we stood facing each other in the barn? All of it, maybe. Not as a story, or even a set of images, but as a sense memory, the weight of her head on my arm, the feeling of being present, briefly, at the center of my life. So many years had passed. The dust oscillated in the sunlight. There was absolutely nothing to be done.

IN THE WEEK OR TWO after we undressed each other in my kitchen, Alice and I saw each other almost every day. It was as if a switch had been flipped. Everything else instantly receded into the background. After that first meal, we didn't go to expensive places. She didn't offer to pay for things with her black card. I'd been shown something, some part of her life, and now it had been locked away again in a drawer. She dressed, like most of my friends, in secondhand clothes. I understood that her battered leather jacket and print dresses were a kind of camouflage. If we were going to be together, I would have to respect the fiction she'd established about herself.

We always went out alone, never with friends. She never invited me to the Knightsbridge flat. Either she'd stay with me or else get a cab, saying she was tired or had things to do in the morning. I accepted that, just as I accepted her reluctance to tell me much about herself. We talked about art, about shows we'd been to see, or cultural trends that she was interested in. The first gift she bought me was an art theory book, which I pored over, underlining phrases about the reification of social relations, and spaces of intersubjective connection. There was something oblique about our conversations, something veiled, these abstractions substituting for more personal topics.

When Alice wasn't with me, I had no idea where she went or

who she saw. I began to wonder if she had another life, stranger than I knew. A gambler or a spy. Often, as I watched her heading away in the back of a cab, I suspected that there was a man waiting for her, a rich young lover, or perhaps not so young, someone she was cheating on with me. Perhaps, when she left me, she changed out of her resewn cotton dresses and went to pay off her credit card by meeting men in hotel bars. Anything seemed possible.

Alice's theory books came at a formative moment for me. I had recently stopped painting, and the change in my art practice had, among other things, led to a break in my friendship with Rob, who'd felt betrayed, as if by abandoning painting I was also abandoning him. For a while he and I had been aligned. Though we wasted a lot of time getting high and chasing girls, painting had been the shared core of our lives. Making strokes, Rob called it. Some days you made strokes, other days you didn't. When it was going well it felt almost mystical. I could lock up the studio leaving something on my easel and when I saw it again the next morning I would have no real idea how it got there. As our ideas evolved, Rob and I had grown embarrassed by our action painting antics, realizing how callow they were. I withdrew into making penitential little abstracts inspired by the landscape of the marshes near where I grew up, muted squares divided into horizontal bands of green and gray and black that I populated with spidery, shadowy verticals, secret representations of myself. Rob was still in love with color and scale, but he was moving on to an obsession with Martin Kippenberger. All his canvases had writing on them, jokes and advertising slogans, and he often painted himself, either as the main subject or some kind of onlooker, a slouching, cigarette-smoking figure in various debauched or abject scenarios, slumped on a sofa or rummaging in his underwear as he sprawled on a bed.

These paintings had been popular with the other students at

our art school, and Rob was being talked about as a rising star. He seemed happy—he'd achieved what we all wanted, the blissful dissolution of art into life, which in his case meant getting wasted and then coming back to his studio and sweating out his debauches in paint. For me it was different. As time went on I began to feel blocked. I'd get down to work and find that something about my composition looked wrong, so I'd wipe off that passage and try something else. Some mornings I started with a painting that was almost finished and by the afternoon there would be nothing left but a few smears.

There are really only two kinds of artist. You're either an intellectual or a savage, and you don't really have a choice about which. Rob was a savage, of course. He liked to approach making things in the manner of a hominid discovering tools. What you have to do, he said, is paint like you've never painted before, like you're seeing color for the first time. I did my best to emulate him, but it was no good. For me, making art was inescapably cerebral. I approached it as a problem, a puzzle that I needed to solve. I was ashamed of that. It felt like a dirty secret, a creative weakness that I had to hide.

I loved painting, but I began to feel that there was also something rotten about it, something shallow and corrupt. I hated its aura of luxury consumption, the knowledge that whatever you did, however confrontational you tried to be, you were—if you were lucky—just making another chip or token for collectors to gamble with. No one around me seemed too bothered. There was some halfhearted academic grumbling about commodification, but most artists were eager to make sales. The London artworld, which had been small and rather dull, was suddenly exploding. You couldn't help but feel excited. Rob reveled in all that, the hype, being part of a fashionable scene. I could never relax and enjoy it like he did. I always had a compulsion to push back.

When I went to shows, I found that I couldn't look at painting anymore. I tried to enjoy it, to take pleasure in color and form, but all I saw were tricks and mannerisms. The drips and spatters and faux-accidental marks seemed calculated and cynical, a way to con some collector into believing he'd bought a flame in a bottle, a trace of the artist's life force. I didn't want to make statement objects for the rich. I didn't want to be shackled to anyone's wall. Finally I admitted to myself what I was really thinking. I no longer wanted to be a painter.

My crisis came to a head about a month before my degree show, the culmination of my time at art school. Without consulting anyone, not my teachers, not Rob or any of my other friends, I destroyed the canvases that I was intending to show and began work on something new, a performance that I thought of as a farewell to painting.

I called it *Unknown Masterpiece*. For the duration of the show I stayed inside a sort of cell, a ten-by-ten cube containing a bed, food and water, basic sanitary facilities and painting materials. The cell was secure. The only way out was through a heavy door. When I went in, there was a certification procedure. I roped in the most authoritative figures I could find, including my tutor and a critic who wrote for one of the monthly art magazines. The certifiers sealed the door with an impressive-looking wax seal. Then I set to work. A camera was mounted inside the cell connected to a monitor in the gallery. It showed a view of me painting at an easel, positioned in such a way that the front of the canvas wasn't visible. Everyone could confirm that I was working, but they couldn't see what I was working on. Three days later, there was another ceremony. I took a Polaroid of my painting and passed the image out to the certifiers through a little hatch. No one but me had seen the painting, and only the certifiers saw the Polaroid. Once they had ascertained that a painting did in fact exist, signing their names to an absurdly formal document, they passed the Polaroid back to me. The feed to the monitor was disconnected and I set to work again, this time with knives and scissors, destroying both the painting and the Polaroid. I had planned on dissolving the shreds and fragments in acid, but the art school's health and safety regulations made that impossible, so I settled for submerging them in a bucket of plaster of Paris. A painting had been made, but now it only existed in my memory, and in the testimony of people who had never seen the original, just a poor-quality reproduction.

It was a refusal, a way to separate myself from all the other artists who were jostling at the money trough for a chance to dip their snouts. Instead of accumulation—of money, recognition, a "body of work," it was deliberate wastefulness, a way to expend my creativity without hope of recompense.

Rob was showing paintings, of course, meticulously copied figures from porn movies and celebrity magazines against abstract grounds of Mod targets or Union Jacks. He'd rendered these things in a deliberately mechanical style, with just a few telltale painterly spatters and drips at the edges. I thought it was terrible work, reheated sixties pop, cynically riding the "Cool Britannia" wave that was fashionable at the time. On the day of the degree show opening, as I was entering my painting cell and waving at the small crowd of onlookers like an astronaut stepping into a space capsule, I saw Rob watching me with a sour expression. He was dolled up like a court jester in a garish lime green suit and matching sneakers, ready to grab some attention and take his rightful place as a Young British Artist.

Inside the cell, I had no idea how my stunt was going to be received. I didn't expect much reaction. It was, after all, just a student show. When I came out I discovered that I'd had a stroke of luck. A famously conservative art critic wrote a weekly column for one of the London papers, in which he excoriated everything fresh and new. All the conceptualists despised him, and he despised them right back, which sold papers, because Middle

England hated conceptual art and liked to see it dragged down. He visited the degree show and mentioned *Unknown Masterpiece* as an example of the "false cleverness" and "denigration of craft" that was ruining contemporary art.

I emerged from my isolation, having painted and destroyed a mediocre self-portrait, to find I was a cause célèbre. The head of the Fine Art Department, who had never previously spoken to me, was waiting outside to offer his congratulations. That evening, as my friends spilled out into the street outside a pub on Charlotte Road, I was introduced to someone I'd seen at openings, a tweedy little man called Jago Purvis who spoke like a minor royal and wanted me to reinstall *Unknown Masterpiece* at a space he had opened a few streets away, behind Hoxton Square. He invited me to a West End member's club and to my surprise, as we talked over a meal and a very expensive bottle of wine, he told me he wasn't interested in objects but in process, in art as an activity, a form of life. Jago wanted his gallery to be radical, to oppose the status quo; in short, he said the kind of things I wanted to hear. If I showed the work with him, there would be a budget and an artist's fee. Whatever he said after that passed me by. I would be getting paid. I would no longer be an art student, but a working artist.

In theory I disdained money, at least in connection with art. Anyone could see that the most important and meaningful work had never been the most popular. The question of whether people bought what you made was—or ought to have been— irrelevant. However, like every other would-be artist I struggled with doubt. To have a commercial gallerist offer me a fee was a validation. The actual sum wasn't that much, but as a gesture it had a powerful psychological effect. We did a tremendous amount of Jago's coke in the bathroom to seal the deal, and I went home with a woman I met at the upstairs bar whose name I'd already forgotten as I stood under the shower the next morning. Rob didn't sell any of his paintings from the degree show. In fact, as I later found out, he put them away and didn't make anything else for some time.

Jago's gallery was young, but he had influential backers and a knack for getting people to come to his shows. The Jago Purvis version of *Unknown Masterpiece* was, from a commercial point of view, a success. It was reviewed in one of the big art magazines, and the remains or relics—the certificates, the broken wax seal, and the bucket of plaster—were sold to a collector. I was asked if I could do the work a third time, at a public gallery in the Netherlands, but I didn't like the idea. The first time I'd made it, the gesture had been full of meaning. I had just burned my paintings and I genuinely felt that I was leaving behind one life and beginning another. In Jago's Hoxton gallery, a shopfront between a café and a betting shop, being locked up in the painting cell seemed like a meaningless confinement. I worked on another uninspired portrait and napped on a camping mat, smelling the stink from my chemical toilet as I listened to cars driving past in the night. Performing it a third time would have been completely empty. I said no.

The show Alice saw, *He's Gone Out,* was my second with Jago, who had invited me to do a joint presentation with another artist he was representing. I remember the opening being packed, or at least sounding like it, a crowd of people moving around and socializing behind me as I stared at the postcard on the wall. By the time I turned round, everyone was long gone and I was alone in the gallery, with an uneasy sense, induced by the performance, that I had done something wrong and ought to be ashamed of myself.

I was pleased that Alice had seen my work, and nervous about what she really thought. She seemed to be impressed by me, and I didn't want her to know how precarious my identity as a "working artist" really was. The money I'd made wasn't nearly enough to live on. I was doing cash-in-hand jobs, painting and decorating, a little studio work for friends, and like everybody else I knew, I was also signing on. Once every two weeks I had to go to the Job Centre for an interview, to prove that I was "actively seeking work." This meant printing out fake application letters and talking convincingly about why my efforts to find employment weren't leading to any actual interviews. Most of the staff didn't care whether you were telling the truth. They were as disaffected as we were. There were similar hoops to jump through to get the council to pay Housing Benefit, which gave me enough to cover my share of the rent on our flat. I'd been fine with this, at least as a temporary arrangement. None of my friends had money. As we tried to organize our lives around art or music or whatever else we were doing, it didn't even really figure as a possibility, so there was no shame in being broke. Yet, as I began to go out on dates with Alice, the humiliation of being unable to pay for things weighed on my mind. As her boyfriend, if that's what I was, I felt like an imposter, a fraud.

So Alice and I made a bubble, leaving our complications outside, and what we mostly did in it was fuck. We spent whole days without leaving my bed, hiding out so we didn't have to deal with my roommates. I had a TV and a VCR, and when we were exhausted, we'd get stoned on cheap Moroccan hash, the kind with bits of plastic in it, and watch films, two or three in a row, mostly European art movies. Those films became another layer of the bubble, an image-world that enfolded us in curtained darkness, offering us the illusion that we'd penetrated to a more deeply felt level of existence. The excitement of discovering them, passed around on fuzzy second- and third-generation tapes, is hard to convey now that you can watch more or less whatever you want at any time. They taught us how to conjure romance out of our squalor, out of used condoms and full ashtrays.

One day, as we lay in bed watching *Scenes from a Marriage,* a film that was making me depressed and fidgety, she told me she had to go away to see her family in Paris.

"Is that where your parents live?"

By this time we'd been together for several months, and it may seem surprising that I wouldn't know something so basic, but the game between us had been played very seriously, and it was the first time I'd ever dared ask her a direct question about her background. I could see her wavering, deciding whether to say more.

"My mother. I won't see my father this time. He lives in the country with his wife."

"So you have a wicked stepmother."

"God, no! That woman is nothing to me."

On the television, Bergman's married couple sat up in bed, shivering on pause, their faces obscured by bands of video static. That woman, Alice explained, was her father's third wife. She was barely thirty. They'd met at a ski resort and now they were renovating a tumbledown château in the Languedoc. The details came in fits and starts. Alice sounded resigned. She clearly thought her father was making himself ridiculous. To me the story seemed like a glamorous fiction, something from one of our movies.

"He must be rich." It was a crass remark, and I regretted it immediately.

"No! He never pays for anything if he can help it."

"And your mother?"

"She lives alone in a very clean apartment in the most boring arrondissement of Paris, in walking distance from the restaurant where my grandmother has her table." I must have looked bemused. She lit a cigarette and waved it at me, an exasperated gesture. I felt like a detective who was about to receive an unexpected confession. I knew this woman in the most intimate way—her smell, the sounds she made when she came—and yet in most respects she was a stranger. "My mother was a bad girl. She ran away with my father, and it didn't turn out well for her. She had to come back and beg for mercy. So now she must show her gratitude and do as she's told. She's my grandmother's servant, basically. The old bitch just clicks her fingers and she has to obey."

None of this made much sense to me. Alice punched me lightly on the leg. "So," she said. "Now you. Where did you come from? Maybe you just dropped like a big strong boy out of the golden pussy of art?"

When I'd stopped laughing, I tried to find something to say. "No. I grew up mostly with my Nan—my grandmother."

"You have no parents?"

"My mum."

She could tell I was uncomfortable. "I want to hear about her," she said. "But only if you want to tell me."

"It's more fun to hear about your family."

"My family is no fun, I assure you."

"You just told me your father has a castle."

"It's not a castle, just an old stone house. It's pretty, though. There's a pool and a vineyard. *She* thinks it's very grand. She wants to play the great lady. For who, I don't know, it's the countryside. No one is there."

"And your father? What does he do?"

"He drinks. He has the cellar full of wine, the study with the leather-bound books, you know. Very civilized. He imagines this girl will look after him in his old age, wipe the soup from his chin."

"And you don't?"

"I'm sure she's bored already. But come on, now you have to say something. We started this bullshit family talk, it's your turn."

It was too hard to go into all the stuff about Patricia and Douglas, but because I owed her something, something real, I told her as best I could about Nan and her pots. Nan was easy to sketch for her, a sharp-faced old white lady with hair that she pushed up into a bun and fixed with whatever came to hand, a knitting needle or a chopstick, once or twice a twig. She'd been an art teacher at a local school, but by the time I was living with her she'd retired, and she spent her days in a shed at the end of the garden, listening to classical music on a slip-spattered Roberts radio and throwing squat little vessels that she splashed with muddy glazes, murky greens and browns that must have pleased her or reminded her of some good feeling that she wanted to recapture, because she never deviated from them. I loved my Nan, despite her starkness, or perhaps because of it, its steadiness, its predictability. Never did a surprise come out of her kiln, never a blue or a rusty orange to meet my eye as I knocked on the door to bring her a cup of tea. Just those browns and greens, the colors of an English forest floor in winter.

I DIDN'T COME FROM A CLOSE FAMILY. For stretches of my childhood I lived with Nan, whose neat little terraced house was governed by inflexible rules and routines, not a place where I ever felt comfortable bringing friends. My social life, such as it was, took place at bus stops, and on windy benches at the seafront. My mum was off being middle-class, in the manner of a character from one of the early-evening sitcoms she liked: gardening gloves and matching china, a strained new accent. She and Douglas (never Doug) lived in the next town over, the last one before the Estuary became the sea, at the end of a row of Victorian officers' houses near the military base where he worked, supervising artillery tests at a firing range.

Douglas was responsible for the great hollow booms that echoed over the marsh, sending the birds scattering and wheeling in the sky. He wasn't a soldier, though apparently he had wanted to be one, his dream thwarted by some kind of medical condition. He was touchy about his civilian status. If I wanted to provoke him, all I had to do was salute or call him sir when he was "dressing me down." The response to such insubordination could be violent, but Douglas knew he had to limit himself. I don't know how far he went with my mother; though cowed, she was not totally supine, at least when it came to protecting me. Those evenings—evenings after an argument—would usually end with him locked in his study addressing the bottle of Scotch he kept in the lower left hand desk drawer, the bottle I often daydreamed about pissing in, before I made my escape to one of the imaginary places I drew in my sketchbooks. My mother, who I always called Patricia, never Mum, to remind her of what she'd forfeited by choosing Douglas over me, would sit on the end of my bed upstairs and plead with me to play the game. *Your stepfather isn't a soldier, he's a scientist.* I'd answer that Douglas wasn't my stepfather. Though technically I was wrong, since he'd married my mother, it was clear to all of us that in some deeper sense it was true. For the time being Douglas was forced to coexist with me, but I played no part in his longer-term plans.

Douglas might have tried to be my dad, once upon a time, when I was little, but after the twins came along there was no place for me. I was a crack in the armor of his respectability, a living, breathing, homework-doing family secret. My real dad was black. Jamaican, reckoned Patricia, though she tended to think all black people were Jamaican. She'd met him at a soul club on Canvey Island. He was a good dancer and took photographs. That was about all she knew. She barely saw him after that first night. He did come to visit once, when I was a few months old. There was a picture of me lying in Patricia's arms. We're outside, on the pier. It's a bright day and she's squinting a little into the sun. There was no picture of him, the man behind the camera.

Douglas, it was understood, had taken my mother in as an act of charity. The trouble was that he could never actually forgive her for what she'd done. He drummed into her a sense of her unworthiness, reinforcing it with tiny reminders, winces and sighs, veiled allusions, stern glances out of the window. My presence gave him the whip hand over her, but while he enjoyed his permanent occupation of the moral high ground, he liked to remember it only when it suited him, when he had some axe to grind or point to score, not to have his wife's past under his nose day and night, tracking mud into the house, scraping its plate with its knife and fork, switching on the TV without permission and using up the electricity. When Patricia was out of earshot, he'd threaten me, whispering and baring his teeth. He had a uniform, as off-duty military as he could make it—corduroy trousers and Tattsersall check shirts, ribbed sweaters with elbow patches, brown brogues polished to a high shine. Everything pressed, everything correct. He was, in his way, a dapper man. Woolly-haired little cunt, he'd hiss. I ought to throw you in the sea.

Sometimes Douglas and Patricia would leave me with Nan, and for a few days she'd look after me. I liked being there. She was gruff but kind. I don't know how it was arranged, but when I was eleven, about to start big school, they decided that I'd stay with her for a longer time. It was supposed to be temporary, to "give everyone a bit of space," but I never lived under Douglas's roof again.

I told Alice all this, some version of it, in fits and starts, in train compartments, lying on a narrow bed in a stifling attic room in Paris. Come along, she said to me, as I was preparing to say good-bye to her for the summer. Why not? Come with me, I don't want to leave you behind. The way I felt at that moment was the way I had always wanted to feel.

I had to get a passport, which I did in secret, not wanting Alice to know that I'd never been abroad. Douglas liked to take his leisure time domestically. Rainy cottages on the Welsh borders, windswept East Anglian beaches. I will never forget the feeling of sitting beside Alice on a train as the landscape of Kent vanished into the darkness of the Channel Tunnel. The relief I felt, all the weight of England lifting from my shoulders.

THERE ARE MOMENTS THAT ESCAPE the flow, grains of memory that get left behind when everything else has drained away. Alice in her underwear, standing before a bathroom mirror, putting on makeup. I'm watching her from the bed. I'm sulking. I think I'm naked. It's hot, certainly, and we have the windows open. I can see irregular chimneys and gray zinc roofs. I hear traffic, sounds from the bistro on the ground floor. We have been arguing.

"It's not worth it." She sounds exasperated. "She'd say something hurtful to you and I wouldn't be able to bear it."

Around this scene very little remains. I can't recall much about the room, or anything else that we said or did beforehand. Just an image, less clear than it once was, its lines cruder and more stylized. Alice standing on tiptoe, her calf muscles tight, leaning in to the mirror to apply mascara, turning her head to look back at me.

Before we left London, Alice told me how it would have to be. It didn't seem like a sacrifice not to meet her family; in some ways it was a relief. She had a friend who was away. We could use her apartment. We'd stay there together, unless Alice's mother insisted that she stay with her, in which case I'd have to sleep on my own. Whatever happened, we'd be together most of each day. After Paris we'd decided—or rather she had decided, and I'd tried to hide my excitement—that we would travel on somewhere else, perhaps to Spain, or to pay a surprise visit to her father in the country. It would be OK for him to meet me. He'd find it funny that she was sneaking around behind her mother's back. In Paris, with the Vietnamese side, it was different. No one could know about me.

I didn't ask why I had to be a secret. It was a conversation I didn't really want to have. She swore it would have been the same with anyone. She wasn't supposed to have boyfriends; it was a condition of studying away from home. One hint of impropriety and her grandmother would send one of her uncles to fetch her back. I promised not to make waves. I felt lucky to be going with her at all, more than lucky: a lottery winner, a man saved from drowning.

Paris was lonelier than I'd expected. Alice's mother wouldn't hear of her daughter staying anywhere but under her roof, and for several days we barely saw each other. For the first time in my life I was alone in a foreign city. I had planned to go to museums and galleries, to commune with all the famous pictures. I had a sketchbook, a camera, everything was ready, but I found I didn't want to look at art, so I killed time, sitting by the river and drinking on café terraces, working my way through an envelope of hundred-franc notes that Alice had given me under the face-saving fiction that I hadn't had time to change money. I felt free and light, but far away from Alice, disconnected from whatever Parisian life had claimed her.

She finally found a way to stay the night, some elaborate story for her mother, and I planned a romantic dinner. I cooked pasta, lit a candle. But she was late, and by the time she arrived, she'd already eaten, so we went straight to bed, leaving the meal congealing in the pan. We fooled around halfheartedly, but she was exhausted; I lay awake, stroking her hair, listening to her breathing. I hoped we'd have a leisurely breakfast. Pastries and orange juice, the *International Herald Tribune,* like a scene from one of our movies. Instead, I woke up to find her out of her bed, swearing and looking for her bra.

She was dressing to go out to Mass, then on to a family lunch. I remember I wanted her to come back and lie next to me on the bed. I knew that once she'd dressed, the visor would come down and she'd have no further use for me until she returned from battle. I didn't want to be on my own for another day, so I asked if I could go with her. I proposed some absurd plan, told her that we could pretend that we just ran into each other. I would be a friend, someone she knew from art school.

She told me I didn't understand her mother. I didn't know what I was getting mixed up in. I should stay out of it. Explain it to me, I said. She said she didn't have time. She was late already and her grandmother didn't like people to be late. Was it me, I asked. Was it me in particular, something about me? She swore under her breath, and her face crumpled. *It's not worth it. She'd say something hurtful to you and I wouldn't be able to bear it.*

The words, then the dress: I watched her unhook it from the hanger and step into it, an expensive gray cocktail dress that she had carried from London in a garment bag. She had a jacket to go over it, a set of pearl studs and a matching pearl necklace. I had never seen her wear such conservative clothes. It was disorienting to watch her execute her transformation.

"My drag," she said, trying to make a joke of it.

While Alice was out that day, I missed her excessively, irrationally, stalking around the little apartment, hating the way I was feeling—like a dog waiting for its owner to come home. She returned early in the evening and I tore off her gray dress at the door and she clung to me in a way that felt somehow desperate, off-kilter, her needy energy matching my own. We clawed at each other as the long summer shadows fell across the bed and afterwards we sat naked at the little square table, sheened in sweat, gulping down wine and refilling our glasses until the very last sharp edges had been smoothed away. I watched a red allergic flush grow on her face and neck as she lit a cigarette and described for me how it had been at Mass, everyone performing their piousness for her grandmother, putting on their most ecstatic faces as they went up to take communion. At lunch, they'd all flattered the old woman, talking about how healthy she looked, how full of energy. They mentioned their children's achievements, trying to melt her heart. Alice put on a high, whiny voice. *See, they've composed a little song for you, Bà. Charles has found a bakery that sells those pastries you like.* Then she lowered her head and folded her hands in her lap, showing me how they had all sat quietly as her grandmother spoke, going round the table and reminding each person of his or her shortcomings. This was normal, apparently, almost a ritual. No one could talk back to her, though she'd say terrible things. One aunt was told that she ought to consider plastic surgery. An uncle who'd suffered a financial setback was called a fool, a failure.

"What are your shortcomings?"

"I take no care of my appearance so I'll never attract a man. I have a bad-tempered face and I should wash it more often because my skin is less clear than my sister's."

"She's a monster."

"You have no idea. She even blames my mother for my grand-father's death. He had cancer. She holds his cancer over her. She brought it up today. She said my mother gave my dad cancer with the trouble she caused, and everyone was very careful not to look at my sister and me."

I still didn't understand why the grandmother was so powerful, why they didn't just ignore her. Alice said that if I was going to make her explain her family, she would have to be high. We lay down on the bed and as I rolled a joint, she told me how her great-great-grandfather had bought some kind of mine, an emerald mine, she thought it was, up in the mountains in an area that later became part of China. He got rich and moved his family to the Vietnamese imperial capital, where he began to buy other businesses. As rich industrialists and devout Catholics, his sons became close to the French colonial authorities, but after the war and the Japanese occupation, the family shifted allegiance and became supporters of the Nationalist government. There was a coup, and the president was assassinated. Without his protec-tion, things became dangerous for them. One uncle, a senior offi-cial, was murdered. Alice's grandfather and grandmother fled to Paris, taking their daughters with them.

In Paris, Alice's mother grew up in a milieu of wealthy Viet-namese émigrés who sat around in each other's immaculate living rooms, grumbling about communism and devising schemes to retrieve their lost assets. She was the youngest daughter and the family rebel. Her parents sent her to boarding school and tried unsuccessfully to shelter her from the corrupting spirit of the times. Believing in the rumors she was hearing about freedom, she ran away with a hippie boy she met when he was busking on one of the quais. This was Alice's father. He wasn't a real hippie, just the mildly bohemian son of an haute-bourgeois family, sowing his wild oats before taking up a career. Later Alice showed me a picture of the two of them at some villa on the Côte d'Azur, her mother in a tight ao dai, her father wearing a floral pattern shirt and white linen pants, sitting together on a big cane chair, beautiful people of the nineteen-seventies. They lasted a few years, long enough to have two children, Alice and her older sister Carine. Then they broke up.

Never having worked, and with no idea how to go about finding a job, Alice's mother was forced to throw herself on the mercy of her parents. Her father was sick, and her mother demanded abject surrender. She had disgraced the family by her elopement, and again by the production of two Eurasian children, but worst of all by her divorce, which put her in a state of mortal sin and prevented her from receiving the sacraments.

"Are you scared of your grandma?" I asked, as we lay in bed. We were whispering, like children talking about a witch.

"Probably less than the others, because I don't want anything from her. If she disinherits me, it would be a relief."

"Why? If you have money you can do what you want."

"They're ashamed of me, but that doesn't stop them wanting to control my life. They're just waiting for me to finish at the Courtauld, then my mother will marry me off. She has a list of boys at the back of her planner. She thinks that if I marry a Vietnamese husband, her stain will wash out. In a generation or two it will be as if it never happened."

"I won't let them."

"What?"

"Make you marry a Vietnamese boy."

"And how will you do that?"

WHEN IT WAS TIME FOR us to leave Paris, Alice's mother insisted on seeing her off at the station, so she had to join the line for the Eurostar to London, then slip away to meet me on another platform. Even after the train had pulled away, it was a while before either of us could relax. The stress had built up and we had some kind of petty fight that left us unable to speak to each other for the first hour or two of the journey.

Those few days had shifted something in a way that wasn't healthy for either of us. It was as if I osmosed her unhappiness, made it part of myself. After that, our roles were set. We were star-crossed lovers, fleeing across Europe, looking soulfully out of the window at the flying countryside as we pondered the unsolvable problems of our lives. We were still obsessed with each other, but almost imperceptibly a cage was dropping down over our relationship, a tragic and mournful tone that we somehow willed into being, its filaments meshing together, hardening and growing, until eventually we found ourselves trapped.

On the train, the hours passed. We ate sandwiches. I made sketches and Alice wrote notes in the margins of a formidable-looking book. Eventually we wedged ourselves into the tiny bathroom at the end of the carriage and crushed and snorted some anti-anxiety pills that she'd taken from her mother's medicine cabinet. Back in the compartment we collapsed against each other, feeling as if we were wrapped in cotton wool, oblivious to the disapproving stares of the middle-aged couple sitting opposite. We were shaken awake by a ticket collector, and eventually got out at a tiny country station, with flowers in hanging baskets and a dog sleeping on the platform. Alice looked around groggily, turning in a slow arc as if searching for something. I asked if we were in the right place. She nodded and said she needed to phone her father to say we were there.

Dizzy and dry-mouthed, I sat at a little metal table outside a bar, while she used the pay phone. The waiter brought us fat-bellied bottles of Orangina. Our bags—my backpack, her sleek hard-shell case—sat beside us in the dust. She came back out and we smoked cigarettes and waited in the shade, watching the fierce sun beat down on the war memorial in the square. "Jay," she said. "Don't expect too much from him. And whatever you do, don't take him seriously."

"You think he won't like me."

"I don't know. She'll like you. It will make her feel very liberal."

"What will?"

She looked embarrassed and squinted into the distance to see if a car was coming. "He'll turn up eventually. He's one of those people, you always have to wait."

In the event it was Alice's stepmother who came to fetch us, waving out of the window as she puttered to a halt in a rustic Deux-Chevaux. Isabelle was an ample woman in her thirties, bursting with social energy. She seemed old to me at the time, part of another generation. She swept towards Alice and they executed some restrained cheek kissing. Isabelle was wearing some kind of long tie-dye robe, very colorful, red and orange. It was funny to see angular Alice enveloped in her embrace, like a swizzle stick in a tequila sunrise.

I folded myself into the front passenger seat and Alice sat in the back with the cases as Isabelle drove us to the house, firing questions at Alice, who put on her dark glasses and responded in monosyllables. Eventually Isabelle got bored and turned her attention to me, asking me about myself in eccentric English. She turned the little car into the driveway and we got out into the scent of herbs and pine resin, the buzz of insects. I looked up at white limestone walls and a row of shuttered windows.

"Cherie!"

Alice's father appeared from the side of the house, wearing a robe, a battered straw hat and tiny yellow briefs, over which a prosperous belly jutted forth like the prow of a dinghy. Alain carried himself with a preening unselfconsciousness I associated with men of his generation, the stallions of the nineteen-seventies. He wore his graying hair long, and his deep tan was set off by a grizzled mat of chest hair. He was friendly, almost as effusive as his wife, shaking my hand and bidding me welcome. It didn't seem to matter that Alice had arrived out of the blue, with a boy in tow. We sat outside by the pool, under a vine that had been trained across a trellis to provide shade. Isabelle made everyone strong Campari sodas and Alain told us about his plans to build a guesthouse on some land further down the hill, the family all politely conversing in their second language to accommodate me. Later we ate dinner, a casual meal that seemed all the more sophisticated for being unplanned, thrown together from the contents of the fridge. I was charmed by Alain and Isabelle, though I could feel Alice's resistance, her unfriendly scrutiny as I laughed at Alain's jokes.

"So, an artist? I always think my daughter will make the perfect muse."

"I'm not a piece of meat, Papa,"

"Of course not. Who said so?"

I wanted to tell him that he should take his daughter seriously, that she was the smartest person I knew, but I didn't. It seemed easier not to antagonize him, so I laughed foolishly and that night Alice turned her back on me in the narrow bed and I lay there, miserable, irradiated in the cold field of her anger.

MY STRONGEST MEMORIES OF ALICE'S father's house are of the pool. It was tiled a vivid turquoise, barely chlorinated, its surface speckled with insects. At night, bats would swoop down to drink from it, black shapes skimming fast and low. I swam lengths, back and forth, twenty, thirty, forty at a time. I had never stayed in a house with a pool before. To glide underwater and then surface to see pines and the back wall blazing white in the sunlight held a value for me that is hard to convey to someone for whom such experiences are ordinary. Swimming had always meant a cold English sea, or the mob scene of the municipal baths. That pool, in retrospect quite unremarkable, even shabby, is enshrined in my memory. As I swam back and forth, Alice would lie on a lounger and read. Sometimes she was joined by Isabelle and Alain and I would pull myself out onto the side, my heart pounding to find all three of them, still as lizards, watching me as if I were giving some kind of performance.

We stayed for two weeks, and gradually wore out our welcome. One day we borrowed the car to drive to a nearby river, and Alice ran it over a rock, which damaged the steering. We stayed up late and woke up late, which irritated Isabelle, who didn't like to find us rummaging around in the kitchen at odd hours. One night I found myself sitting outside with Alain, who had opened a third bottle, and wanted company. Around us, the insects were making a racket. The night was fragrant. I felt good, confident of my place in the world. I had privately decided that Alice's judgment of Alain was overly harsh. He was, she had warned me, a cynical man. He'd expected to live off Alice's mother, who had been brought up like a princess, and was dismayed to find that her family disapproved of their relationship quite as much as his own. Such immigrants, though not exactly "boat people," ought to have been overjoyed to see their daughter moving up in the world. Instead Alice's grandfather had made it clear that in order to win the approval of his in-laws, Alain would have to make something of himself, which was precisely what he had hoped to avoid. When the expected funds were not forthcoming, he packed his bags.

Seduced by his charm and sophistication, I saw none of this. That evening he decided he wanted to show me his collection of African masks, and took me into his study, where they were hanging on the wall. He had, he said, been on a jeep tour of the Dogon country with his second wife. Very good memories. He had not found the people primitive at all. Alice had mentioned the second wife, whose father sat on the board of one of the big French banks. Her money had allowed Alain to embark on a haphazard career of investments and business ventures. After some years of turmoil and a second divorce, Isabelle had entered the picture and whisked him off to the provinces. The Dogon masks had long faces, with slits and circles for eyes. They stared down at us judgmentally.

"So," he said, making his way round the desk. "Alice says you are African, a little bit."

"My dad was Jamaican."

"Ah yes. Bob Marley."

"I didn't grow up there."

"Maybe this is why your skin is so white."

"I should go to bed, Alain."

He waved away this suggestion. "Tell me, you like my daughter?"

I said that of course I did. He nodded, and put out a hand to steady himself on the back of a chair. He was drunker than I'd thought.

"Is she good?"

"What do you mean?"

"I always wondered. I look at her, I can't decide. Maybe she is a little cold."

I wasn't sure that I was understanding correctly. He slapped me heartily on the back.

"Come on, you can tell me. We are men."

I didn't know what he wanted. To provoke a reaction, maybe.

"She looks like her mother, you know. When she was young.

That girl's pussy was so tight. It was like being, you know, in a fist."

He grinned at me, showing his teeth, and I saw something truly debauched in his face, something I didn't want to confront. I walked out. The last I saw of him he was sprawled on his office chair, staring at his hands, turning them over, the palms, the backs, as if looking for something.

Upstairs, in the tower, I told Alice I wanted to leave. I didn't say why, but she seemed to sense that something had happened. The next morning, Isabelle drove us to the station. The atmosphere in the car was frosty. She let us know in small ways that we had disappointed her. We weren't the smart young people she had hoped for. Alain hadn't appeared to say goodbye. He was feeling unwell, Isabelle said. He needed to rest.

I THOUGHT TRAVELING TOGETHER HAD sealed something, but when we arrived at St. Pancras, Alice said she was going back to Knightsbridge to sleep. I watched her wheel her case down the platform towards the taxi rank, then sat on the tube, heading in the other direction, wondering if I'd done something wrong.

When you fall in love young, you imagine that the object of your desire is both finite and infinite, a magical and unfathomable creature who you will also be able to know completely. I wanted to crack Alice open like a geode, to expose all her crystals, her stars. It was hard to accept that she had anything in her life that didn't concern me; it made no difference that I was hiding parts of my life from her. I'd missed my signing-on date, and my money had been stopped. It had been fun to have her hundred-franc notes in my pocket, but that wasn't my reality. I spent a morning staring at a worn patch on the carpet of the dole office, waiting to be seen. I told the man some story. I'd been ill. No, I didn't have a doctor's note. He stared at me through his smudged glasses and tugged at his tie. It was exhausting, grubbing around for money, and I didn't want Alice mixed up in it. She belonged to something else—train windows, the azure blue pool—something precious that I wanted to protect from contamination. So although I imagined some kind of total union between us, I felt I had to defer it until I could show myself in my true colors, like the pauper who reveals at the end of the story that he is actually a prince.

Despite my worries, that year we were at our best. We started going out, wafted on a discreet current of Alice's money. I met her friends and she met mine. That was when people would run our names together, when we'd receive joint invitations to openings and house parties, before we locked ourselves away. I had a friend with a studio on the top floor of a building on Regent's Canal. We would go up onto the roof and look out at London's future and its Victorian past, the skeletal gas holders by the towpath, the distant clusters of bank buildings in the Docklands and the City. We spent a lot of time at a bar in the basement of an electrical appliance store. You went through a display of fridges and dishwashers and down a flight of stairs. It was always loud and packed, and no one cared if you were in corner making out or doing drugs. One night we were on the dance floor, spangled in some kind of disorienting glitterball lighting, and my vision began to behave strangely, flipping on and off like a shutter effect in a movie. Alice was grinning at me and I was yelling at her that I loved her. She cupped her hand over her ear and shrugged, pretending she couldn't hear a thing.

The East End artworld was small in those days, and clustered tightly. There were three or four pubs that "everybody" went to and dozens more that they didn't. In one of the chosen pubs, the landlady, Sandra, had a coterie of favorites, mostly well-known young artists, who she'd fuss around with trays of snacks. One night we ran into Rob in the saloon bar. Apparently he was one of the few, for though it was a Friday night and the pub was full of people, he was holding court at a table by the fire, making conversation with some other local faces over a plate of cocktail sausage rolls.

The landlady shooed some other people off their chairs, and we joined Rob's table. I made the introductions and he looked Alice up and down. Outstanding, he said, nodding approvingly. I could see that Alice found him offensive. Almost immediately, another man leaned forward and engaged her in conversation. I went to the bar so I didn't have to listen to him flirt.

I was getting used to the particular challenges of being with Alice. Wherever we went, there was always some sullen boy shooting her unhappy looks and trying to take her outside for a conversation. Even in sweatpants, with unwashed hair and a cigarette in her mouth, men turned to watch her or catcalled her on the street. Alice moved through the world as a promise and a disruption, and for me, barely out of my teens and possessed of a sort of chivalric high-mindedness, it was both thrilling and threatening to be her man, the one expected to care enough about the other men but not too much, to manage all those reactions. "Don't worry about him," Alice would say, when she'd disengaged herself from some admirer. So I wouldn't, or at least I'd try. I tried to trust her, and—what was harder—myself, to feel sophisticated and a little blank, like a character in a New Wave film.

"Your friend thinks I'm a bitch, by the way."

Later that night, we were eating at a Turkish café in Dalston.

"Rob? No. Why would he?"

"Because I didn't laugh behind my hand and bat my eyelashes. He's impressed with you, though. He thinks you did well to pull such a—how you say—a fit bird."

"No. He's not like that. He's OK, honestly. It's just his manner."

"Will you tell him what it's like to fuck me?"

"No, of course not."

"Why not?"

"I'm sorry. I don't want you to feel . . ." I hunted for the right word. "I'll tell him not to mess around with you. I don't like it."

"But you don't mind that he's jealous."

"You're with me. It's not important what he thinks."

Another night Alice and I walked into Sandra's pub, to find Rob telling a dramatic story to a group that included a big gallery artist whose work was selling for hundreds of thousands of pounds. She was laughing at whatever it was he was saying to her, twisting up her mouth in a crooked smile. I nodded to a couple of other friends. At the far end of the bar was Jago, nursing a pint and a large brandy. "What happened to him?" Alice asked.

I shrugged. Whatever it was, it didn't look good. He had a black eye, and his face was bruised and puffy. A grubby dressing was taped over the bridge of his nose.

Jago and I had become friends, in a way that went beyond our relationship as artist and gallerist. He and I had recognized something in each other. We were both strivers, always afraid that we'd end up back where we came from. Jago's cut glass accent and fogeyish style, signals in the complex semaphore of the English class system, were not as straightforward as they seemed. He let everyone think he was a toff, slumming it in the East End. Actually he was a lower-middle-class boy who'd attended a minor public school on a scholarship, and his Brideshead persona was backed by nothing more substantial than a couple of tweed suits and a winning manner. His conservative presentation masked something wild and self-destructive, a darkness that I shared. We would sit up late in his tiny studio, propped up on cushions round a low coffee table, doing drugs and talking about art, or sometimes just doing drugs, doggedly trying to get as high as we could on whatever was to hand. He'd painted the whole place a shade of light gray. Walls, floorboards, even the ceiling. It was a rule of his never to live with any object that he didn't find beautiful, and what little money he had went into the gallery, so as a consequence he had very few possessions. It was an oddly double existence, a rigorous, almost Spartan life that included every kind of excess.

I clapped him on the shoulder. "What happened to you?"

I saw that he was several drinks deep. He was slouched purposefully against the bar, as if determined to hang on as long as possible.

"Oh, hello Jay. You know, fell down the stairs."

"Did you get mugged?"

He nodded. "Down by the railway arches."

"What on earth were you doing over there?"

He tapped the side of his nose. "Loose lips sink ships. Let's just say it was a pleasure, up to that point."

"Are you OK, though?"

"Oh, absolutely, old chap. Wounded pride. By the way, if you're looking to see a man about a dog, he's over there."

He pointed out an older drinker in a Crombie coat, talking to another man near the door. They both looked vaguely familiar. I wasn't going to pass up the opportunity to score, but at that point I remembered that, as usual, I didn't have any money. Alice gave me her bank card and I went off in the direction of Liverpool Street station, where there was a cash machine.

Sandra took a dim view of dealing in her pub, so Crombie and I went for a little walk. When we came back, Alice told me she wanted to go home.

"Are you sure? I mean, I just got all this gear."

"You and Jago don't need me tonight."

We went outside to look for a taxi. Almost instantly, her magic powers conjured one out of the night. She kissed me and hopped in. As I went back into the pub, I realized she'd slipped her card back into my pocket.

That night, cross-legged around Jago's Noguchi coffee table, we got to the stage where we were rolling our eyes and grinding our teeth, and our conversation degenerated into rants and disjointed exclamations. Jago had a theory that to get ahead in the artworld you had to be an actor.

"The thing is, old chum, I can tell who I'm playing, but I can't with you."

"I'm not playing anybody."

"Stuff and nonsense. You just don't want to admit it."

He kept on—such and such was a romantic lead, so and so a jester—and to change the subject, I asked him about the mugging.

"Did you see who it was?"

"No. I think he hit me with a brick. Someone found me and called an ambulance."

"Jesus, Jago."

"Oh I'm all right. They took some pictures, put me in one of those contraptions, you know, a big metal tube, to see if there was any swelling."

"How long ago was that?"

"A few days. Apparently I was lucky he hit me in the face, rather than the back of the head. My poor old nose protected me from brain damage."

"Should you really be doing all this powder?"

"Now you say it, they did tell me to go easy for a while."

"Jago. What were you doing down there? Were you drunk?"

"Well, yes, obviously."

"And you were just wandering around?"

"If you must know, I was getting what's known as a lick and a suck."

It was, he explained, a sort of package deal. For twenty quid you got a hit on a crack pipe and a blowjob. I was at a loss for words. Jago had a sort of dirty mac vibe, but I thought it was ironic, part of his schtick, like betting on the dogs or eating his breakfast every day at the same greasy spoon on Bethnal Green Road. I knew he was a regular at one of the lunchtime strip pubs on Brick Lane, and carefully stored in an archive box in his living room was a collection of vintage pornography, but that didn't make him any different to a dozen other artists I knew. I used to defend Jago when women said he was sleazy. I'd tell them he was very shy, that he had problems making relationships. Despite his charm, there was something blocked about him, something furtive and arrested. He wasn't a bad-looking man, and plenty of women would have been interested, but somehow he found all that impossible. He claimed that the reason he slept with prostitutes was that he didn't have to feel ashamed for asking someone to touch him.

"Why, Jago? Why not just have a girlfriend?"

"School," he said, as if I ought to understand.

I CAN SEE IT, wafting through the years, hanging in the air like the smile of the Cheshire Cat. Rob's expression as he watched Alice upstairs at Fancy Goods. The hint of desire that crept around the corners of his mouth, the ground shifting under my feet.

We were deep into one of those grim London winters, when the light fails in the middle of the afternoon and the city seems as if it's blanketed in despair. Alice had gone to Paris for the Christmas holidays and I'd been spending a lot of time brooding, wondering if she had someone over there, some ex-lover, an imaginary charmer that I pictured as the actor Jean-Pierre Léaud, irritating star of many of the French films we'd watched together. One freezing day, I was cycling down Hackney Road, sprayed with water by passing cars, when someone shouted my name. Rob was wrapped up in a massive but rather grubby down jacket. He had the look of a disreputable polar explorer. Enfolding me in a bear hug, he told me he had something special he wanted me to see and asked me to meet him later at an address on the canal.

It was already getting dark when I turned down a side street, my bike juddering over patches of old cobble. Following Rob's directions, I found a small factory of the kind that used to be everywhere in that part of London, from the time when workers turned out textiles and ironwork, glass and rubber goods, all the myriad requirements of the Imperial metropolis. Deindustrialization had emptied out most of those buildings, and though many of them were being converted into studios or lofts, some still lay empty, providing shelter for various marginal activities. This one looked unpromising. Blackened by a couple of centuries of soot, it slumped over the water, walls bowed out, the ground floor windows boarded up with mildewed particle board. Against the wall was an old bedframe and a pile of rubble. A wooden sign above the door had partly rotted away, making the proprietor's name illegible. You could just read the phrase FANCY GOODS.

In front of the building lurked an enormous pothole filled with muddy water. Someone had laid a plank across. I wheeled the bike over this makeshift drawbridge and shouldered open the door. Inside, the only illumination came from a standard lamp, the kind that usually sat in people's front rooms, a wooden pole topped with a pinkish tasseled shade. In this weak circle of yellow light, a long-haired man in overalls was attacking the uneven cement floor with an angle grinder, making sparks fly out into the darkness. As I propped the bike up against the wall by the door, Rob shuffled out of the gloom, wearing a headlamp and staggering under the weight of two black plastic sacks full of building waste. I took one from him and we dumped them on the pile outside.

"What do you think?" he said. "Isn't it beautiful?"

Rob was squatting the building with some other artists, none of whom I knew. They'd broken in, then made some kind of deal with the landlord, promising that whenever he wanted to start redevelopment, which was not scheduled for at least two more years, they would get out. In the meantime, he'd agreed to leave them alone. The plan was to live on the top floor and use the other two floors to mount shows. Rob showed me round with an almost comical pride. It smelled of decaying wood and canal water. Long fingers of freezing air seeped in from outside, hovering over the icy concrete. He led me up a creaky flight of stairs with gaps in the treads and a missing handrail that had been crudely repaired with a timber plank. On the two upper floors, steel-framed windows pierced the walls. The windows were filled with scuffed glass bricks, murky with decades of city grime, and the daylight that filtered through was no more than an anemic glow. You can get up on to the roof, Rob said, if you climb carefully.

I was spending vacant hours in my studio, listening to music and doing unsatisfactory drawings, diagrams really, abstract maps that all ended up being about Alice. I had an idea that I could make a sort of schematic of our relationship, transforming its amorphous emotions into something comfortingly technical. I knew I was being self-indulgent, but somehow it suited me to pine for her. I wanted to rot, to smoke in bed and think mournful thoughts as I waited for her to come back, but there was only so much lying around I could stand. While Alice was in Paris, I ended up spending much of my time at Fancy Goods with Rob, helping to repair the broken staircase, chipping away at the ragged ribbons of pigeon shit that were caked across the floorboards upstairs, the signature of generations of birds that had roosted on overhead pipes and ducts. I spent New Year's Eve sitting round a gas heater with Rob's friends. We got drunk, and for an evening I imagined we might turn into one of those legendary art collectives; one day I would be a face that young artists pored over, in the way that I pored over faces in old group photographs of Surrealists or Situationists, trying to divine what it must have felt like to be in some kind of remarkable creative fellowship with others.

When Alice came back, she was curious about how I'd been spending my time, and I took her over to Fancy Goods to see. I expected her to find it all too dirty and disorganized, which shows how little I understood her. As she watched Rob and his friends unloading sheets of drywall from a flatbed truck, her eyes sparkled. At once she got involved in a conversation about the utilities. The plan was to hang track lighting from the beams downstairs, but the only electricity was coming from a dubious hookup into a building next door and it kept cutting out. When this happened—if someone tried to use a power tool, or plugged in Rob's toaster oven—you had to break in, which involved crossing over on the roof and letting yourself down through a skylight to reset whatever fuse had tripped. To my surprise, Alice told them she could help. And she did. Somehow, within the constraints of our tiny budget, she found two Polish guys to rewire the place. One of them, Filip, became the regular Fancy Goods technician, part of the group that hung around cooking big pots of pasta on the gas ring. Filip and his friend, whose name disappeared from my memory years ago, strung cable through the building, giving each floor a few outlets. Alice also solved the trickier problem, persuading the electricity company to restore supply, so our new wiring could run straight from the mains. Our installation wasn't pretty—or legal—and it wouldn't have withstood any great strain, but at least we could use a drill without plunging the place into darkness.

Alice even sourced some secondhand track lights. I borrowed a friend's van, and together we went to pick them up from an industrial estate out along the Thames Estuary, near where I grew up. It felt strange to see Alice against that familiar flat landscape, the fields and marshes and red-roofed housing developments. I remember the seller flirted with her and made her tea in his office while I loaded the lights. Back at Fancy Goods, Filip and his friend rigged them up, and suddenly the dungeon-like ground floor became a place where you could imagine showing art. Alice became the heroine, the Marianne, the Joan of Arc.

There was something very deliberate about the way she threw herself into the life of the Fancy Goods collective. She would take on the worst jobs, the ones that other people tried to avoid.

She sat on the phone and begged materials from builders and art supply companies. When the landlord turned up, she made him coffee and sent him away happy, promising that he'd give three months' notice if he needed to take possession.

I worried that she was being exploited, and told her that—in my opinion—she was doing more than her fair share; I received a typically Alice answer, a worked-out theoretical position that seemed only tangentially related to what was actually going on. Art, she said, was about social relations as much as objects, much less (a phrase she coated with such disdain that it stuck in my mind) retinal pleasure. Galleries and studios were places of experiment, where artists could do something that she seemed to think of as a kind of social repair, a way to renew the bonds between people through shared experience and the giving of gifts. She wanted Fancy Goods to be a kind of utopian laboratory. It was a vision I found moving, though I wasn't sure that Rob's group of lads would be interested in putting it into practice.

I was pleased that Alice and Rob were becoming friends. It now seems foolish that I would push them together, but I almost demanded they get over their initial dislike. That year, the three of us spent a lot of time together. I remember a picnic on one of the beaches on the south coast. Rob drove us down there in a borrowed car, stealing glances in the rearview mirror as Alice and I fooled around on the back seat. Complacently I thought of myself as the hinge, the fulcrum about which our little system turned.

The weather grew warmer. With some lubricant oil and a crowbar, we managed to force open the upstairs windows, stirring up the stale winter fug with a trickle of fresh air. Rob got a residency, and while he was away, Alice and I lived in his room. The squat had to be occupied at all times, in case the landlord changed his mind, or some other group decided to try and take it over. The other person who normally stayed there was also traveling, so we agreed to hold the fort. It was our first experience of cohabitation.

Rob had covered the walls of his room with dark red flock wallpaper that he'd bought at Brick Lane Market. It was, he said, the stuff they used to sell to Indian restaurants. He'd made a sort of stage set, with old-fashioned lamps and thrift store seascapes that he had overpainted with his own figures. It seemed like an adventure, sleeping in Rob's gaudy room, but I'd underrated the strangeness of being alone at night in such a large and noisy old building. The only toilet was all the way downstairs, an epic journey through primal darkness. Rob kept an iron bar by his bed. More than once I woke up groping around for it, thinking someone had broken in.

The creaks and groans and rattlings would have been easier to get used to if they weren't mingled with other sounds, the scurrying and rustling of rats. When we woke up, we often had to clean feces off the table and the gas ring before we could make tea. Eventually someone got a rescue cat, a grizzled old ginger tom, and for a while the situation improved, but the cat got run over, and within a week the rats were back, chewing through wrappers and plastic bags, scratching and chittering overhead as I tried to sleep. I was relieved when Rob returned.

THEN IT WAS MY TURN to go away. I had a show at a public gallery in Vienna, my first outside the UK. I was excited, and I hoped Alice would come with me, but she said that there were too many things to do at Fancy Goods. The trip to Vienna turned out to be important, not for anything that happened there, but because of the journey itself. I'd never been in a plane, and I didn't feel ready to fly. I wasn't afraid, exactly, and later on I did fly without incident, but foreign travel was still very new to me and I wanted to experience it physically, to feel the changes as I went from one country to another instead of jumping instantaneously, which was how I naïvely imagined air travel. Originally I wanted to walk to Vienna, but I abandoned the idea as impractical. The compromise was to cross the Channel, then take a sleeper train overnight from Belgium through Germany to Austria. Because of the Schengen Agreement, once I'd left Britain there were no border controls, no officers passing through the carriage and looking at passports. I'd expected something different, versions of the scene from old movies, the compartment door sliding open, the passengers handing over their documents to an unsmiling uniformed man. I found myself wondering, if countries could agree to remove their borders, what kind of existence did those borders have? They came into being every time an identity was checked, then disappeared again. I'd been reading about colonial administrators marking frontiers on maps, Sykes-Picot, the partition of India. Imaginary pencil lines. I didn't know what I wanted to do with these thoughts. In Vienna, someone gave me a sticker from an activist group called Kein Mensch ist Illegal—*no one is illegal*. I stuck it over the logo on my laptop.

I had been invited to do a performance I called *Natural Rhythm*. My arms and legs were attached to ropes, connected to a pulley system. I played a solo on a drum kit, the movements of my arms pulling the ropes tight, causing weights to rise up and down as I tried to keep time to the amplified ticking of a metronome, a rhythm that gradually got faster and faster, until it became inhuman, impossible to match. The Austrian audience watched intently as I strained and stretched like a human puppet, working myself into a frenzy that climaxed as I broke the kit and twitched on the floor, tangled in my rigging.

On the way back to London I stopped in Berlin, where I did the drumming performance again at an artist-run space in Kreuzberg. I stayed on a few days, and ended up joining some people who were doing graffiti in one of the empty buildings along the old line of the wall. To get in, we had to climb over a fence topped with razor wire. My new friends threw a scrap of old carpet over it, and went up using a grapple and a length of rope, like pirates swarming a ship. It was impressive, and afterwards I began to take an interest in climbing, the physical act of passing over barriers. When I walked past a high wall, I would instinctively look for footholds.

Number five in Sol Lewitt's *Sentences on Conceptual Art*: irrational thoughts should be followed absolutely and logically. Number six: if the artist changes his mind midway through the execution of the piece he compromises the result and repeats past results. I had pinned both these aphorisms to the wall of my studio. I liked their scientific tone. At the time my heroes all came from the same moment in the nineteen-sixties and seventies, when artists were producing typewritten lists of instructions, and carrying out actions that often required enduring stress or pain. Around that time I tried performing actions in public, small gestures that were strange or disruptive. I crawled along a street, drawing a straight line with a piece of chalk, dividing one side from another. I held up mirrors to passers-by and asked them to describe themselves. Sometimes I recruited friends to hold a camera and document the reactions. Both Rob and Alice helped out at one time or another. People had negative, even violent responses to what I was doing. I was searched by police at Liverpool Street station, where I was standing on a box dressed in a suit and tie like a commuter, with a briefcase in my hand and an old-fashioned dunce's cap on my head. They told me that I was behaving antisocially, and if I did it again I would be arrested.

Like the action at Liverpool Street, the drumming performance was about shame and discomfort. I wanted to explore the way I'd been made to feel as a child, mostly by Douglas and Patricia. The performance at Jago Purvis, where I stood and stared at the wall, had been a reconstruction of one of the more traumatic events of my teens, when Douglas locked me out on the balcony of the house he shared with Patricia and the twins. I was thirteen, already living at my Nan's, but I'd gone over for Sunday lunch. He and I had some kind of argument and he put me out there as a punishment. It was an absurd little terrace with a couple of plant pots and a low rusty railing, just a flat space on top of the bay of their dining room. It was February, and sleeting. I was so angry that I didn't move. I didn't pace about, or bang on the French doors. I didn't want to give Douglas the satisfaction of seeing me exhibit any emotion. I just stood there with my back to the door, shivering uncontrollably as I looked out over the black water of the Estuary. Finally Patricia came and let me back in. "He's gone out," she said. She put me in a hot bath and fed me milk with brandy in it, but as far as I knew, she never remonstrated with him, never stood up to him for what he had done.

When I was with Alice, my art was a kind of self-therapy, a way to map the particular channels of my unhappiness. I didn't make those pieces because I thought my experiences were special, or even interesting to others. Calling it a compulsion would also be wrong. It was just where I seemed to be going, the road I was traveling on. I did *Natural Rhythm* at Jago's gallery, and several other places. The idea of being constrained or impeded was something I played with. There was a Japanese action from the fifties in which an artist thrashed around in a pool of mud, fighting an unwinnable battle with it, until he was exhausted. I admired that. I wanted to make art from struggle, the struggle of staying alive every day. I thought a lot about drowning, asphyxiation.

WHEN I GOT BACK TO LONDON, something had subtly shifted at Fancy Goods. Before I left for Europe I'd said I didn't want to put any work into the first show. Rob cajoled me, and eventually I agreed to pin one of my relationship diagrams to the wall. The reasons for my ambivalence were complicated, and it's hard to reconstruct them. I think it was because I didn't like some of the other work. There were a couple of friends of Rob's who made what I thought of as "loft art," large flashy abstract paintings intended to catch the eye of unsophisticated collectors. That kind of cynicism repelled me, and it didn't seem like a good context for anything I wanted to do. I thought of myself as part of the FG collective, but my negativity had been noted. Though I was away for less than two weeks, when I came back it was as if a circle had closed and I found myself outside.

Alice, on the other hand, was enjoying herself. I was uneasy at the way that Rob and his friends seemed to be pushing her into subservient roles—as organizer, assistant, den mother. I was already feeling excluded, and something frightened me about the little smiles that played across Rob's face when Alice was around, as if they had shared some intimacy while I was away.

One afternoon we were upstairs. I was helping to address invitations for the first show, waiting for Alice to be finished so we could go to the cinema. I remember I wanted to take her away from the group for a while, to have her to myself. There were half a dozen of us, chatting and listening to music as we worked. It must have been a few weeks before it opened.

Rob turned to Alice and made some joke about her aunt's porcelain collection, about how she was the girl who lived in a museum. I had heard her talk about this collection, which sat on glass shelves and had to be treated with enormous care, but I'd never seen it, because I'd still never been to her apartment.

"I'm sorry, Rob, did Alice show you the porcelain?"

"Yeah, why?"

My humiliation was intense. Unable to think of anything to say, I got up and went outside. I expected Alice to follow me and explain herself, but she didn't, and after ten minutes of angry pacing, I was forced to go back inside. As the other members of the collective avoided eye contact, I picked up my bag and mumbled some excuse about needing to get home. I was wheeling my bike out into the street, when Alice came downstairs and asked why I was "in such a bad mood." I don't know if she intended to be provocative, but her tone made me furious.

"You'd take him to where you live, but not me? You've never— I mean, you treat it like it's a fucking state secret."

"Don't overreact."

"Don't tell me how to react."

"Let's not do this here. Sound carries upstairs. They can all hear us."

We walked away towards the main road. Eventually we found a bus stop and sat in silence on a sloped plastic bench.

"I don't understand you. You're making me feel like a mug."

"Like a what?"

"A fool, an idiot. I thought I was respecting your privacy. It's—I mean, like, where did you two—I mean, did you really take him to your flat?"

"Yes."

"Well that's just fucking perfect."

"Jay, stop. It's not a big deal. Why make it into a drama?"

"You two just found yourselves on the other side of the city, and you dropped in to the top secret hideout which I've never seen, so Rob can—what? What did you two do together?"

"It's just a flat. A horrible, stuffy flat with wall-to-wall carpet and dusty old vases on shelves."

"How did it even come about?"

"It just happened. I ran into him at this thing."

"What thing?"

"Stop interrogating me, Jay."

"I'm not interrogating you. It's a simple question."

"I don't have to tell you everything."

"Now I really think you have something to hide."

"Oh, grow up."

"Grow up?"

"Just back off, OK? You don't let me breathe."

She was looking up the street, and I followed her eyeline, to see a black cab coming towards us, its yellow light on, as if she'd summoned it. She jumped up and hailed it.

"So that's it?" I asked.

She gave me a sarcastic peck on the cheek. As I watched her drive away I wondered if we'd just broken up. Dejected, I went home and got drunk with my housemates, then fell asleep in the living room in front of a TV show about teenagers with superpowers.

EVENTUALLY, Alice did take me to her apartment. After our argument at Fancy Goods, there were several excruciating days of silence, then she called. I carried the phone into my room, passing the extension cord under my door and closing it so I couldn't be overheard.

"Come over."

"Where?"

"Jay, just come."

"Why?"

"Do you want me to hang up?"

"You'll have to tell me your address."

And so I took the tube to Knightsbridge and walked along streets of mansion blocks and trim townhouses with ornate Dutch gables and forbidding black doors. I found Alice's building and pressed a buzzer on a highly polished brass plate. After an interval there was a burst of static and a click, and I pushed my way into a hall tiled with black and white marble. I rode up several floors in a stuttering elevator with a brass scissor gate that clattered as it opened and closed. Stepping out again, a muffled silence enveloped me. A Persian runner stretched away along a gloomy corridor hung with hunting prints. There was a faint smell of bleach, and I began to feel slightly nauseous, as if my body were trying to warn me of something. I found the number, pressed another bell, and after a moment or two heard the sliding of a dead bolt. Alice opened the door.

"Abandon all hope," she said, smirking awkwardly. As I stepped inside, my feet sank into the deep-pile carpet of the vestibule and something metaphysical closed around me, a feeling that my reality had just forked, and the life in which I hadn't crossed that threshold was now utterly irretrievable. Maybe it was the flat's dead acoustic. Everything was double-glazed, padded, hushed and dampened. I pretended to myself that I wasn't afraid. I even complimented Alice on the silence. How nice, I said, hearing one of my mother's banalities in my mouth, that you couldn't hear the traffic. If I'd known how that place would break me, I would have fled.

Even with the windows open, that flat was stuffy. The air just would not circulate. I'm sure it must be a trick of my memory, but I picture all the rooms as a single shade of gray-green, the color of decay. That first afternoon we sat on green wooden chairs and drank green tea out of pale green cups. Slouching on her throne like the disaffected princess of an undersea kingdom,

Alice opened her arms in an ironic gesture of welcome. I half-expected gills to open at her throat.

"I'll show you round," she said. "You can see exactly what it's like."

She took me into the little dressing room she was using as a study, a narrow space dominated by a looming row of closets with mirrored doors. She'd wedged in a flimsy-looking table with a white plastic top, and a swivel chair. On the table there was a task lamp and many piles of books. The room was very neat, precisely organized in a way that suggested care and concentration, but as I looked around, I felt sad for Alice. There wasn't a place to pin up a drawing, nowhere to make a carefree mark. It was an inhibited life. She could have packed it away in half an hour, and afterwards no trace of her would have remained.

"Does she ever come here? Your aunt?"

"Not for a long time. She used to visit London to gamble, but I think the club she liked closed down. These days she usually flies to Macau."

"So who normally lives here?"

"Nobody. When I arrived, I had to throw out all the food in the cupboards. The spices, everything. It all had sell-by dates from, like, the eighties."

I followed her into the bedroom, which was stark and neglected, but less cramped than the study. The bed was unmade, and there was a tangle of dirty laundry on the floor. As I looked around, I understood why she'd never brought me there. It wasn't some boudoir, some private sanctuary. Alice wasn't keeping any secrets. There was nothing to reveal, unless it was her emptiness, her lack of autonomy. There was nothing in that flat she was allowed to change or make her own. Later, naked, we smoked out of the window, sending our ash floating down into a gloomy inner courtyard several floors below.

THE FIRST OPENING at Fancy Goods took place on a warm summer evening. Hundreds of people showed up, spilling out onto the street. There were so many bodies upstairs that you could see the floor bowing under the weight. Downstairs, a pile of amps and a rat's nest of cable occupied the middle of the floor. We had bands playing art punk and electropop; when the first act started up, the whole building began to vibrate. We had set up a grill, selling burgers and kebabs, and for days afterwards the building smelled of charred meat, blended with the white paint we'd used to freshen up the walls. I wanted to be helpful, to mend a few fences with the rest of the crew, so I volunteered to run the bar. I spent the evening pouring drinks into plastic cups and fishing cans of beer out of a cooler, trying not to think about structural collapse and fire hazards.

Despite an idealistic press release, written by Alice, that mentioned participatory experience and seeking a relational exterior to capitalist modes of exchange, it was, in most respects, a show designed to sell art to art collectors. The hang was, in my opinion, a mess. At the last minute a lot more people had been invited to participate, and it was hard to make out any coherent thread that bound the whole thing together. The ground floor had a lot of tiny works—a little pile of colored marbles in a corner, drawings on torn-out notebook paper attached in a haphazard way to a pillar. Upstairs were several gimmicky paintings done by Rob's loft-artist friends. Rob was showing his overpainted charity shop seascapes. He'd mounted them on a structure made out of old furniture, the heavy brown kind that was being turned out of houses back then. It was a sort of hut, like a shack or a beach cabin, festooned with paintings. It was definitely the best work in the show.

Jago had brought collectors with him, a wide-eyed older couple who he helped out of a cab, solicitously squiring them through the scruffy throng of drinkers. I recognized a couple of other young dealers, also with clients, expensively dressed people who stood out against the crowd. London's most famous collector showed up, a legendary figure who was reputed to have the power to single-handedly make an artist's career. He was only there briefly, keeping a car waiting as he scrutinized Rob's seascapes. He was a big ungainly man, and I watched him eye the rickety stairs suspiciously. When the first band started up, he left, without attempting the climb. The loft painters, whose work he missed, were devastated.

From my station behind the bar I saw Alice fall into conversation with a smart young guy in a blue silk suit. He was conspicuously handsome, and if he wasn't wealthy, he certainly dressed the part. As they came to get drinks, I heard them speaking French, laughing together at some joke. She introduced him as a gallerist from Paris. We're going on to dinner, she whispered excitedly to me, when her new friend was momentarily distracted. I think he wants me to guest curate a show. Later, she came to say goodbye. "You're welcome to join us," said the gallerist, his tone implying the opposite.

"I'd love to," I said.

Alice flashed me a fierce look. "I'll call you tomorrow, OK?"

As usual, I tried not to succumb to jealousy. She was going to a business dinner, that was all. I stayed at Fancy Goods until the party wound down, then carried on back at Jago's, a binge that took us well into the following day; the most efficient way I knew to avoid confronting strong emotions. When I next saw Alice, she didn't want to talk about the dinner or the gallerist. Her silence had a bitter edge, from which I deduced that the man had made a pass instead of offering her work.

I had begun to store up small resentments against Alice. When we were together I felt as if I were holding my breath all the time. I didn't want to provoke an argument, because she was better at arguing, more committed to her positions, always able to tie me in knots. Of the two of us, I knew I was the one who needed our relationship more, and I was afraid of unbalancing its delicate mechanism. I had cast myself in a ridiculous role, a sort of middle manager, adjusting to each new crisis, rushing around and sending memos to other departments to keep the enterprise running. In none of this did I see Alice, not really. I was so preoccupied with trying to maintain our love affair that in a certain way I forgot to have it.

That show at Fancy Goods changed things for a lot of the participants. The famous collector bought Rob's installation, and overnight he became an artist to watch, on the radar of people who could make painters rich. Jago sold my diagram to the wide-eyed couple, hinting to me that I ought to make more like it. This, of course, made me swear to myself that I would do no such thing. Other artists also attracted attention, and for the short time it lasted, Fancy Goods could claim to be the most important—or at least the most fashionable—artist-run space in London.

Later that year, I did another performance at Jago Purvis, part of what Jago billed as an art cabaret. Everyone associated with the gallery did some kind of turn. It was supposed to be improvised, amateurish, one part Dada to one part music hall. I sang a Christmas carol, wearing a supermarket plastic bag over my head. The carol was one of Douglas's favorites, and reminded me of the terrible atmosphere that descended on their house during the holidays, when he drank more than usual and was in a mood to dwell on the failures and indignities of the dying year. I had cheated so I could breathe, but visually it had the intended effect. I looked as if I were choking as I struggled to sing, the plastic taut against my open mouth. The audience was disturbed, clapping uncertainly, happy to hurry on to the next act, a famous old ham of a sculptor reciting a poem full of bitchy inside references to other people in the room. Afterwards, to my astonishment, Jago was contacted by a curator from one of London's most prestigious public galleries, offering me a solo show. It was an institution that had a reputation for radicalism that went back to the seventies, when it had supported various kinds of confrontational performance art. The curator told me she had been following my work, and believed I stood in that tradition. They looked forward to seeing what I would do.

It was a break, a jump of several rungs up the art ladder. Alice was excited, and encouraged me to think confrontationally. At the time I was reading a lot, and getting fired up by political ideas. Most of my art friends didn't care about politics, but I was becoming preoccupied by all the intersecting causes of the nineties left, the Zapatistas, corporate branding, globalization, the predatory behavior of the International Monetary Fund. It seemed possible that we were on the cusp of a change—the millennium was approaching and all sorts of utopian ideas were in play. That summer Alice and I were part of a huge protest in London, a masked carnival that turned into a battle, as the crowd tried to storm the London Futures Exchange. I remember samba bands and mobile sound systems, protesters dressed as clowns, mocking the ranks of riot police in their sinister black body armor.

All this was on my mind as I planned my show. I wanted it to be a statement about capital, about the dirty money that flowed through the artworld. The trouble was I hated most protest art. Giant puppets and street theater seemed naïve, and meaningless in a gallery. Instead I decided I would diagram the various connections of the host institution, make visible the network of commercial and cultural obligations that lay under its supposed radicalism. When I presented this to the curator, she poured cold water on the idea, saying that institutional critique had already been thoroughly explored. I could, she thought, be more effective if I took another approach. After a meeting in the gallery, I was left alone in an office, and I stole some papers, including correspondence with the agency that supplied their cleaning staff. I discovered that the cleaners were being paid below minimum wage. I began interviewing workers who were in menial roles, and researching members of the "patron's council," a board of collectors who helped guide the institution, including the wives of investors with interests in such things as arms and fossil fuels.

Instead of giving a performance, or making some kind of exhibition or installation, I imagined a stage and a microphone, a platform for all the people the art audience didn't usually hear from: cleaners, security guards, installers and technical crew, workers in the back office, as well as the people whose money made the wheels turn—if any of them would agree to participate. It would be a democratizing gesture, cafeteria workers and rich donors standing up and saying what art meant to them. The only visual element would be a banner that I had salvaged from the summer protest, picking it up off the street in the aftermath of the police charge. *The Earth a common treasury for all,* it read, a quote from the leader of the Diggers, seventeenth-century radicals who had tried to set up a community on common land in Surrey.

When the gallery people found out what I wanted to do, particularly my intention to share information about the exploitation of the cleaning staff, they lost their minds. At a meeting, the director raised his voice, calling me "a childish little Trot." The curator hung her head as her boss came round the conference table, looking as if he were going to physically attack me. When I tried to take his photograph, he swiped at the camera, which smashed against the wall. The show was canceled, and they tried to make me sign a document saying I wouldn't talk to the press. I refused, and immediately put a statement online with a picture of the broken camera. Some other artists circulated an open letter, and the controversy made the pages of *The Guardian*. Soon afterwards, a young tabloid journalist turned up on my doorstep, tugging at his greasy collar and asking leading questions. Was I an anarchist, he wanted to know. Did I advocate violence against the police?

For a week or two, while the drama unfolded, I felt good. People were congratulating me on my uncompromising stance, discussing the issues I'd hoped to raise—about equity in the artworld, the use of culture to launder money and reputations. Then, once the scandal had run its course and attention moved on, I began to wonder what I'd done. Several people told me that I'd been stupid. The director of the institution was very powerful, and he would do his best to block me in any way he could. Though he denied all my claims about what had happened at the meeting, including breaking my camera, the revelations about pay had damaged the gallery's reputation, and he had personally come out of it looking very bad. He put the blame on the employment agency, saying all the usual things—he was shocked, no one in management knew anyone was getting less than minimum wage, it wasn't the institution's fault because the cleaners weren't directly employed by them—but mud had stuck to him, and there had even been calls for him to step down.

I pretended to take all this in my stride, but really I was nervous. What had I expected to achieve? Had I just destroyed my career? I'd come to a strange and difficult place in my work, where I found many more questions than answers. I started to withdraw, spending a lot of time on my own, refusing all offers. At around this time, other things happened, a confluence of events that swirled together, exerting a gravitational force on my relationship with Alice, a well from which none of our light would escape.

The first was the premature closure of Fancy Goods. Though the landlord had promised he wouldn't redevelop the building for at least two years, his schedule changed and he told the collective that they had to leave. Alice was bitterly disappointed. There was some talk about finding a backer and moving the project into a commercial space, but she was the only one who really wanted to try. After his sale to the powerful collector, Rob had found representation, a young rival of Jago's who'd opened up in Clerkenwell. He was content to move on. One by one the other artists melted away.

Then Alice had a bike accident. Someone doored her as we were riding along Old Street and she almost fell under a bus. I was ahead of her, and I didn't see it happen. When I realized she wasn't behind me, I turned back, only to find a scene of chaos, drivers getting out of their cars, Alice sprawled like a broken doll in the roadway. An ambulance came and she was taken to the Royal London with a concussion and, as it turned out, two badly broken wrists. I felt terrible. I was the one who'd persuaded her to start riding a bike in the first place, something she hadn't done since she was a child. She'd been nervous, but also proud of herself, enjoying the freedom, the nimbleness of slaloming through the London traffic.

She kept the accident secret from her family, because she was afraid that it would give her mother an excuse to call her home, or, just as bad, come over and start prying into her life. She could barely bathe and dress herself, and I started staying with her in Knightsbridge, cooking for her, cutting up her food, trying to keep her from falling deeper into depression. Though she was in pain, and had been prescribed strong medication, she enjoyed being taken care of, and I enjoyed doing it. She did physiotherapy, squeezing squash balls and pulling at elastic bands. Little by little, she got better.

My money situation was bad. I wasn't making anything that Jago could sell, and since the debacle with the art institution, I didn't have any other income. I couldn't pay rent, and my housemates finally got sick of my problems and told me to go. Instead of getting another place right away, Alice said I could stay with her. Neither of us wanted to see anyone, and there were only so many movies we could watch in a day. We had Alice's credit card to keep us afloat, and almost no obligations, so we began to pass the time by getting high. I'd always liked drugs, and though she didn't tolerate alcohol very well, Alice liked them too. Her circle of Parisian friends was very straitlaced, but in London she'd immediately gravitated towards a party scene, and the lingering pain from her bike accident meant that she was often most comfortable when she was stoned.

At first, it was just for fun. Then we developed something like a plan. When I have a setback, my instinct is always to push harder. Because things had gone wrong with my art career, the answer was to become a better artist. When I was still a painter, I would have tried to work on my craft, to improve some skill— line or color or composition. Hiding out in Alice's flat, I wanted to push myself, but if technique or craft wasn't what made someone a good artist, what did? The conventional answer was that a good artist was someone who had good ideas. I wanted to perform experiments, to open up a richer mental world for myself. If I had better access to my subconscious, maybe I could produce images that others couldn't, or if not images, then configurations, juxtapositions, trains of thought. Alice didn't have the same enthusiasms, but she was happy enough to go along for the ride. There was a trustafarian in Notting Hill who was connected in some way to the Goa trance scene, and Alice knew, I'm not sure how, a woman who ran a sort of agency, doing house calls with a little briefcase. Between them they gave us access to an alphabet soup of chemicals, many of them related in some way to MDMA. We took MDEA and MDA and 2C-B and 2-CE and on one occasion, something called DOM that lasted for so long that I began to fear we'd done something irreversible to our brains. We smoked Salvia and ate mushrooms and took acid trips that sent us to a Blakean heaven of refulgent skies and prophetic emanations.

I tried to explain to Jago what we were doing, how we were trying to sharpen our perception. He was skeptical. The world, in his opinion, was quite sharp enough already. He thought I was confused. Art was about structures. "What has the derangement of the senses got to do with anything? Just make me some fucking pictures and stop living off your girlfriend." I was lying on his floor in a state of semi-collapse, a rime of powder round my nostrils. I laughed so hard I almost threw up.

What came out of our experiments? Sex and broken glass. I remember being inside Alice but unable to look at her face, because eyes and mouths were growing all over it. I remember smashing wineglasses and trying to screw up the courage to walk over the kitchen floor in my bare feet, like a yogi. Submerged in the bath, we stared at each other like crocodiles, and she held my hand while I went so far out that I forgot my name, didn't know I was the kind of thing that even had a name. We smoked DMT and bargained with entities that shared no human characteristics with us, inorganic lifeforms that seemed to have an independent existence, into whose world we had dropped, unannounced, like clumsy aliens landing in a busy shopping mall. The entities found us curious but inconsequential, and for the short time we were with them, it seemed to us that the drug had literally transported us to another place.

We tried recording some of this stuff, but the traces were dis-

appointing, unfocused Polaroids of body parts, pages of meaningless scribbles that no longer contained the key to all mythologies.
When the strength in her wrists came back, Alice showed me
some illustrations in a book about Brion Gysin, and I built a
dream machine out of a lightbulb and a record deck, a device
that pulsed light on our closed lids, sending us into a trance. She
had read somewhere that the world is colorless. Color is in your
mind, she told me. I tried to imagine that, but it scared me, the
thought that there was nothing out there but a raging electro-
magnetic sea.

For several months, there was never a time when we weren't
high. We smoked weed from the moment we woke up in the
morning, moving about our pale green undersea world like
unquiet ghosts. Occasionally the real world would intrude, but
usually it felt as if we'd slipped through the cracks, the difference
between inner and outer space collapsing until reality was purely
a function of what we'd ingested that day. At first it seemed excit-
ing, as if we'd found an illicit truth, a doorway into a place that
was inaccessible to ordinary people, but gradually the returns
diminished, and instead of beauty and wonder, our artificial paradise began to feel like a trap. The empty rooms smelled moldy.
The walls spawned stains and discolorations that might or might
not have been tricks of the mind. I would find Alice scrubbing
away at a door frame or a patch of carpet, convinced that we'd
caused some damage her aunt would notice.

We slept erratically, sometimes staying up for days at a time,
leaving only to get food or to score. Sometimes I couldn't stand
it and went out to a climbing wall, where I'd cling to holds high
above the ground, chemical sweat sheening my body. More often
I was too wasted or apathetic to make the effort. Alice was slipping too. She stopped washing her hair. Sooner or later it would
clean itself, she said. She rarely changed her clothes. I gave up
worrying about trying to get her to eat. I made food for myself,
pushed plates of leftovers into the fridge for her to pick at. Some-

times she would put on enormous dark glasses and take a taxi to a Vietnamese supermarket in Soho, where she'd buy big foil trays of nems or summer rolls; for a few days we'd survive on those, until we couldn't stand the taste anymore and had to think of something else. After one of these expeditions she cut all her hair off, squatting on the bathroom floor and shaving her head clean with a razor. Some guy had catcalled her. She said she didn't want to be looked at anymore. Afterwards she lay sobbing on the bed, folded up like an insect. "Do you still like me?" she wailed. "Do you find me disgusting?" I told her she looked fine. I didn't want to be repelled by her. I wanted to love her, desire her, but somehow all that was getting lost. She was painfully thin. Her hips jutted out, two wings or stumps framing the concavity of her stomach. She wore ancient colorless sweatpants, and always the same stained tee shirt with a picture of a cartoon alien. Her skin was greasy. She stank of cigarettes. I didn't want to touch her. I tried to push my disgust down deep, hoping it would dissipate of its own accord, so I would never have to admit that my love for her was less than perfect.

After a while I gave up all thoughts of sharpening my perception. Jago had been right. The world could cut you; better to take the edge off. We would smoke heroin and watch movies, surrounded by a litter of scorched foil. When we were high like that, plot made no sense to us. We couldn't follow all the talking. What we liked were images, jump cuts, sudden and violent events. At the end of *Pierrot le Fou,* Jean-Paul Belmondo wraps dynamite around his head and blows himself up. We rewound that scene and watched it again and again, savoring the way it mirrored our own frozen cool. Despite its temptations, heroin never consumed us like it did some of our friends. The drug we really fell for was ketamine. We'd snort lines and feel ourselves rising up out of our bodies, immaterial presences looking down on the puppets sprawled out below.

Our mental state became more fragile. Alice would collapse on the sofa, crying and saying she wanted to kill herself. I would tell her to be quiet because I was trying to work; my work consisted of rearranging things on a table and staring at the empty pages of my sketchbook. We'd started out doing the same drug at the same time. Now we'd fallen out of sync, doing hits of this and that whenever we felt like it. Sometimes I'd walk into the living room and find her in one of her gray moods, smoking a cigarette and staring into space. She would turn round with an expression of irritation, directed not at me, or not particularly at me, but at something I was reminding her of, some annoying fact about her life. I would try to work out what she had taken. A suspicion developed between us, a need to assess and interpret before we could interact. Her hair grew back slowly. She looked like a gaunt boy.

Scoring was my job and it took up a lot of time, sending me all over the city. I would put on headphones and sneak out into the world. Jago connected me to a guy from Green Lanes called Emir and there was a Bangladeshi bodybuilder called Mukul who lived in Limehouse in some kind of new development where you never saw anyone else. Sometimes, when I couldn't get what we needed from my regulars, I went elsewhere—to the guy who sat in his BMW in the parking lot of a supermarket in Shepherd's Bush or the guy who lived in a little terraced house in Walthamstow where the whole downstairs living room was taken up by a jacuzzi and half the upstairs was a grow, the walls papered in silver foil. There were several people I knew casually from the art scene, like the Crombie coat man, and a guy I only went to see twice, because he lived behind an improvised barricade, put up after some people had broken down his door. The second time I went there, he made me stand in a tiny galley kitchen for half an hour while he was resupplied by his dealer, whose face it wouldn't have been healthy for me to see.

Scoring gave me excuses to be away from Alice. I would walk

around, drink a coffee or sit and nurse a pint in a bar. One night Jago had an opening. Alice didn't want to come out, deep into a wrap of K and a reality TV show. I tried to hide my relief, and headed east. That night Jago got into a fight with a Russian provocateur who made a habit of disrupting artworld events. It was rumored that he'd done prison time in Germany for spray-painting a dollar sign on a Malevich. He and his partner, who I think was German, used to turn up and shout slogans, sometimes throw things. Often she'd try to distract people while he dropped his trousers and took a shit on the floor. This was his party trick, his statement about art and money. Most gallerists knew to look out for the two of them, but sometimes they still managed to evade security. At Jago's opening, the woman got onto a chair and started shouting about Neoliberalism, as her friend began to wrestle with his belt. Together Jago and a friend picked him up by the waistband of his trousers and threw him out. He tried to get back inside, but Jago defended the door, poking at him with a striped golf umbrella, which he wielded like a fencer.

It was like a scene from some Swinging London comedy. It was also the last time I saw Jago alive. We heard the terrible news from Rob, the only friend who ever came over to Knightsbridge to visit. He would turn up and persuade us to go outside; the three of us would do simple things like see a movie or walk in Hyde Park, and we were always grateful and excited to see him because he saved us from each other. Ordinarily he phoned, but that day he arrived unexpectedly, finding us lying in our usual litter of pizza boxes and ashtrays. As usual, the curtains were drawn and the VCR was on. Without preamble, he sat down and told us why he was there. No one had seen Jago for several days. He'd missed meetings and the gallery had been shuttered. Some of his friends had persuaded his landlord to open the door and they'd found him lying on the floor of his living room.

Eventually there was an autopsy, and it was determined that

Jago had asphyxiated. He'd been taking GHB and had stopped breathing. A rumor went round that the police had found evidence of other people being there with him. Dirty glasses, something like that. It seemed that when Jago had gone into a coma, he'd just been abandoned. I don't know what I found worse, the thought that he'd been left to die, possibly by people we knew, or that he was on his own doing that shitty drug. Jago was a lonely man and his plans had always involved gathering people around him. Whether he'd been alone or with others, it was an ugly death.

The funeral was a very Jagoesque affair. Friends decorated his coffin, and I helped carry it through the streets near his gallery, followed by a motley parade of artists and a Salvation Army brass band. The image I try to retain is that of him defending his gallery floor from the shitting Russian, the swashbuckler with the umbrella rather than the furtive little man standing under a railway arch in the East End darkness.

ALICE AND I HAD A MISERABLE MILLENNIUM. Jago's death hung over us, and we probably wouldn't have braved the chaos in the city if we hadn't needed some relief from each other. I was both angry with Alice and desperately worried about her. I wanted to reset things, to return to the way it had been when we first met, and just being with her felt like a blessing, but I had no idea how. So we dressed up and went to a big dinner that a friend of Rob's was holding at his studio. At midnight we were on a roof, looking out at London, trying to spot signs of the end of the world. Would the millennium bug crash all the computers? Would planes fall out of the sky? Nothing seemed different. To my surprise, Alice said she wanted to experience the crowd. Rob said he would come too. The three of us ended up on Blackfriars Bridge. A dramatic fireworks display had been planned. A famous Chinese artist was to send some kind of pyrotechnic dragon down the Thames, or over it, no one really knew, but in any case there had been a technical error and it hadn't worked. There was no dragon, just throngs of drunk people, seething and surging on the narrow roadway, packed so tightly together that sometimes we were lifted off our feet. It was on the edge between exhilarating and terrifying and I remember holding on to Alice, trying to shield her, as Rob did the same on the other side, the two of us gripping arms, forming a kind of ring round her. I have a strong image of Alice's face, her mouth open, lips drawn back over her teeth, screaming or laughing, I can no longer remember which.

AT HOME WE STOPPED TOUCHING. We slunk around, and if one of us accidentally brushed the other, they flinched. The future seemed empty, leeched of serotonin. The days emerged and dissipated like bubbles on a pond. One day Alice went out and spent a thousand pounds on an ugly cocktail dress, a sort of tunic with a guitar embroidered on the front. For a day or two she wore it as we watched movies. Then she fell asleep while she was smoking a joint and burned a hole in the front. It lived for a while bunched up on the bathroom floor. One day it disappeared. I suppose she put it in the trash.

Rob kept up his visits, appearing at our door like a messenger from the upper world, a reminder of life. His new gallery had decided to launch him with a solo presentation, and one day he came over to deliver an invitation. The show was called *Business,* and the card reproduced a painting, done in muted Morandi-esque tones, of the inside of a shoe repair shop, a mess of leather scraps and machinery. It was obvious we would have to go to the view, though everything in me resisted it. That day, I convinced myself I felt unwell. Only when I saw Alice getting ready, applying makeup, trying on outfits in front of the mirror, did I peel myself up from the sofa. I knew I would feel worse wondering what she was doing than if I had to talk to our friends, most of whom I hadn't seen since the cancellation of my show at the art institute. I dreaded the inevitable questions about what I was working on, where I was showing next. Most of Jago's artists had moved on to other galleries. No one had contacted me.

Alice appeared, casually beautiful in a suit jacket and jeans. I told her how good she looked and she thanked me politely. I was irritated at her formal tone. I wanted to touch her, kiss her. This was the girl I was with, not the wan creature in the stained tee shirt. On the tube I put my arm around her, but she disengaged herself, pretending to be engrossed in her book. I arrived at the opening feeling prickly and miserable.

On the street outside the gallery, bikes were attached to every lamppost and railing. There was the usual scrum of people holding bottles of art-brand beer. I smiled and nodded at people I knew, trying not to get trapped in conversation. Together, Alice and I pushed our way inside. It was too busy to see the work properly, but I picked up a press release from the counter and read it while Alice chatted to a girlfriend. *A young artist paints where the urban poor shop,* it began. There was some stuff about how he was embedding himself in the fabric of the underclass, and some more stuff about how he was transforming abjection into tiny moments of transcendence. The show consisted of a dozen or so biggish paintings of the inside of various Hackney businesses, with the emphasis on old-fashioned ones, the kind that were being rapidly displaced by the people packed into the gallery. Apart from the shoe repairer, I remember one of the twenty-four-hour bagel place on Brick Lane, a pound store, a fishmonger.

I looked at the gallery-goers, socializing in front of these images, the lives of others transformed, not, as the press release claimed, into tiny moments of transcendence, but trophies for people who would never dream of stepping inside the places they depicted. It was nauseating, a poverty safari. It wasn't that the painting was technically bad. Quite the opposite—Rob had always been a good painter, and the text had surely been written by the gallerist. I suspected that the subjects weren't particularly important to Rob; he would have been happy making a picture of whatever was in front of him—a pint, a slice of cake. His love for painting was simple and consuming. He liked everything about it, the smell of the thinners, the scratchy sound of the brush against the canvas. The other part, the part I was involved with, the struggles with politics, the questions about the purpose of art; all of that meant very little to him. If fashions had been different, or he'd been born in a previous century, he would have been content to paint portraits of the local aristocrat, or take an easel to the countryside to capture the way the afternoon light fell on some nearby mountain.

Alice found Rob, and he threw his arms round her, greeting her with a whoop of joy. He kissed her on both cheeks and she beamed, the kind of smile I hadn't seen on her face in months. The involuntary thought crossed my mind that they looked good together. He glanced over her shoulder and waved to me. I waved back, shaking a packet of cigarettes, miming that I was going outside to smoke. For a while I stood outside the gallery, talking in a desultory way to various acquaintances. I left soon after that, falling back on my excuse about feeling sick. Alice went on to the gallery dinner. She didn't come home that night.

Soon afterwards Alice told me that Rob had asked her to sit for him. I remember I was in the living room, in my underwear, packing the bong for my morning hit. She emerged, perfectly made-up, dressed to go out. When she told me she was on her way to Rob's studio, I felt a pang of jealousy that I struggled to suppress.

"Do you have a problem with it?" she asked.

"No. Why would I?"

"I don't know. I thought maybe you didn't want me to do it."

"I don't mind."

"I won't do it if you don't want me to."

That was my chance. Looking back, it was blindingly obvious. She was telling me what was about to happen, and asking if I wanted to stop it. It was my chance and I didn't take it.

"Go ahead," I said. "Say hello from me."

For the next few weeks she made regular visits to Rob's new studio in Hoxton. She would come back in a good mood, ready to be sweet to me. This made me happy, and in return I tried to do better, clearing up, cooking, looking for ways to make amends. I stopped getting high during the day, and things seemed to be improving between us. I told myself we were entering a new phase, that we could start treating each other how we wanted to be treated. I was going to propose that I look for somewhere else for us to live. She could keep a fake presence in Knightsbridge to satisfy her family, but we'd finally set up the life I wanted us to have, as an East End artist couple.

I would ask how the portrait was going, and she'd reply in vague terms. I told her I was curious to see it, even suggesting that I go over for one of the sittings, but she said Rob didn't like other people around when he was working. I found that strange, since I'd often hung out in his studio, and as far as I remembered, he had no problem painting with an audience. I told Alice about my plans for our future, and was disappointed at her lukewarm reaction. She said that she thought it would probably be a good idea if I moved out, but didn't commit to the other part, the part where she came with me. Somehow I skated over that. I told myself she'd come around.

My curiosity began to curdle. Every few days I would ask if the portrait was finished. Alice would equivocate, and because she seemed to want to keep it from me, my anxiety grew. Somewhere, dimly, I knew what was going on; I just needed to confirm my suspicions. So one day I just turned up at Rob's studio and rang the bell.

He looked surprised to see me, a little nervous.

"I wasn't expecting you. Did we have a plan?"

No, I said. I'd just been passing by. He let me into a bright, clean space, with fresh white walls and skylights in the ceiling. It was, I remember, a beautiful studio. The contrast with the undersea gloom of the Knightsbridge flat couldn't have been greater.

"Cup of tea? Beer? I've got a couple in the fridge, I think."

At the far end, an assistant was stretching canvases.

"That's Carlo."

I shook Carlo's hand. We drank tea and looked at the painting Rob was working on. It was a huge canvas, more than twelve feet long, much grander than anything I'd seen him make before. He'd only just started on it. There were some roughly sketched figures, and a kind of border, like a proscenium arch in a theater. I asked about the scale, and he said his dealer had suggested it.

"I'll make some smaller versions too, so I have something to offer at various price points."

I said nothing to that. Seeing my sour expression, he frowned and shrugged.

"I'd ask what you think but there's not really much to see yet."

I tried to make positive noises, mumbling something about how the composition looked promising. He asked if I was feeling better.

"Better?"

"I haven't seen you since the opening. You didn't make dinner."

"Yeah. No. I wasn't at my best."

"The show sold, by the way."

"The shop pictures?"

"Yeah. People really like them. I already did some more. Carlo?"

The assistant was directed to bring out some examples. He

propped them up so we could look at them. There was a pie and mash shop and a butcher. I did my best to formulate a response, but I couldn't hide my impatience.

"What I really want to see is the portrait of Alice."

"You do? I'm not sure it worked, to be honest."

"I want to see it, Rob."

"I don't think it's ready to show."

"Alice said it was finished."

"Well, it's my picture, not hers."

"And she's my girlfriend."

He sighed. "Why don't you take ten, Carlo. Go for a coffee."

Carlo left and Rob slid the picture from a rack, carrying it over to an easel. I remember he couldn't really meet my eye. He took a step away, lit a cigarette.

He had painted Alice from the waist up. She was sitting sideways on what looked like a bed, her head turned towards the viewer. She was wrapped in a white sheet, holding it round herself with one hand so her bare shoulders were exposed. It sagged down low over her back, revealing that underneath she was naked. He had taken care with the delicate line of her collarbones, the nape of her neck. She wore an unfamiliar startled expression, a wide-eyed stare that made her look unlike herself; I took this as Rob's invention, some way he wanted to see her. Her cheeks were flushed and her mouth was slightly parted, her lips in an intense, purplish hue. They looked swollen, almost bruised. It had none of the satirical energy Rob usually brought to his figures. It was an unmistakably sexual portrait, a lover's portrait.

"I see," I mumbled. What else could I have said? It was the realization of all my worst fears.

Rob made a little halfhearted gesture with his cigarette, then ashed it on the floor. I stared at the picture a moment longer. When I turned to him, he took an involuntary step backwards.

"I see," I said again. "I see how it is."

I pushed past him and left. When I got home, Alice seemed nervous. I expect he'd called to warn her. I said nothing, trying to act as if everything was normal. I'd brought home ingredients for a meal, so I busied myself in the kitchen, cooking a dish I thought she'd particularly like. She ate a little, and pushed away her plate.

THEY CHOSE THEIR MOMENT CAREFULLY. I'd been invited to do a panel discussion in Newcastle and the gallery had booked a hotel for me, so Alice knew I would be away overnight. I was excited. It had been a long time since I'd been asked to participate in anything like that, and it felt like a good omen. When I said goodbye, Alice barely responded, but that wasn't unusual. As I sat on the train, I felt a profound sense of relief at being away from my life in London. Watching the countryside go past, the flick flick of pylons at the side of the high-speed rail tracks, I did some writing in a notebook, a sketch for a project, a motivational list of tasks I wanted to achieve when I got back. *Move, stop doing drugs, go to the climbing wall twice a week . . .* After the panel, I ate Indian food with the curators and the other artists. The gallery director said she was interested in working with me, floating the idea of a commission. I went to bed feeling happy, and the next morning I texted Alice from the train to say that I'd be home soon. I asked if she wanted to go out to dinner that night. My treat. She didn't answer, and I remember feeling disappointed, but I didn't give it undue weight.

When I got back to the flat, I knew at once that something was different. Alice's shoes were gone from their usual place by the door. Not just one pair, but several. I looked around and found other things missing: clothes, her laptop. I called her phone, waited a few minutes, called again. I texted. *where r u call me*. That evening, I phoned round to some of her friends, to ask if they'd seen her. No one seemed to know anything. Her best friend Charlie was evasive, saying she was busy and it wasn't a good time to talk. It occurred to me to phone Rob, but it felt humiliating to have to ask him where Alice was, and I suppressed the idea.

I went to bed late, unable to sleep. Alice still wasn't picking up. The next day I called Charlie again. I said I knew something was going on, and she had to tell me what it was. She said she didn't want to get involved. What did that mean? Where was Alice? She said I should probably speak to Rob.

In those situations, people take sides. No one seemed to want to be the one to break the news, and I left a lot of messages that weren't returned. Finally a mutual friend took pity on me. We sat in a pub and she explained that Alice and Rob were in Greece together. They'd gone to stay with a schoolfriend of Alice's. She thought it was unfair that neither of them had mustered up the courage to face me.

I knew the place she meant. Alice would sometimes talk about this friend, whose family had a beautiful house on an island close to the mainland, a weekend resort for rich Athenians. She had described the house, which stood on a hill overlooking the sea, its limewashed walls, the bougainvillea tumbling over the door. I imagined it in terms of paint pigments. Titanium white. Cadmium red. Cerulean blue. Alice loved the place, but she always said it would be impossible for us to visit, because her mother and the friend's mother knew each other, and she would never be able to stay there with a lover. I'd accepted that as just another of the limitations imposed by the secrecy of our relationship. It had always felt humiliating to be kept secret, and to discover that she would blithely go to her island with Rob made it hard to deny what I'd always suspected—that Alice had imposed limits on me that didn't apply with someone else.

Afterwards, as I turned over why she'd gone, I blamed myself. She had more or less invited me to stop her sitting for Rob, and I'd done nothing. Was that because I didn't love her enough? Was I just too weak and pathetic to fight for her? For the next few weeks, that house on the island was more real to me than my actual surroundings. Overlaid on the dead Knightsbridge streets, I saw fragments of Greece, a country I had never visited. White walls. A blue sky hard as enamel. I saw Alice pushing open a set of wooden shutters, her feet bare on terracotta tile; Alice in the morning light, sun streaming through the window, looking back and smiling, not at me. I tortured myself with graphic images of sex, and, what was almost as painful, with romantic scenes, dinners at harborfront tavernas, walks among ancient ruins. Finally I called Rob's number and left an incoherent, angry message, making threats and calling him names.

After that, I let myself fall apart. I took all the rest of the mushrooms in the freezer and endured a terrible, nightmarish trip, most of which I spent locked in the bathroom, hearing Douglas laughing at me from the other side of the door. I considered various ways to kill myself, conjuring Jago out of the darkness. I imagined dramatic scenarios of denunciation and revenge, in which Alice and Rob would discover just what they'd lost by leaving me. What I really wanted was to disappear, to become nothing. I imagined scattering into dust, so that experience could pass through without touching me, like a comet traveling through the solar system.

ONE AFTERNOON someone knocked on the door. I ignored it but they carried on, until eventually I heard a key turning in the lock and a woman who looked like a tougher, more imperious version of Alice walked in, a statement bag thrust out in front of her like a search warrant. There was no way to finesse it. I'd been lying on the sofa in a sort of nest I'd made of Alice's old clothes, doing drugs and watching black-and-white comedies. The apartment was filthy, stinking of weed and dereliction.

"What are you doing here?" I asked. The woman ignored me, stalking around and examining things. I realized this must be Carine. In Alice's telling, her sister was a sort of Valkyrie, whose hobbies were competing in endurance sports and reading quarterly earnings reports. She certainly didn't seem like someone who believed in doing unnecessary emotional labor. "You need to leave," she said, without bothering to introduce herself. "I've told the building management you will be out by the end of the week."

I opened my mouth to say something. She held up a finger. "Please don't. It's not like you're even paying rent. And you better clean up before you go. You're lucky my sister phoned me. If my aunt's agent finds you here, he'll have you beaten and thrown in the street."

"You spoke to Alice?"

"She wants you out, that's all she said. She had some idea that I ought to give you money. I told her not to be stupid. How much have you taken from her already?" I didn't know how to answer that. She waved a hand. "Actually don't bother telling me. I don't care. You can leave the keys in the box downstairs. If there's anything missing, I won't hesitate to involve the police." She looked around again. "Someone will be back on Friday to look over the place. If you're still here, it will go badly for you."

She turned on her heel and went to the door.

"Tell Alice hello," I called after her. "Tell Alice her black boyfriend said hello."

After Carine left, I lay down on the couch again and tried to work out how many hours of watching time there were in a week, how many tapes I'd have to rent to get to the end.

ONE MORNING, I woke up in the barn with a terrible headache. The wind moaned in the treetops, the beginnings of a summer storm. My mouth was dry and my chest full of mucus. I felt dizzy and short of breath. I drank some water and stumbled back to bed. For some hours I drifted in and out of sleep as the attic room slowly warmed, and a fly or bee, some drowsy heavy thing, knocked irregularly against one of the windows.

Every day I spent there, the outside world grew a little more distant and insubstantial. I knew I was allowing myself to fall prey to something; a dream of ease and softness; a trap. As I lay on the bed, my fever coming in waves like the gusts of wind shaking the branches of the trees outside, I realized that Alice was sitting at the little table, working on a laptop, a pile of papers on the floor near her feet. I watched her through half-closed eyes. She was dressed, as usual, in running clothes. Her mask was pushed down under her chin. She tapped at her computer, occasionally picking up a document, tracing down columns of figures with a finger. She seemed anxious, as if she didn't like what she saw. I looked at the face that had launched a thousand of my twenty-something ships, tracing what had changed and what had stayed the same, marveling that she was actually there, present in the room, that she was frowning at her screen in the same way she always used to frown at screens, that this expression had persisted through all the time we'd been apart.

I fell into a dream and my mind picked up on some echo or rhyme with the turn I'd made off the public road into wherever I was, that green world of Alice's, and I caught, quite distinctly, the smell of Isabelle's old car, the faint smell of gasoline and plastic, the turn into another driveway, the sound of gravel. I found Alice asleep in her childhood bedroom, a lavender and pink confection that seemed peculiarly lifeless and old-fashioned. The dressing table had rosettes stuck around the mirror, prizes from riding competitions. There were porcelain dolls and a hand-tinted engraving of the Sacred Heart. Above the bed was a needlework sampler in a gilt frame. *Aimer c'est vouloir le bonheur de l'autre.* Her suitcase was open on the floor, vomiting tee shirts and underwear over the rug. I said that the case seemed out of place and Alice told me it wasn't surprising, because we were in her mother's room. She was the one who won prizes for riding. She was the reader of the row of children's classics.

I opened my eyes. Everything was close and still. The roof beams drove hard stripes across my field of vision. It must have been late afternoon. I took small gasps of air, trying to fill my lungs. I turned on my side. Alice was leaning over me, ministering angel. She was very close, her hair down, brushing my face, asking if I was all right, did I need anything. Yes, I said, yes, but I forgot what it was I needed, I always forgot with Alice. She reached up to open the window; light came pouring in like syrup. My breathing eased and I lay back in bed. I closed my eyes. When I opened them again, Alice had gone. The storm was over. She had left a window open, allowing a breeze to circulate, just strong enough to ripple the pages of a book on the table, a tiny movement in an otherwise still scene.

I stood up. I felt strong, and very hungry. I ate an apple and a piece of stale bread, then a bowl of cereal. I could hear the scream of a hawk as it hunted in the meadow. Suddenly I couldn't hide in the barn any longer. I had to go outside. I was choking, stifling. I needed to breathe fresh air. So what if there were cameras in the trees? Maybe I was still feverish. Certainly I wasn't thinking clearly. I dressed and pulled on a pair of shoes. I listened to see if I could hear anyone coming up the path. Not a sound. So I stepped outside, into the light.

I MIGHT AS WELL HAVE BEEN ALONE in the huge parkland. It was like one of those fantasies about being the last human on earth. I took the path that led gently uphill, and soon was lost in a green world. The gravel track petered out and my feet sank into springy moss. I had the sensation of walking over the back of some ancient creature as it breathed ponderously in its sleep. Gradually the path climbed upwards through tall birch trees, their slender trunks wrapped in papery white bark. I worried that I was pushing myself too hard, but at first I felt fine, better than I had in a long time. I wanted to find a viewpoint, a place where I could get a sense of the property. It didn't seem possible that Alice's cottage could be the only building on such a huge tract of land. I thought it must be a guesthouse, an adjunct to some larger house elsewhere.

The uphill climb was strenuous, and I began to feel my limitations. I found a fallen tree and sat down against it. I thought I might fall apart, crumble into dust. I pictured myself as one of those skeletons found by questing heroes in adventure stories, a sign or warning, the remains of the last person to get that far. It was not an anguished experience. I felt prepared, even happy to lay my burden down. After a while some force or current reanimated my limbs and I got up again.

I took it slower, putting one foot deliberately in front of the other. After ten minutes or so, I walked out into an open space and stopped dead, confronted with something that my mind found impossible to process. It was as if I'd come upon a portal, a point where the world was touched by some other nearby reality. The birch glade had been sliced up like a vertical louvre, the filigree of branches and dappled light superimposed on another near-identical version of itself, segments or splinters of a second forest transposed or rhymed with the first, or—that was it—reflected.

As my eyes adjusted, I realized that I was looking at an installation of mirrored slabs set into the ground, their surfaces reflecting the surrounding trees. I experienced an odd sense of disappointment. When, for a moment, you suspect that you've come to the edge of reality, you find out how you really feel about the world. I once dropped acid and watched a hole open up in the tiled wall of a bathroom. Beyond it lay a cartoonish magic kingdom, all primary colors and fluffy clouds, filled with playful but also slightly sinister creatures who invited me to cross over and join them. I told them I'd rather stay where I was, and though I felt a pang of sadness as the hole closed back up, it wasn't a hard decision. I was at art school, there was a party going on downstairs, and in general my life seemed full of potential. There in the glade, things were different. I discovered that my desire to leave was very strong. I would happily have crossed over to another world, no matter how strange or unwelcoming.

I spent a long time circling the installation, looking at it from all angles. The mirrored glade was a pure and perfect gesture. Had I been walking around a gallery, waiting to be impressed, it might not have had such a powerful effect, but coming on it by surprise was overwhelmingly emotional; I could feel tears welling up in my eyes. Gradually I worked out how it was done. Each pillar had three faces. There were twenty of them placed in a spiral. Even my deep ambivalence about everything to do with art couldn't erase the pleasure it gave me.

I sat in the glade for a long time, then walked on uphill through the woods. There I came upon a monumental steel sculpture, a giant red twist that had nothing to recommend it beyond its size. It seemed heavy and inert, and I passed by without stopping. Further up, I scrambled over gnarled roots and slabs of rock, finally hitting the ridgeline, where there was a high chain-link fence. Reaching this boundary was almost a relief. I'd begun to fantasize that Alice's domain was endless. I followed the fence, looking for a gap in the trees. Eventually it was interrupted by a steep stack of rock, a promontory that formed a natural barrier. I climbed up it, not feeling the slightest bit fatigued, and stood looking out over the treetops, a green wave that fell down and away from me into a valley, an almost perfect round bowl with the lake at the bottom. I could see the cottage on the far side, the boathouse, the jetty, a wedge of acid green lawn, but nothing else, no sign of the mansion that ought to have existed there.

I realize that I've fallen into referring to the house as a cottage. Had I seen it on a city street, it would have appeared as what it was, a large property with many bedrooms, but in those surroundings it was completely lost, the lawn a little green slice of civilization cut out of a forest that, from above, seemed almost primeval. It's hard to convey how it feels to look out across a vista like that and realize that it is all private land, when you have been living only a few hours away in a city where people are swarming on top of each other, breathing secondhand air.

It was as if, through walking, my blocked energy had begun to flow. I felt high, exalted, eager to spend the rest of the day exploring. I ventured down near the lake, and even risked traversing a stretch of clear ridgeline on the hill behind the house. I saw no sign of cameras. I should have been more cautious. I was ambling along a path when a figure stepped out in front of me.

"Don't move. Put your hands up. I said hands up, motherfucker!"

He had a military rifle, an AR-15 or something similar, one of those sinister mass-shooter weapons that are marketed to American men like motorcycles or small-batch whiskey, signifiers of rugged individualism. The rifle was all I could see at first, its black bulk magnified by my fear, the muzzle wavering slightly as it pointed at my chest. The man holding it was slightly built, with a pandemic beard and a mop of curly brown hair. He wore wrap-around dark glasses and a white N95 mask; the effect was both futuristic and slightly obscene—the white pouch nestled in the pubic beard, the oil-slick lenses that made it hard to discern a human face. He was trussed into some kind of body armor, a black vest with Velcro straps, hiked up tight under his chin. The clothes underneath weren't military, rolled-up skinny chinos and some kind of long white linen shirt that flared out under the tight vest. He seemed nervous, keyed up. I stood very still and raised my hands.

"Now turn around and put them behind your back."

"Who are you?"

"Comply or I will not hesitate to shoot you."

Reluctantly I did as I was told. The man seemed unstable. I felt that he was looking for an excuse to shoot; it seemed possible that I was about to die.

"I've had eyes on you for an hour, motherfucker."

"OK. Be calm. Just stay calm and tell me what you want."

I could feel him moving about behind me, his breathing ragged and irregular.

"Who are you?" I asked.

"Who am I? Think you can sneak in here, you tweaker hobo motherfucker? Think you could just rob the place? I bet you did. Fucking tweaker. I'm going to settle you once and for all."

I looked up at the sky. I told myself I was OK with it. Now or another time. If it was now, I could accept it. I felt him behind me, and a zip tie was looped around my wrists. As he cinched it tightly, cutting off the circulation to my hands, my calm faltered. It was hard not to be afraid. I tried to concentrate on the trees, to take in the detail of the leaves, the way they shivered as the wind moved the branches.

"This is private property, fucko. I'm calling the cops."

The cops. He wasn't going to execute me. My relief almost overwhelmed my ability to speak; my voice, when it came, was a low croak. "You don't need to do that."

"Oh yeah? You worried now?"

I glanced round to find him fumbling with his cell phone. Spooked by my movement, he raised the rifle again.

"You must be Marshal."

"How do you know my name, asshole?"

"Educated guess."

"Shut up."

I flinched. "Marshal, you don't need to point the gun at me. I'm a friend of Alice's. My name is Jay. Alice knows I'm here."

"She what?"

"She let me stay here, up in the barn."

"Bullshit. There's no one on the property but us."

"I know."

"I mean, there's me and my guys. A bunch of guys. Fuck, I can't get bars."

"Just take me to the house. Alice will explain."

"You don't know Alice."

"Just take me to Alice."

"You don't know her."

I looked round again. He was gripping the rifle loosely with one hand, the phone to his ear. I considered running. We were surrounded by trees. I doubted he'd had much practice with his weapon, but I still didn't like my chances. How far would I really get?

"Marshal, let's just go down to the house. Alice will explain."

His shoulders sagged a little. Even with the mask and shades obscuring his face, I could tell that he wasn't sure of himself.

He was stressed and exhausted. This was not something he was trained to do. He stuffed the phone into one of the pockets on his vest and motioned for me to walk in front of him.

"Don't try to be smart," he said.

We started off towards the house.

Our progress through the woods was painful and slow. The zip tie dug painfully into my wrists and I stumbled frequently, unable to right myself without twisting and staggering. More than once, I heard Marshal curse under his breath. He didn't seem like the type to have good trigger discipline and I worried that he would trip and discharge his gun. It would be too stupid to die by accident, shot in the back. I looked down at my feet, trying to be precise about where I trod. I was relieved to see the house appear in front of us. We were approaching from the back, past the concrete cap of a septic tank and a row of air conditioners humming loudly in wooden enclosures. A short flight of wooden steps led up to the deck. As we got close, Marshal began to shout for Rob and Alice and Nicole. So much for his "guys." I actually laughed, a sound that came out as a bark, an uncontrollable spasm of stress. Marshal told me to go up onto the deck and kneel down.

"I'm not kneeling down."

"Shut up and comply. Rob! Are you in there?"

Reluctantly, I walked up the stairs onto the deck. Marshal followed close behind. The first person to appear was Alice, who screamed and ran back inside. There was the sound of an upstairs window opening.

"Marshal? What the fuck are you doing?"

"I captured an intruder!"

I caught a glimpse—of hair mostly, a mass of tight curls falling over a woman's face.

"Why are you dressed like that, Marshal?"

"Never mind. You need to call the cops."

She was young, not far into her twenties. She pushed her hair back and secured it with a headband. Her features were regular and sharp, a long straight nose, a full mouth, her skin a deep coppery black. She looked frankly terrified.

"Marshal, honey, are you OK? Why do you have a gun? Are you upset about something?"

"Nicole, just call 911. Don't be afraid. I have him fully restrained."

She disappeared. After a moment or two I saw Alice peering nervously round the side of the building. Now, Alice, I thought. Now would be a good time to say something.

"It's OK," she called out. "I know him."

Marshal turned towards her. "Seriously?"

"Marshal, you're scaring me."

"This a friend of yours?"

"Alice?" I called out. "I'm sorry about this."

"I'll deal with it, Jay. Marshal, could you put the gun down and let him go?"

Finally, Marshal lowered the rifle onto a strap attached to his ballistic vest. He took off his glasses and mopped his face with a bandanna, lifting up his mask to wipe around his chin. It was a warm day and he was sweating profusely.

"I got a call about him earlier this morning, so I went on recon."

"You went on what, now?"

It was Nicole, who'd appeared beside Alice. She was wearing a flower pattern kimono, as if she'd been upstairs napping. "What the hell, Marshal? Where did you get all that military shit?"

"I have a cache, Nicole. I told you about my cache. Did you call the cops?"

"No, of course not."

"Why the hell didn't you follow my instructions?"

"Because I don't want the cops here."

Alice came closer. Over her athleisure clothes, she was wearing an apron, dusted with flour. She looked at me anxiously. Her back to Marshal, she mouthed "sorry."

"Marshal, I told you he's my friend. Let him go."

I twisted round to show her my zip-tied wrists. "Could you get him to take these off?"

"Oh my God. Look at his hands! Marshal, his hands are purple."

Marshal still seemed unconvinced. Alice raised her voice.

"I said I knew him, didn't I? Let him go! Right now!"

With a rip of Velcro, Marshal opened one of the pockets on his vest and drew a hunting knife with a serrated blade. He went behind me and cut the ties. As I massaged my swollen hands, I suddenly felt cold. I observed the phenomenon as if from a great distance, feeling totally disconnected from the body that was beginning to shiver, at first slightly, then violently, uncontrollably. Alice hurried towards me and put an arm round my shoulder. "You better come inside."

Marshal barred the way. "You want to bring him into the house? Are you insane? He could be infected."

"He's not."

"How would you know?"

"Because he's been here over two weeks."

Nicole looked at Alice. "I don't understand what's happening."

"I'll explain. Come on, Jay. No, not you, Marshal. First you leave that thing outside. I will not have it in the house."

"That 'thing' is for your protection."

Alice lost her temper. "Get rid of the gun, right now, and stop making a fool of yourself!"

"You should be thanking me, Alice."

I listened to the argument as if it were taking place on TV, something in which I had a mild interest, but didn't fundamentally concern me. As Marshal carried on talking, justifying himself with some kind of extended metaphor about wolves and sheepdogs, Alice steered me inside and sat me down on a high-backed chair at the head of a long wooden table. I looked around vacantly at a large eat-in kitchen. Over a fireplace hung a messy figurative painting that even in my dissociated state I recognized as the work of a famous nineteen-eighties Neo-expressionist, an artist whose work I'd only ever seen in museums. Distractedly, I took in other details. A battery of copper pans hung on hooks over a massive brushed-steel range. On a marble-topped island, an iPad sat on a stand, open to a *New York Times* recipe page. On the floured surface in front of it was a ball of dough. Alice had been baking bread.

Nicole noticed that I was shivering. "Do you want, like, a brandy, or something?"

I nodded. She started opening cupboards. I looked at my hands on the wooden surface of the table and they did not belong to me. The thought about belonging did not belong to me. Marshal sat down grumpily at the far end of the table, still wearing his N95. "I'd feel more comfortable if he masked up," he said, to no one in particular.

Alice was standing nearby and for a moment I thought she was going to strike him. "You are talking about feeling comfortable right now? You are seriously talking about your personal feelings of comfort?"

Marshal shrugged. "I'm just saying."

"This is Jay. You know the barn on the other side of the lake? He's staying there."

Marshal looked sharply at her. "What do you mean, he's staying there?"

"What I said."

"Alice, I had an agreement with Greg. An agreement. You understand what I'm saying? He was very strict."

"Jay's—a friend of mine. It was an emergency."

"A what? No one else on the property, that's what I promised Greg. No one."

Nicole handed me a glass, smiling quizzically. "I thought I saw someone in there once, when I was out running."

I sipped the brandy, feeling it catch at the back of my throat. "That was me."

"But why?" Marshal was almost apoplectic, waving his hands at Alice. "Why would you invite him without telling me? Greg called me. Do you have any idea what systems he has installed here? Motion detection, infrared. If I don't phone him back soon, God knows who he'll send out to deal with it."

Nicole frowned. "What do you mean?"

"A security team, Nic." He let out an exasperated sigh. "He has former spec ops guys on retainer. This person, whoever he is, should count himself lucky it was me that brought him in." He turned to me. "They would have taken you the fuck down, buddy." He jabbed a finger at me. "The fuck down."

I stared back blankly. Nicole shook her head at him. "Why would you talk like that?"

"I'm sorry." Alice was trying to smooth over the situation. "This was not what I intended. I get what you're saying and if there's a problem with Greg just give him my number. Tell him it's my fault."

"I'm the one who has to answer to him, not you, Alice. He and I have a relationship."

"I'll talk to him."

"And to remind you, it's a relationship all of us benefit from. Directly or indirectly."

"Marshal, I get it. But we also need to talk about the gun."

"I cannot believe you hid him in the barn. How could you be so stupid? You asked him up here from—from where?" He turned back to me. "From where?"

"He's an old friend from London. He was delivering food."

He scrutinized me. "And you were delivering—what, pizza? You are an old friend from London who just turned up with a pizza?"

"Groceries."

"And she believed that line of bullshit?"

I shrugged.

"Sure she did. I'm sorry. Alice, you know the delivery guy? Your 'mate' who just turned up out of the blue? Am I in a fucking porno movie right now? That is the script of a fucking porno."

"Watch your mouth."

"Oh, I'm sorry. It's just I find it kind of ridiculous that the delivery guy has been holed up in the barn for weeks."

"Marshal, why do you have that gun?"

"For situations like this. When naïve liberals demonstrate that they don't have a lick of sense."

"He's my friend. You could have killed him."

"We are in a global pandemic. We are on the verge of catastrophic social breakdown. And you seem to think you're on vacation. I don't know where to begin with this. It was incredibly irresponsible not to tell us about him."

"He's not a threat."

"I'm supposed to take your word for that, when you believe his garbage line about turning up here by accident? I mean, a pizza? Seriously, Alice. Live in the real world."

"It was groceries."

"Whatever."

"So what are you saying?"

"That he has some kind of agenda? Duh. And why are we talking like he's not here? Time to speak up for yourself, buddy. What do you want?"

"Can't you see the state he's in?"

"What? What state? Hey, are you in a state?"

I'd had enough of him. "Fuck you," I muttered.

"Fuck me? Very nice." He turned back to Alice. "Very nice, your friend. Your friend who is exposing us all to the goddamn plague. We agreed we weren't going to put the pod at risk. We were all very clear about that. This is—I don't know. It's the selfishness. That's what gets me. I don't know what to say to you."

"I didn't put you at risk."

"Because your friend has been here for weeks."

"Yes."

"But you were exposed to him when he arrived."

"We were careful. He already had it. He wasn't contagious."

"How can you say that? Are you a doctor? Are you a fucking doctor, Alice?"

Alice screamed. "Marshal, why are you sneaking around with a gun?"

"What's going on?"

Those nasal Manchester vowels, still intact after so many years in America.

Rob was never a gym rat, and he had the kind of stocky build that made him look heavier than he was, but when I'd known him we were both young, and our nights of drinking and days of junk food were usually sweated off on some dance floor. Occasionally he'd stare at himself in the mirror and dislike what he saw, and that would set him off on a sort of reverse binge. For a few weeks he'd lift weights and eat healthily, and soon enough he'd look, if not exactly fit—he had a pale complexion and reddish hair and there was always something slightly crepuscular about him, something hostile to sunlight—then at least not actively unwell. In the doorway I saw a hulking man with rounded shoulders. He had a full beard, and like most people in those first months of the pandemic, he needed a haircut. Dressed in painting clothes, he stood in the doorway, wiping his hands on a rag. He looked around the kitchen, at Marshal, still in his body armor, then at me. For a moment his expression was blank. Then he frowned, trying to place the face.

"Hello Rob," I said.

It took him another moment. Then his eyes widened and his mouth went slack. "I thought you were dead." His voice came out as a whisper. "Everyone thinks you're dead."

Marshal and Nicole were making identical movements, their heads swiveling from side to side like spectators at a tennis match.

"Is it you, Jay?" he asked.

"It's me."

Marshal was almost plaintive. "You know this guy too?"

Rob ignored him. "Why are you here?"

"I don't know, Rob. It wasn't planned."

Marshal's phone rang. He stepped out onto the deck to answer, and I could only catch fragments of conversation. "No, it's all fine . . . yes, totally . . . I'm sorry, it was a misunderstanding. It won't happen again . . . He's about to leave . . ."

Alice was going through the story again, how I'd turned up with a delivery, and she'd let me stay in the barn. She left out the part about me living in my car. Marshal ended his call and came back inside to listen. As Alice spoke, Rob stared fixedly at me, trying to excavate something, to tunnel beneath my surface with his eyes. When he spoke, his voice was hollow. "Are you here to kill us?"

The room went silent, as if someone had unplugged the audio. Everyone stared at Rob. I saw firstly that it was a serious question, secondly that he was high. His eyes were bloodshot and his pupils were dilated. He was twisting his painting rag compulsively in his hands.

"No," I said. "You don't have to worry about that."

"This is super weird," said Nicole.

Marshal took a step forward. "Rob, is this man a threat to us? Why would he want to kill you?"

Alice sighed. "Sit down Marshal. We used to date. A long time ago. Rob's just worried that certain chickens are coming home to roost."

"You used to date the delivery guy?"

"He wasn't always a delivery guy."

"You've been with Rob ever since I met you."

"This was before. A long time ago. In London."

"Just a minute." Marshal's eyes narrowed. "Were you an artist?"

I nodded.

"And you were friends with these guys in the nineties."

"Yes."

"Oh my God! I think I know who you are!" He turned to Nicole. "You know who that is?"

"No."

"Jason something. Gaines. Gates."

"Who?"

"He did this series of actions called—what were they called? *Drifting,* something like that. Then he disappeared. Just vanished."

"The seventies guy? The Dutch guy?"

"No, later. My God, Alice, this is amazing."

I felt disoriented. For years, I had lived away from the art-world. Now this man I'd never met, a New York gallerist, was saying my name as if someone ought to know who I was. I'd never exhibited in New York. When I was younger, I met a few American artists, mostly people who'd come to London to show or study, but I never even visited the US until much later, when I was, in a quasi-literal sense, someone else. The papers I was using had a different name, a different place of birth. I had not been Jason Gates in over a decade.

"I'll leave," I said to Rob. "You don't have to worry. I'm not here to cause trouble."

"No you won't," said Alice.

"What?"

"You're staying."

Rob looked confused. "Here? In the house?"

"He can sleep in the barn."

Rob turned to me. "Why did you have our groceries?"

"That's my job."

"Delivering groceries."

"Yes."

"In America."

"Yes."

"I don't understand. Why would you do that? Is it for a piece?"

"No, just for money."

"You live here?"

"I've been here a long time."

"Are you legal?" asked Marshal.

Rob was staring at me suspiciously. "How did you know we were here?"

"I didn't."

"Pull the other one. This doesn't happen by chance. What do you want?"

Marshal nodded. "Exactly! That's what I said."

"I don't want anything from you, Rob."

"You sure about that?"

"Like I said, I'll go. I was in a bad way. Alice was kind. She let me stay. But I've imposed on her hospitality too long."

Alice shook her head. "You're not going anywhere. You still owe me an explanation. You need to tell me where you've been."

Rob was twisting his rag in spasmodic little motions, as if wringing a chicken's neck. "Alice, I think we need to talk. This— I don't think this is what you think it is."

I got up unsteadily from the table. "I don't want anything from you, Rob. I don't want to hurt you. I don't want your money. I'm not running any kind of scam. I never expected to see you again."

Alice turned to her husband. "If he goes, I'm going too. Back to the city. You can carry on here if you like, but I can't be here any longer."

Rob groaned. "What the hell is going on? I don't understand."

He looked over at Marshal, and seemed to notice the vest for the first time. "Why are you wearing that?"

"He has a gun too," said Alice. "I made him leave it outside."

"What kind of gun?"

"It's a rifle. A SIG Sauer MCX with a folding stock."

"A what?"

"It's called being prepared, man. We don't know how far this thing is going to go."

"What thing?" asked Nicole.

"The pandemic. It's all going to come apart. Armageddon time. The boogaloo."

"What the fuck, Marshal? You are spending way too much time on the internet."

"And you're not? Why won't any of you take this seriously? I don't know why I can't get through to any of you. The center. Cannot. Hold."

Alice turned to me. "I think we all need to talk, work out what to do."

I sat back down. I felt exhausted.

"Are you OK? Maybe you should eat something."

"Something sweet," suggested Nicole.

Alice came back with a chocolate chip cookie. I chewed the cookie. The sweet chocolate mixed together with the brandy and I began to feel a little better. The other people at the table were glowering at each other, Rob clinging on to his rag like a child with a blankie, Marshal widening his eyes at Nicole, doing some kind of what-is-going-on mime with his hands.

"Why don't you go back up to the barn and rest. I'll come find you later." Alice's tone was hostess-bright. "You can have dinner here and then you can tell us what you've been doing all these years."

I stood up again.

"Hey," said Marshal. "I'm—like, I didn't know, OK? I'm sorry."

I nodded.

"You're Jason fucking Gates. That's incredible. Really."

I gave him a weak thumbs-up and went outside. As I began

walking to the barn, Marshal and Nicole came out onto the deck, continuing some argument they must have started inside. They were raising their voices, arguing about the cops, why she hadn't called, why he thought they'd make anything better. As I got closer to the lake, the sound was muffled by the trees.

BACK AT THE BARN, I lay down on the bed. My body felt as if I'd gone over Niagara Falls in a barrel. Drained of adrenaline, I was jumpy and scattered. The prospect of having to tell my story over dinner was weighing on me. At the best of times I found it hard, almost painful, to talk about myself. In the world I used to inhabit, the world in which I'd known Alice, everything was discussed and analyzed. People were articulate about their emotions; it was a kind of social currency. Many men, particularly older men, find such talk intolerable, and will go to great lengths to avoid it. I've worked alongside men for weeks, sometimes months, without finding out a single piece of personal information, or being asked one question about myself. Silence can be a kind of courtesy, a pact not to put each other under pressure or extract anything but the most basic obligations.

I heard Alice's voice, calling me from downstairs.

"Are you OK?"

"Yes."

"How are your wrists?"

"Sore. I'm sore all over, to be honest."

"You want to stretch it out a little? I thought we could go for a walk."

Of course it's one thing not to speak about your feelings, another to be afraid of them, or act without understanding why.

We followed the path up the hill. Under the trees, it was already cool. The mass of green leaves murmured and shifted over our heads. Only in the mirror glade could you still feel the day's heat, the ground slowly exhaling. The pillars cast long shadows, their westward faces blazing with light like beacons, alien signaling devices. Alice walked around the perimeter of the installation. Slivers of her, multiplied. I wanted to take her hand and cross over into the mirror world.

"They're beautiful, aren't they?" She turned to me, then frowned. "Or maybe you don't approve."

"Why wouldn't I approve?"

"You were always very critical of beautiful things."

"I was?" I was genuinely confused. "I thought I was beauty's biggest fan."

"I'm sure there's a lot we remember differently."

"I remember taking beauty very seriously."

"You took everything very seriously."

"But I didn't think—I mean, I wasn't against beauty. I was never against beauty."

"What was that slogan you used to repeat?"

"That wasn't me. That was your slogan. From one of your relational aesthetics books."

"Really? Fuck retinal pleasure? That was what you were about, though. The battle you were fighting."

We walked along in silence for a while. "So," I asked. "When you sneak off up here to see me, what are the others doing?"

She thought for a moment. "I suppose Rob is passive-aggressively lying on the couch in his studio. He knows that's what will piss everyone off the most. Marshal will be on a call, or mixing one of his weird fitness drinks. I don't know about Nicole. Hiding out somewhere. 'Doing self-care' is the phrase she uses when she doesn't want to be around the rest of us."

"Sounds fun."

"It's terrible, if you want to know. Everyone is on edge. I wish we could go back to the city."

"Why don't you?"

"Because Rob has to make these paintings."

"Why?"

"He just has to."

"Why does anyone have to make a painting?"

She sighed deeply. "Jay, I can't do this with you. It's not that it—the way you're talking—isn't important. But it's not about that. It's not helpful to talk like that."

"Like what?"

"Like it's about art. He has to make the paintings because Marshal already advanced him money for the paintings."

"So art doesn't really come into it."

"Jesus, Jay. You turn up here like a ghost, and suddenly we're back in this conversation. The same old conversation."

"I didn't mean to sound judgmental."

"Well you did, OK? What I don't understand is why you even care."

"Why shouldn't I?"

"I don't know. I don't even know if you do. I heard that after we left you were doing really well, getting shows, and then you just dropped out. You stopped being an artist."

"Who said that?"

"You disappeared, Jay."

"Disappeared. That's quite a word, coming from you."

"It's not the same thing. We moved to New York. You vanished."

"From a certain scene, maybe."

"You vanished. People would call us, asking for news. No one knew where you were. No one has heard from you, Jay, not for years. People write theories about you on the internet."

It was the first I'd heard of that. We stood in silence, listening to the small sounds of the forest. A bird called plaintively from the lake, answered by its mate.

"So," she said. "You're still making art."

"I didn't say that."

"OK, then. You're an artist but you're not making art."

"Maybe. I know how that sounds."

"Where have you been, Jay?"

The sun had almost set. The tips of the mirrored pillars were still dabbed with orange light, little molten drops gradually being squeezed away.

"I moved around. I was in Asia, then Europe for a long time. Then I came here. But what about you? Did you fulfill your dreams?"

"What dreams?"

"I thought you were going to be a curator. Directing a museum, running a biennale."

"I had a gallery for a while."

"Why did you stop?"

"Oh, you know. Rob takes up a lot of light and air. When he started selling, it began to seem, well, not the best use of my time. Money passes through Rob's hands, but he has trouble keeping track of it. Someone had to take charge."

"So that's you."

"That's me. I put out fires. I negotiate with Marshal. I am Rob's envoy to the mortal world."

She checked the time on her phone. She had to go and start dinner, she said. If she didn't, no one else would. She asked if I'd walk down with her, but I wasn't ready for the house. I told her I needed a moment. We said goodbye at the barn. When she'd gone, I went upstairs and lay down, just to think things through—how to start, what to say—and I must have fallen asleep, because the next thing I knew someone was calling my name from outside. I looked blearily out to see Nicole standing under the window, her hair up in a scarf, her hands jammed into the pockets of a hoodie. I ran downstairs and pulled open the barn door.

"Hello."

"Alice said you might have fallen asleep."

"Have I missed dinner?"

"Oh no. But it's almost ready. I came up to fetch you."

It took a few minutes to get myself together. I brushed my teeth and put on a clean shirt. When I came down, Nicole was waiting, leaning on the car.

"This your ride?"

"Fancy, huh?"

"I've seen worse. It would get a person back to the city, for example."

"You thinking of leaving?"

"Maybe. Marshal has his theories, and he can definitely be, you know, argumentative, but I have never seen him like he was earlier. He scared me."

"Did you know he had the gun?"

She shrugged. "I mean, I knew he had something. Not all that—the armor and shit."

"He seems kind of tightly wound."

"You could say so. Look, we ought to go. Alice is cooking a fish stew. She says it has to be served as soon as it's done."

"That's funny."

"Why?"

"Alice never used to cook."

"She's kind of a foodie, actually."

We walked down the hill towards the lake. The heat had gone out of the air and the sky above the trees had a faint orange tint. As we walked, she asked me which company I'd been driving for. She knew about the app, how it worked, how routes were assigned. She had friends who were drivers. I had the impression I was being probed, my story delicately stress-tested.

"So you from England too?"

There was an unspoken supplement to her question. It was the reason she'd walked up there, to look me in the eye and work out what my deal was, away from whatever performance she thought I was putting on for the others. I nodded.

"And you know these good people from back in the day."

I nodded again.

"But you didn't take the same path."

Growing up where I did, with no other Black people around, I dressed and spoke like my white friends, most of whom were outcast seaside Goths. I wore charity shop overcoats and skinny black jeans; I liked synthesizer bands. When I got to London, to do my foundation year at art school, I never tried very hard to fit in to any of the Black scenes I drifted through. That didn't stop me hating the suspicion I aroused, the out-group signals I gave off by the way I used or didn't use my hands when I talked, the words I didn't know, the dances. At a sound system party some girl told me I talked like a taxi driver. She meant I talked white, the particular working-class white accent of the Essex sprawl. I wondered where Nicole ranked me in the freemasonry of the diaspora. It was obvious she thought I was running some kind of hustle.

We crunched our way down the slope towards the lake, and got to the flat part, where the gravel gave way to tarmac. I asked her if she was an artist.

"I suppose so. I mean, yes. Trying to be. But I work for Marshal too, helping organize parties, dinners, you know."

"What do you make?"

"Working for Marshal?"

"No, what kind of art."

She looked embarrassed. "It's kind of post-internet? I mean, I don't have a studio up here. I'm just kind of doing stuff on a tablet. Nothing important."

"Is it important to you?"

"Yeah, I guess."

"Well then."

She winced. "The weird thing is that Marshal's very excited that you're here. He can't stop talking about you."

"And Rob? How's he taking it?"

"Not too well. After you left he and Alice had a fight, and he stomped off back to the red barn."

"The red barn is where he's painting?"

"If he was painting, Marshal wouldn't be having a nervous breakdown. No, Rob just goes there to get high and look at shit on his laptop."

I glanced over at her. Her face was studiously neutral.

"How long have you all been here?"

"Too damn long."

We made our way past the boathouse and the little dock, and began to climb up the slope towards the house. I could see lights on downstairs, figures moving about.

"So have you and Marshal been together for a while?"

"Lord no. About six months. This whole thing—the pandemic—kind of accelerated us. We weren't even living together before we came up here."

"Really?"

"It was kind of an on-off thing."

She seemed like she needed someone to talk to. She described a dinner, how he made a point of sitting beside her, swapping place cards with someone else, being very charming. "So of course I ended up going home with him."

"And he offered you a show."

"Oh we are cynical! No, he didn't give me a show. Not that he doesn't look out for me. He's introduced me to a lot of people."

The lights were blazing, and for a moment we stood outside, listening to someone's Bossa Nova playlist filtering through an open window. Nicole seemed to be as reluctant to go in as I was. She turned to me and gave me a straight look.

"Don't judge me, OK? I can see you judging me. When the city shut down I didn't have anything coming in. All my little hustles dried up. At this point I haven't paid my rent in two months. Coming up here with Marshal didn't seem like the worst option."

We pushed open the back door.

Alice was in the kitchen, presiding over a large pot, from which emanated a delicious odor of saffron and tomato. Seeing us walk in together, she frowned. Nicole immediately asked if she needed a hand, and was given the job of slathering garlic butter onto a loaf of what I presumed was the bread she'd been baking earlier. There was a brightness about the way the two women dealt with each other, an edge of tense politeness. They had been thrown together, and would not naturally have been in each other's company; they were trying to make the best of it.

Alice poured me a glass of wine, lightly touching my shoulder as she leaned over me. I looked around, at the chandelier hanging over the table, the fruit ripening on the counter in a big art pottery bowl, trying to remember when I'd last been in such a quietly luxurious room. For a moment there was calm, then Marshal bustled in. He headed straight to the pot, whipped off the lid, and started poking around in it with a fork. Alice was irritated.

"Marshal, I'm cooking."

"I know, I know. I'll be out of your way in a second."

"But we're almost ready to eat."

"Yeah. It's just, well, is there cheese in that?"

"It's bouillabaisse."

"How did you source the fish?"

"Oh my God, Marshal."

"No, it's a serious question. I don't want to have to do any more chelation."

"None of us want that. The fish is clean. I got the fish from the place that does the good fish. There are no heavy metals in the fish. Now could you step out of the way? I need to drain the potatoes."

Marshal held up a military-looking flask containing some kind of gray liquid.

"I'll probably just do this, as a boost."

Alice gestured in his direction with a big two-handled colander, eloquently conveying how little she cared about his boost. He ignored her and sat down at the table next to Nicole, slinging an arm around the back of her chair.

"Is there wine? Oh, you're already here. Hi."

Seeing me, Marshal's face fell into what appeared to be a sincere expression of anguish. It was the first time I'd seen him without his mask. He had small features, a delicate mouth and nose, all set quite close together, as if someone had pinched them out of clay.

"Look," he said. "I feel terrible about earlier on. I really want us to reset." I caught Alice rolling her eyes as she spooned the potatoes into a serving dish. "I'm truly sorry. That's what I want to say. I'm sorry. I wouldn't have approached it like that if I'd known who you were."

"Who I am?"

"I mean, you're a legend. How was I to know?"

"And that's what saved me?"

He laughed, as if I'd made a joke. Seeing that I wasn't smiling, he stopped.

"I wasn't going to shoot you. I mean, come on."

"You looked like you wanted to. You were imagining what it would be like to pull the trigger."

"That's not fair. Sure, I was adrenalized. But I was in full control."

Nicole turned to him. "Do you realize how psychopathic you sound?"

"Honey!"

"Don't honey me. I'm serious."

"It turned out to be a false alarm, and that's great. I hate having to repeat this, but we are not in normal times. I know I gave Jason a scare and I'm truly sorry. I wish I could take it back, but I also think you're being just a teeny bit complacent."

I saw a rapid succession of emotions pass over Nicole's face, among them barely filtered rage. Marshal, fully focused on me, seemed not to notice.

"I'm glad we're getting a chance to talk," he said.

"Don't ever point a gun at me again."

"Of course not. I'm sorry. It was an honest mistake. If possible, I just want to draw a line, make a fresh start."

I said nothing. Marshal swallowed his glass of wine and refilled it. We sat in silence, listening to the music, which was playing over some kind of speaker system built into the ceiling.

"So you came here straight from the city."

I was tempted to ignore him, but it seemed pointless. I was at dinner. People talked to each other over dinner.

"I left about six weeks ago."

"And you were sick."

"Yeah, I got kicked out of where I was living."

Nicole frowned. "Why?"

"My roommates—well, the landlord. No one wanted to take the chance. They told me I had to go. I didn't have many options, so I drove up here."

"While you were sick?" Marshal was interested in this. "Where have you been staying?"

Alice answered. "He was sleeping in his car."

Marshal looked at me with the abstract concern of a man hearing news of famine or far-off war.

"So you're basically homeless."

I looked at my hands, irritated that Alice had brought it up. What was I doing there, really? I didn't know those people. I didn't even know Alice, not in any way that mattered. She was a woman in branded yoga clothing, cooking fish from the good fish place. She was a stranger.

Nicole asked if I could tell her how the city had felt. Most of her friends and family were still there. She, at least, seemed grounded in a reality I could recognize.

"Very empty. Sometimes it felt like the end of the world."

"That's exactly what my grandma says, though I think she maybe means it more literally than you. She says we're entering the time of tribulation."

Marshal poured himself another glass, jiggled the bottle at me. "When they brought that ship, the hospital ship? That was the red flag. I said to this one, just pack a bag, babe, let's get out of here. No way I wanted to risk getting locked down in a plague city."

"So the four of you have been up here for a while?"

"About two months."

"Without seeing anyone else?"

"Not until you. We make the occasional supermarket run, that kind of thing. Fully masked, of course. So, I mean, it's not like we haven't set eyes on other human beings. But, cards on the table, what I wanted to say, this house doesn't belong to me. And the owner was very strict about who he wanted on the property."

Alice interrupted. "Could we not, Marshal? Could we save that whole side of things for later?"

We went on, making Covid small talk and waiting for Rob to appear for dinner. I helped set the table, filling a jug with water as Alice folded napkins and Nicole took the garlic bread out of the oven. The food was ready to be served. Marshal leaned back in his chair, lifting up his wineglass so we could work round him. In his opinion "the situation" was going to get a lot darker. It was almost certain that the pandemic wasn't a natural occurrence. The "whole story about the wet market," for example, was "obvious bullshit."

Alice and Nicole looked as if they'd heard it all before. "Just do some research," he said to me, as if I'd expressed skepticism. "There's a level four lab there."

I asked what that was.

"Where they do the most hazardous stuff. I tell you this was not an accident. It is a Chinese bioweapon."

Alice swore under her breath. "Oh my God. Would you listen to yourself? This kind of garbage is why I wanted to leave. It's not safe to walk down the street because morons hear your conspiracy theories and think Asians are spreading disease."

"Conspiracy theories? I'm sorry, but you have to pursue the truth regardless of where it leads."

"What do you know about the truth? You're just reading Facebook posts."

"They can't censor everybody."

"A woman had acid thrown in her face."

"This is bigger than all of us. You can't tell people not to ask questions about a world-historical event. I think it's going to get worse, actually. I think we'll end up going to war. We have to be able to discuss it without getting censored. It's a fundamental right."

Before Alice could say whatever she was about to say, Rob walked in. His hair was wet, and he seemed bedraggled, as if he'd taken a shower and hadn't fully dried off before putting on his clothes. He was wearing a white linen shirt and beige drawstring pants, colors that emphasized the doughy pallor of his skin.

"About time," Alice muttered.

"Sorry love. I'm starving. What's for dinner?"

He seemed nervous, his bonhomie ginned up, overdone. He stuck out his hand, but before I could shake it, he withdrew it again. "You've changed, mate," he said. "I wouldn't have recognized you. You look . . ." He trailed off. "You look like you've been outdoors a lot."

He pulled up a chair and Alice started serving the food. I was acutely aware of the penumbra of money that surrounded us, of the heft of the silverware, Marshal's complicated diving watch, the mid-century dining chair that was so perfectly supporting my back. We talked, in a disjointed way, about trivial things, a show Marshal and Nicole were streaming, the deer Alice had seen outside the window while she was cooking dinner. Rob said very little, concentrating on his food. From time to time I caught him watching me, a sour expression on his face. Soon enough, a silence fell. Alice wiped her mouth with her napkin and said that she knew we had a lot to discuss, and everyone needed to understand more if they were going to make informed decisions. It was evidently time for me to talk. "So," she asked. "Now you get to tell me where you've been."

IT WAS LIKE A JOB INTERVIEW, the four of them looking at me over the table, their expressions ranging from mild interest to frank hostility. I told myself that only Alice was important. It didn't matter what the others thought. So I told Alice how, looking back, I found it hard to disentangle the choices I'd made freely from what had been forced on me by circumstance. I described moving out of her aunt's flat, gathering up my few possessions, cleaning and scrubbing the place until the cleaning became compulsive, in some way interesting to me, the idea of erasing my presence, leaving no trace. Until I began to speak, I'd forgotten how it had felt to throw my stuff into the dumpster in the building's basement, the sense of lightness, of bringing something to an end.

I didn't make any effort to explain the context to Marshal and Nicole, and neither did Alice or Rob. They were left to follow along as best they could. I described how I took a small bag containing the few things I wanted to keep and moved to the cheapest rented flat I could find, a one-room studio on the thirteenth floor of a tower block in Newham. It had rough gray carpet tiles, the kind usually installed in offices, and a little kitchenette at one end: some chipped wooden cabinets, a Formica counter and a wobbly electric cooker. The wind moaned at the windows and from the outside walkway you could see across the city, an arc of roofs and streetlights that I found soothing: other lives, at a safe distance from mine. I kept the place almost empty, sleeping on a futon that I rolled up every morning and stored in a closet.

There I experimented with renunciation. I gave up drugs, alcohol and meat. One day a week I fasted, drinking nothing but water. I tried more extreme things, such as taping black plastic over the windows and living in darkness. I spent whole days wearing headphones and wax plugs in my ears, trying to experience a world without external sound, the pure frequency of reality. I was trying to catch myself being; that's the best way I can explain it. I was trying to spot the moment when I happened, to engineer a way to bump into myself.

For money I took a job at an art mover, helping to pack and ship work for galleries. The other movers were also artists, and they liked to swap gossip and opinions, to make themselves feel closer to the action than they actually were. Through them I learned that Alice and Rob were in New York. I wasn't sure how I felt. I was saved from the anxiety of running into them, but the thought of Alice embarking on a romantic new adventure convinced me that I had to do something drastic. I was determined to copy her by leaving behind the person she had left, to break myself in some way and begin again.

"It was about me." It sounded involuntary, words that weren't so much spoken as drawn out of Alice like a breath. Rob stared at her over the table, a look of cold fury on his face. I heard the same thing he heard, the shocking intimacy of it, his wife and her ex-lover continuing a conversation that had been going on for weeks without his knowledge.

"No," I said. "It's not that simple."

I'd started, and now they would have to follow where I led. I told them that I'd only showed one artwork during this period. It was a sculpture, called *The Name of the Bow Is Life*. A strip of flexible metal about five feet long was attached to a wall at chest height. At one end was fixed a large knife, more of a machete, a big rough agricultural thing. The metal strip was pulled into tension by a nylon cord, whose ends were also attached to the wall, curving it backwards into a wicked half-moon. The blade of the knife lay against this bowstring, shielded only by a strip of cardboard, as insubstantial as I dared make it. Were the cardboard to be removed—or slip—the knife would cut through and sweep in a long, vicious arc across the room, or possibly fly off the metal strip and bury itself in the opposing wall. It was a way to freeze the potential for violence and hang it in a gallery, to make people feel what it was like to live under threat. A foolhardy curator put it into a group show, then watched, terrified, as the crowd at the opening jostled around near it, talking and holding drinks. It was removed the following morning. People told me it was the most terrifying artwork they had ever seen.

Most of my work at that time wasn't intended for anyone else to see. I did actions, often formulating rules that I would follow for a set time, without telling anyone else. Part of it was pure experimentation, seeing how it would feel to behave within certain limitations or follow certain routines. I would go to a particular place at a particular time of day. I would do something or refrain from doing it. Sometimes I took photos, trying to document my work, but sometimes that seemed like a betrayal of a process that had to be completely private to function. There was a sort of koan of Marcel Duchamp's that I wrote out and pinned on my otherwise bare wall, a line about whether one could "make works of art that are not works of art." It was my only attempt at decoration, and though I wasn't sure I understood it, it seemed like a key, an arrow pointing the way forward. In a very precise sense I knew I had to work in vain, in a way that wasn't about accumulation or achievement. That seemed very hard to do, maybe too hard.

I realized that my work—and not just my work, everyone's

work, the work of all artists—was an alibi for the desire to put a frame around a certain part of life, to declare that inside the frame was art, and outside was not. The inside followed certain rules, was worthy of a certain kind of attention. I wondered what an art would look like that didn't sit inside a frame, that bled out into life's messiness and uncertainty. Art that didn't have a border.

Because you fall away from the purity of your best ideas, my work became, for a while, about borders in a more literal sense. I had already done an action in which I drew a chalk line down the middle of a street between two galleries, forcing visitors to cross my arbitrary frontier. Now I made a number of other lines, some public, some private. I made borders around administrative buildings, courts and police stations. I experimented with lines that were gradually erased by foot traffic, and lines that melted or were washed away. I went on a residency in Spain, and photographed myself up in the mountains, carrying an old suitcase, first on one side, then the other side of the Franco-Spanish border. Then I took a third photograph, in which there was just the border marker. I had made myself vanish.

"I know that work," said Marshal. "It was in your book."

As far as I knew, I didn't have a book. Alice said she thought she'd seen the photos in a magazine, part of an essay on art and disappearance.

"There was another one," added Marshal. "A still from a video. Something about sailors."

I'd come to think of my art as part of my inner life rather than something that ever had an independent existence. For everyone else around the table, this kind of conversation—about ideas, influences—was the most natural thing imaginable, but I had the sensation of being stretched like a fence wire, as if my present were being ratcheted tighter and tighter, reattached to my past. They brought out more wine, and I told them about *Crossing the Line,* a single-channel video work I'd made about shipboard hazing rituals. I'd done some filming at the Greenwich meridian line, a video of myself walking along it with exaggerated care, my arms outstretched like a gymnast on a balance beam. Visiting the naval museum, the rooms full of model ships, I'd got interested in the initiation rites that used to take place when sailors crossed the equator. There were stories of people being waterboarded, slathered with tar, dragged through the sea and assaulted in various other brutal and carnivalesque ways by characters dressed up as King Neptune or Davy Jones. So much violence to mark the crossing of an imaginary line. I'd re-created one of these ceremonies, with myself as the unlucky sailor and friends as masked tormentors. It was shot like amateur camcorder video, shaky and jumbled. The effect was confused, nightmarish.

I made other films, and performed other actions that I documented with more or less rigor. There was a series in which I climbed over walls and fences, inspired by my Berlin graffiti friends. There was a video of me making a human-shaped hole in chain-link with a pair of bolt cutters. I produced maps of disputed border areas in other parts of the world—the Korean DMZ, the Line of Control in Kashmir—with dotted red lines indicating routes where they could be crossed on foot. On some of them I stenciled the phrase *to get to the other side.* A curator from a small public gallery in Bristol came to visit me, sitting on my carpet-tiled floor, drinking green tea and leafing through images. After an hour or so, she invited me to make a show.

To Get to the Other Side was a sort of redemption, and I worked hard to make it as good as I could. I surrounded the gallery with a version of an eruv, a wire perimeter that some Orthodox Jews erect around their neighborhoods, inside which certain Shabbat prohibitions can be ignored. I arranged the work I'd been making throughout the space, the photos, the maps, with the *Crossing the Line* video looping on a big screen in a darkened room. It was a critical success, and because of the wider political climate—this was soon after 9/11—the subject matter was topical. I was offered other opportunities. Gallerists got in touch about representation. My upward trajectory went vertical when it was announced that I'd been nominated for a big art prize, one of the few awards that impinged on the consciousness of the non-art public. Suddenly I was being asked to speak to the media. A newspaper wanted to send someone to profile me. A columnist wittily termed me "art's illegal migrant." I began to push against this story, to look for ways to short-circuit it. I caused problems for the prize administrators by refusing to be photographed, eventually compromising by wearing a mask of the face of one of the famous Young British Artists who courted that kind of publicity. When I agreed to speak, I tried to avoid describing my work, saying that it had to stand for itself. I talked earnestly about politics, in a way that journalists found irritating. What kind of statement are you making, one asked. I said I wanted to be outside the space of statements, to exist in the space of events. In her article, the journalist described me as "pretentious and vague." Around that time I found an entry I'd made in a notebook: *The only duty the artist has is to become more completely him or herself.* I crossed that out and wrote: *The only duty the artist has is to forget himself, to forget he ever existed.*

At the awards ceremony, I sat through an elaborate dinner and made halting conversation with a famous film director who was seated at my table. The prize went to another of the nominated artists, and I found, to my shame, that I was disappointed. I'd expected to be relieved, happy to be free of the distraction. Instead I had to accept that I was ambitious, that I craved recognition.

The story of the prize interested Alice and the others. As I spoke about the work I'd made, Nicole paid close attention. I could see her picture of me changing, my status rising in real time. Marshal kept shaking his head, as if he couldn't believe what he was hearing. "I was so happy for you when that happened," Alice said. "I thought of writing, but I didn't think you'd want to hear from me."

Suddenly I felt very tired. My personality was like a muscle that I'd not used for a long time, easily strained by the ordinary serve and return of conversation. Maybe it was the virus. Maybe I was just exhausted from the violence and fear of the day. Suddenly I found myself struggling to follow the thread. "I don't think I can do any more of this tonight," I said. "I have to sleep."

"Have another drink," said Marshal. "You're just getting going."

"No."

I must have sounded abrupt, even aggressive. I was suddenly suffused with shame, as if by talking so much I'd betrayed myself, revealed too much. Alice told me brightly that she understood, I should go and rest. She reminded me that now everyone knew about me, there was no point in hiding up at the barn. I should come down to the house for breakfast. She and Nicole and Marshal said good night as if I had been a charming dinner guest. Rob, who sat slumped at the far end of the table, gave me a brief nod.

THE NEXT MORNING, I knocked at the kitchen door, and Marshal let me in. He was making some kind of complex smoothie, with fresh fruit on a cutting board and tubs of esoteric ingredients arranged in rows on the counter. He asked if I'd slept well, and offered me a glass.

"Look," he said, over the whine of the blender. "I want to apologize again. I was out of control. Nicole's so mad at me. She's totally right, of course."

"Sure," I said. I didn't want to get into it with him. During the night I'd been jerked awake by a vivid flashback of the muzzle of his gun pointing at my chest.

"Here," he said. "Positivity in liquid form."

I sipped. It tasted of banana.

"You see?" Marshal nodded affirmingly. "I think it's great you've come, actually. You'll give us some fucking perspective. We've been totally cut off—well, me maybe less than the others. What I'm saying is I don't think these guys really appreciate how intense it is out there. You know. You've been on the front line. An essential worker."

I shrugged.

"I just feel like someone here has to be thinking about security."

"Because?"

"Because, well, I don't know about you, but from where I'm standing . . ."

He trailed off and looked at me significantly. When I didn't bite, he changed the subject.

"Anyway, how are your wrists. Are they OK?"

I told him my wrists were fine. We took our drinks outside and found Nicole sitting cross-legged on the deck, wearing yoga pants and a Nirvana tee shirt, holding her phone up to her face.

"No, Grandma, I haven't. There isn't one nearby. I don't think they're even holding services."

As she saw us coming she got up and moved further away. "I'm not making excuses," she said, as she climbed down the steps off the deck. "I'm just saying." I watched Marshal watching her. He shook his head. "She's fucking gorgeous, man, but she's a handful, you know?"

When I didn't respond, he started scrolling through pictures on his phone. "Look at this." He turned the screen towards me and I saw a picture of the invitation card to my final show. *THE DRIFT-WORK,* it said in a plain sans serif font. Then, underneath: *The only thing left behind by the artist is the scene of his disappearance.*

"I found it on an auction site. They wanted a good amount of money for it."

I stared at the image. It felt unfamiliar, unconnected with me. Marshal was scrutinizing me intently, as if gauging my reaction.

"This is weird for you, I guess. Coming full circle."

There was a movement at the kitchen window. I saw Rob watching us balefully, wearing a robe and holding a cup of coffee. Marshal waved at him.

"Not as weird as it is for him." He kept his voice low. "I mean, you and Alice were together. It looks—well, you can see how it looks, her stashing you away up in the barn."

Nicole came back up the path.

"Hi honey," Marshal said to her, brightly.

"Hi Marshal. Hi Jay."

"Grandma OK?"

"She's fine. She worries, you know."

Marshal explained to me. "Nicole has a big family. Very close."

"Not that big."

Changing the subject, Nicole sat down with us at the table and asked where I'd been staying in the city. I told her Jackson Heights and Marshal started talking about Indian restaurants. I said that I'd picked up deliveries from one of the places he'd mentioned. He gave an embarrassed laugh.

"You must be, like, the only artist who knows how to ride one of those electric bikes."

Nicole looked at him sourly. "You'd be surprised." She turned to me. "Marshal is what you could call an art diaper baby. His dad had a gallery, and so he's grown up thinking the only people who make art are the ones he meets at parties."

"That's not fair. That makes me sound elitist."

"You are elitist, Marshal."

"Jesus, Nicole. Have you not had coffee?"

He explained, somewhat grumpily, that his father had been a secondary market dealer in the eighties and nineties. A different world; men who wore bow ties and gold-buttoned blazers, rooms full of eighteenth-century furniture. He talked about artists whose work his father had sold, and despite myself I was fascinated. Famous European Modernists; Dubuffet, Miró; what it was like to grow up with that kind of art as part of your everyday life. Rob ambled out, still in his robe. I noticed he was sweating, though the day hadn't really warmed up. He listened as Marshal told me that for a few months, they had a Klee hanging over the mantelpiece in their classic eight on the Upper West Side.

"Can you imagine?" Rob turned to me. "We had one of those string pictures of an owl." I smiled, but he didn't return it. "I think," he said, "that you and I ought to have a word."

We left Marshal on the deck and walked down towards the lake. When we were no longer visible from the kitchen window, Rob produced a pack of cigarettes from his pocket and offered one to me. I shook my head.

"Suit yourself." He lit up and took a couple of nervous drags. "I told Alice I'd given up."

I felt for him. In the weeks I'd been in the barn, I'd had time to prepare, to equip myself for this moment. He'd been completely blindsided. As he sucked on his cigarette, he seemed to be trying to gather his forces, staring down at his bare legs, scuffing a shower slide against the dry grass. Finally he looked up.

"So, man-to-man, why are you here?"

"I told you the truth. It was pure chance."

"You think I was born yesterday."

"I can't blame you for being skeptical. I don't really believe it myself."

He took a few more drags, then dropped the cigarette into the mud. "I suppose what I want to know," he said, grinding it out with his heel, "is are you here for her or me?"

I said I didn't understand.

"Well, if you're here to take a shot, go ahead. Or do whatever. Fucking stab me, whatever it is you came to do. Just get on with it. I can't stand the suspense."

"I didn't come here to hurt you."

"So it's her, then."

"I didn't come here for her either."

"She's my wife. You were together for, what, a few months? That was twenty years ago. I've been with Alice twenty years. Do you know what that means? We have lived a whole lifetime since we last saw you."

"And you love her?"

"Of course."

"And you're faithful to her."

"None of your fucking business. Is she faithful to me? Maybe that would be more interesting to talk about. What's your opinion on that?"

"She doesn't seem happy."

"Fucking perfect. That's fucking perfect. And I expect you've been giving her a shoulder to cry on, up there in the shed. Look, I don't know what your deal is. To be honest, I don't know who you are. Are you Jay Gates? You look like him, or a beaten-down version of him, but that doesn't mean anything. How can I be sure you're not just some psycho who saw party pictures of us on the internet?"

"You know that's not true."

"You've conned my wife, but that doesn't mean you're home and dry."

"I don't want anything from you, Rob."

"So what's your angle?"

"No angle, I keep telling you."

"If it's money, I'll give you money. I can sign a sheet of litho paper right now and make twenty grand. And then another and then another. I can just sit down at a table and make money. How about that? All I have to do is fucking sign my name."

"I don't want anything from you."

"You sure about that? A hundred percent? You sure you're not just a little bit jealous? You never thought I'd be the one, did you? The one with the big career."

"I don't know what you mean by that. You were a good artist."

"But you thought you were better. Go on, admit it."

"I see you've decided it is actually me. Not an imposter."

"You thought you were better and now you're nothing. So why don't you take—sure, why not, twenty grand, take twenty grand and get in your little delivery truck and fuck off and leave me and my wife alone."

Twenty grand. My value had gone up.

NEAR WHERE I GREW UP, there was an island called Foulness, an Old English name that meant something like "bird headland." It was owned by the Ministry of Defence, and sometimes my stepfather Douglas ran ordnance tests there. One day, when I was seventeen, he drove me out to the bleak spot where the causeway joined the island to the mainland, a stone path that was only exposed at low tide. He switched off the car engine in the parking lot. Gulls wheeled and cried overhead. By the path that led onto the causeway was a sign with various regulations and prohibitions, and a red flag fluttering on a pole, a warning that tests were currently under way.

"I will pay you a thousand pounds to leave," he said.

"I beg your pardon?"

"You heard."

"A thousand pounds?"

"Yes. To go. Right now. I have it in cash."

"Why would you do that?"

"Will you take it?"

"Why does it matter? I don't even live with you. I live with Nan."

"Does she let you call her that?"

"What?"

"It's common. You ought to call her granny, or grandma."

"Winds you up, does it?"

"Watch your mouth."

"A thousand pounds."

"Cash."

"You must really hate me."

He thought for a moment. A low boom echoed over the water from the range, sending up a cloud of birds.

"You want to know why?"

I nodded.

"Because every time I look at you I'm reminded of some black man's cock inside my wife."

I was only seventeen, and I could play tough, but the ugliness of those words hooked itself into me. I wondered if he was about to hurt me, and if so, how badly. He was wearing old-fashioned leather driving gloves, the kind with string backs. He was flexing his hands in the gloves, as if rehearsing my strangulation. If he was going to do it, I wanted him to get on with it. I wanted it over with. I stared out of the window at the disconsolate marsh and told him he was a cheap bastard. What could I do with a thousand pounds? Pay rent for a few months? I said if he offered me ten I'd get on the next train to London and he'd never see me again.

"You little bastard."

He lunged towards me; I flinched; he pretended he had only been opening the passenger door.

"Get out."

"You don't have it, then? You don't make that kind of money."

"Out!"

"You just wanted to see if I'd say yes."

He turned onto the road with a screech of tires. As he drove away, the wheels of the Cortina threw up mud. I began the long walk back to my Nan's.

LOOKING AT ROB, I remembered all the things I'd had to forgive him when we were friends. The arrogance, the moral laziness. After he ran off with Alice, one of the ways I'd found to get over what had happened—how hurt I was, how much I missed him— was to dwell on his bad sides. Soon enough it became hard to remember the rest. I flashed back to the times when we'd been a double act, clowning around, getting wasted and making a spectacle, always with one eye on who might be watching. Once, during the time of Fancy Goods, we had a pitch at an artist's street fair, a tongue-in-cheek version of the kind of English village fête that had a lucky dip and a cake stall and a booth where you could throw wet sponges at the vicar. It was around the time that the film *Titanic* came out, with the sexy bohemian painter toughing it out in steerage while the rich girl in first class is getting bored at the captain's table. We dressed up in smocks and berets and got drunk on filthy Czech absinthe that had the color and taste of mouthwash, selling sketches of passers-by under a sign that read PAINT ME LIKE ONE OF YOUR FRENCH GIRLS. I remember Alice striking silly poses for us, Rob throwing up behind some bins.

So, I wondered, was Alice using me to get back at Rob? Was I his punishment for abusing her, or taking her for granted?

"Hello? Anyone at home?"

I realized I'd drifted away. Rob was still standing there, waiting for an answer to some question. What was the question?

Twenty grand.

"I don't want your money."

"So just go, then. Leave me alone. You and Alice have done whatever. You've had your fun. I've got enough on my plate without this. If you don't want money, I don't see what else you think you're going to get."

"We used to be friends."

"So? We used to be friends. Or I used to be friends with someone called Jay. Maybe you're him, but maybe not. Maybe you just used to be him. I don't really care."

"I'm going to stay, for now at least."

"No you're bloody not."

"It's not really up to you, is it?"

He stepped towards me, then thought better of it. I walked away onto the wooden jetty that led out over the lake, listening for the sound of his heavy tread on the planks behind me. I hoped he wasn't going to make me fight him. Two middle-aged men wrestling, the indignity would have been too much. But he didn't come, so I sat down on the jetty and looked across the water. He was right, of course. The people whose names we carried didn't exist anymore. And maybe it really was time to leave.

Alice had made her choices long ago, and I'd made mine. Nothing was going to change.

"Jay?"

There she was, as if I'd summoned her, jogging down the hill, her hair falling over her shoulders.

"What did Rob want? I saw him stalking off up the path to his studio."

"To give me money."

"Money?"

"He said I was conning you. He offered me twenty thousand dollars to leave."

"Seriously? The bastard. He has no right."

"I don't blame him for being suspicious."

"He has no right to do that. And he's in no position to lecture anyone about keeping secrets."

I wondered what I was to Alice. Who was she running towards, when she put on her track shoes and followed the path round the lake? How did it feel to go back after she'd seen me and sit down in the kitchen with her husband and her friends?

"What are you thinking about?"

"You know, the old days."

"Ah, those."

"I don't blame you. I want you to know that. I don't blame you for what happened between us. I wasn't good to you."

"No, you weren't."

Overhead in the trees, some bird was crashing about, making a racket. We looked up, trying to see what was going on. Alice sighed.

"I know it was cowardly, the way I ended it. But you were so intense. I was scared of how you were going to react."

"I would never have hurt you."

"I was more worried about what you'd do to yourself."

She sat down beside me at the end of the jetty. Alice took her shoes off and dangled her feet in the water.

"Look," she said. "Since we're talking, I need you to understand something."

"What?"

"I always thought you'd killed yourself. No one heard from you after you left. No one had any news, so I assumed the worst. And it made me very angry."

"Why?"

"I thought it was because of me."

"I wouldn't have done that."

"How was I to know? I've carried it around, Jay. For years. And then you just turn up. I mean, it's—I don't know. It's turned everything upside down."

"For me too."

"I don't think you understand. It was unfair, what you did. To put it all onto me. How could you make me responsible for something like that? We weren't even happy together. I didn't know how to leave you. I was too timid. Was that my fault? I was very young, Jay. I just wanted to be happy. It's not wrong to want to be happy."

It had never occurred to me that Alice would feel responsible for anything I did after she left me. By the time of my "disappearance" she was already in America.

"I just wasn't any good," I said. "Not for you. Not for anyone."

"I never thought that."

"No?"

"It was just that you were so serious. I always felt I was walking on eggshells. The way you sneered when something fell short of your impossible standards."

I didn't know what to say. She carried on.

"I was happy to hear you were doing well. I thought that meant I'd managed it OK, but then you vanished. I thought you were capable of anything, and the longer it went on, the sicker I felt. I was eaten up by guilt."

"It wasn't about you."

"So you say. But that doesn't change anything. For years I've had your death on my conscience."

"After you left I did a lot of thinking, and—I decided I had to go, but it wasn't directed at you."

"Well, wasn't that your problem? You were always so in your own head. When I finally realized what was going on it was like a bell I couldn't un-ring."

"What do you mean, what was going on?"

"That you barely even saw me. Nothing was directed at me. It was all projection. When you were talking to me, you were really just talking to yourself, some fantasy you had. And then when I deviated from it, you punished me."

"Alice."

"You're saying I'm wrong? You never seemed to see me. I'm not sure you even liked me. When Fancy Goods was repossessed. It was—I won't say everything, but it was important to me. You knew that, but you didn't seem to care how sad I was. You didn't seem to notice. You always behaved like you were above that place, that it wasn't quite good enough for you."

"I thought they were exploiting you."

"Maybe. I didn't feel that way. I was excited to be a part of something, while I still could. You could be so patronizing, and you didn't seem to understand that I was on a clock. Any day my mother was going to tell me I had to come home and get married. She had a boy lined up—I never told you that, you would have been so angry. She made me meet him each time I went to Paris."

"Including when we were there together?"

"Yes. I had to go have lunch with him. I can't remember what I told you. He played tournament badminton, can you believe it. That's what I would have been doing at the weekends. Wearing a sun visor and clapping from the stands. My whole life was about to get taken away and I needed someone who was going to help me and you didn't seem to grasp that."

"How could I? I didn't know. You never said anything."

"Well, maybe I thought you should have understood. You kept saying you loved me, but you can't love someone unless you love yourself, Jay, and you never did. It was really hard being around your self-hatred. You were so unsatisfied with everything, and so proud and humiliated and angry about being humiliated. Rob—well, Rob was just Rob. It was all much more straightforward with him. He looked at me one day and said do you want to get out of here and I said yes. He said OK where do you want to go, and that was that."

"So if I'd asked you to run away, would you have gone with me?"

"I don't know. Maybe. But I couldn't wait around for it to happen. You were so stuck."

"I used to think of you, out in the world somewhere. Living your life. I never expected you'd stay with Rob."

"And yet I did."

"And you had a daughter. That's amazing to me. Does she look like you? You haven't shown me a picture."

"I guess. I see a lot of Rob in her." She made no move to get out her phone.

We sat and looked out at the lake. The sun had gone behind a cloud and it felt cold. Alice turned to me and kissed me, very lightly, on the mouth.

"Friends?"

"Sure."

She got up and slipped her shoes on. "I'll see you later, OK?"

I watched her walk along the jetty to the shore. In the beginning I'd wanted the cosmos to punish Alice for leaving me. I'd wanted her to weep bitter tears of remorse. I'd wanted—what had I wanted? Not to hurt her. Yes, to hurt her. To leave a mark on her, because I was afraid of being forgotten. So what did it feel like to discover that my wish had been granted? It felt wretched.

. . .

I WALKED BACK ROUND THE LAKE, trying to govern my self-disgust. I should leave, I thought. It was time to leave. On a whim I cut up through the trees, heading for a part of the property I'd not explored before. I walked for a long time, then, one after the other, I found two more giant sculptures, an arrangement of long white slabs like gravestones, and a towering mobile, almost as high as the tree canopy, made of oxidized steel disks hanging from a curved stalk. I was too preoccupied to pay much attention to either.

When I drove out of the city, I was so sick that I thought I was about to die. I had a dream of tall trees, clouds moving slowly across the sky, a place where I would take my rest. This was that place. It had been given to me for that purpose, but somehow I'd recovered, which meant that instead of an ending there would be—something else. I visualized packing my belongings into the car, but it didn't seem like something that could actually happen. I'd spent so many days consumed by memories of Alice; a past I'd thought completely unrecoverable had become so vivid to me that it was as if I'd turned my back on the future, which didn't just seem unknown in the ordinary way, unpredictable or yet to manifest, but absent, nonexistent, devoid of content. Again I returned to the suspicion that I was dead, and had somehow failed to notice.

I climbed up to the sentinel rock to take a look at the valley, and to see if I could spot the steel disk sculpture amidst the trees. Walking back down towards the mirror glade, I heard a noise. Somehow the prospect of meeting anyone was intolerable. Instinctively I backed away and crouched behind the trunk of a large conifer. Pressed up against the tree, I heard the sound of running feet coming to a halt, the ragged breath of someone who had pushed hard uphill. Risking a glance, I saw Nicole pressing a button on her watch and pulling out a set of earbuds. She began to take little paces back and forth, clasping her hands behind her head. Her body glistened with sweat.

I turned away, and stood with my back against the trunk's rough bark, waiting for her to go. I could hear the crunch of twigs and leaves under her feet, the sound of deep recovery breaths, in through the nose, out through the mouth. After a while I heard more sounds on the path. A heavier, slower tread. This person was larger, out of shape. When they reached the glade they were gasping. I heard them cough and spit on the floor.

"I thought you were going to let me catch you," Rob said, and I heard a familiar whiny note in his voice. Rob, always the birthday boy.

"Why would I do that?"

"Well, it would be fun, for one thing."

"Are you OK? You're not going to have a heart attack, are you?"

"I'm just getting my breath back."

They were very close by. I could have stepped out from my hiding place and confronted them.

"You got any water?" he asked.

"No, I always wait until I get back."

"Fuck. I'm parched. I tell you one thing, I didn't mind coming in second place. You in those running shorts, it's better than telly."

"Give me a break, Robert." Her voice was modulated, precise; a cautious tone for handling volatile men.

He sniggered. "Oh no, not the full name! You're killing the mood."

"What mood?"

"Tell the truth, are you going to sit for me?"

"Again? I told you it's really not where I'm at right now."

"Don't be ridiculous. You know I have women literally begging me to let them take their knickers off and stand on a wooden box in my freezing cold studio."

"Not me."

"I'd warm it up for you. For you, I'd warm it up."

"Still not me. Not the one you're looking for. Why not ask Alice?"

"Oh Jesus, I've painted Alice a hundred times. I can't look at her anymore. It has to be you."

"I have my own work, Rob."

"And that too. You should let me see your—whatever you're doing. I could help you out."

"Give me a crit? A few tips?"

"Exactly. Come on, everyone wants you to do it. Even Marshal, and he's a jealous little fucker."

"Marshal said that?"

"He wants me to make paintings. And if I say I want to make a painting of you, he's going to tell you to do it."

"Marshal doesn't get to tell me what to do."

"Oh no? And who pays for all your fancy dinners? That pant-suit you were wearing the other night?"

"Nice. Very classy. So what does Alice think of you proposi-tioning all these women to take their clothes off in your studio?"

"She's a big girl. She knows how the game is played. Come on, Nicole. See how hard I'm working. I need you."

"So you've got your breath back?"

"I most certainly have."

"Race you to the house then."

"Oh, come on. No. Don't do that. Fuck."

There was the sound of feet on the path. I heard Rob pac-ing about the glade, spitting on the ground. I peered cautiously round the tree. He was drenched in sweat, his thinning hair plas-tered back on his scalp. His running clothes, a sagging tee shirt and baggy ball shorts, gave him the look of a superannuated teen-ager, the kid who'll never make the team. He was pacing around in angry little circles, exposing a white globe of belly as he wiped his brow with the front of his shirt. After a while he jogged off down the hill.

·   ·   ·

LATER THAT AFTERNOON I WALKED round the lake to the house. I found Nicole and Marshal on the deck. I sat down at the table and Marshal opened up the canvas umbrella to shade us from the sun. I could see Alice moving about in the kitchen.

"Do you keep in touch with the art scene?" Marshal asked. When I said I didn't, he was incredulous. "Not at all?"

I said it was years since I'd even been inside a gallery.

"But you were living in New York," Nicole pointed out. "You weren't even tempted?"

Alice came out with a jug of lemonade. A fly buzzed around us. Nicole's suggestion that she go and fetch Rob was received in silence.

Nicole started quizzing me, saying names that presumably belonged to fashionable artists. How about museums? Had I been to MoMA? To the Guggenheim? As I shook my head, she put a hand over her mouth, a gesture that made me smile. To her I was a freak of nature.

"Did you just stop liking it?"

"Not exactly."

"You wanted to do something else?"

"No, not really. I could never think of anything I wanted to do more than make art."

Marshal showed me another image on his phone, a scan of a page from one of the monthly art magazines.

"Do you remember this?"

I did. Soon after my prize nomination, the magazine had asked me to contribute to a series of statements or sentences about art. My text was only a few lines long.

Good art is objective

It is risky yet disciplined

It has literal social meaning: no metaphors, no re-creations, just the indexical present

The artist should be anonymous

What had I meant? I looked at the words on the page. Such confident declarations. It is, it has, the artist should. The tone was abrasive; I did not recognize myself in it. To me objectivity had simply meant the opposite of subjectivity. Instead of an art of self-expression, I wanted an art which was just another thing in the world, that didn't try and tell a story, or draw attention to its maker. And anonymity? I used to take the 55 bus from Hackney into the center of London. On the roofs of the bus shelters along the route, someone had placed or thrown spiky little sculptural creations, humble caltrop-like objects that seemed to be made of plastic straws and gum. I liked them. I used to sit upstairs so I could look out for them. Knowing the name of the maker wouldn't have added to my pleasure. The experience was complete as it was. Only in the system we have, where everyone is expected to be an entrepreneur of the self, is anonymity a kind of death. There are reasons for an artist to take credit for their work, mostly to do with money. Few of those reasons add anything to the experience of the art itself.

I said some version of this to Alice, Marshal and Nicole. I told them how in the year or so after Alice and Rob left, I thought a lot about anonymity and personhood. I was fascinated by fake identities, or how one would go about losing one's identity, becoming inscrutable, unreadable to all the systems of identification. The so-called Global War on Terror was intensifying, and people were expected to be transparent: for security's sake we all had to make ourselves available for inspection whenever required. I made a short film, based on an action by a British conceptualist of the sixties, in which I cut up and chewed my passport, sealing the pulpy remains in a vial, which I then tried to present at immigration to board a Eurostar train to Paris. I was arrested. The whole thing was taken very seriously. The destruction of the document was, I discovered, a criminal offense. Later I appeared in court, and received a small fine.

There are many ways to disappear. You can die, of course. That is the most literal. You can be marginalized or rendered invisible in some way, perhaps because you have no papers, or you're incarcerated or have nowhere to live, no address. Or you can leave. You can make vanishing into a project.

This was how I began *THE DRIFTWORK*. The invitation card that Marshal found online had a numbered list on the back. It was structured as a sequence of three pieces, which I originally called *No Trace Piece, Return Piece* and *Fugue Piece*. Eventually I dropped the artspeak word "piece," so the card, as printed, read:

1. *No Trace*
2. *Return*
3. *Fugue*

In *No Trace* I recapitulated the experience of leaving Alice's aunt's apartment, scrubbing and wiping down everything. This time I did the same with my Newham flat. I didn't video the work or anything like that. The only record was a text, describing what I had done. At the same time I paid a service that advertised its ability to remove unwanted internet content, giving them the task of erasing as much of my digital footprint as possible. They took down pictures, news items, entries in databases. None of this was documented, so there was no real way for an art consumer to ascertain whether it had happened or not, or to work out what had gone. It also existed only as a description, just a paragraph of writing, an unverifiable claim that something had taken place.

Return was more elaborate. As I started to describe it, Marshal nodded vigorously. It was, he said, a seminal work. The phrase startled me. I'd had no idea it was remembered at all.

Return had something in common with my earlier work, in that it required a set of witnesses. *THE DRIFTWORK* was backed by a gallery, and they advanced money for train tickets and hotels, so that three artworld authorities—a museum curator, a critic and an elderly conceptual artist—could meet me for dinner in a restaurant in the 6th arrondissement of Paris. I chose the location because it was opposite the building on rue des Grands-Augustins where Picasso had painted *Guernica,* a studio that he in turn had chosen because it was the setting for Balzac's story "The Unknown Masterpiece," whose title I had taken for my degree show. I liked the combination of fiction and reality, the art-historical aura. The restaurant was an old-fashioned establishment with white tablecloths and a menu of traditional dishes. I treated my authorities to a good meal, refusing to discuss the reason I had brought them there. Instead, I made conversation about Paris, their memories of seeing or making art there. Having evoked the past, I paid for dinner and then placed my newly issued passport on the table, along with my wallet, bank cards and my driver's license. I opened my pockets to show that I had nothing with me—no money or papers. Then I showed them my "survival kit," a small backpack with such things as a pocket-knife, a poncho, matches, a length of string and an old-fashioned magnetic compass. It was as if, in the middle of a large city, I was swapping the tools of civilized survival for those of the wilderness. The authorities had questions, of course, but I didn't answer them. Instead, I invited them to meet me at another restaurant in London the following week. We took photos, shook hands, and left.

I walked out of the restaurant, which was right by the river, crossed over and began to head north through the city in the direction of Calais and the English coast. Sometime later that night, already cold and tired, I made it to a truck stop in the outskirts, a bleak and windswept lot where I hitched a ride with a Spanish driver, a talkative man who also paid for a meal. I arrived at the coast the next day. There was an element of theater in what I was doing, but it was still illegal. A boat was waiting for me at a marina in a coastal town between Calais and Boulogne. It was a little cruiser with a cuddy cabin, over forty years old and not in the best shape, but mechanically sound and stocked with fuel and supplies. In it I crossed the Channel back to England.

Along with so many other things, I had Nan to thank for my sailing proficiency. At a time when I was particularly lost and unhappy, she signed me up for classes at the local boat club, and insisted I keep on going even though I hated the atmosphere, the men in windcheaters and deck shoes, flashing their watches as they propped up the bar, the wives and daughters pretending they hadn't been eyeing me up when their men weren't looking. I dodged a couple of fights and earned sailing and navigation certificates, even crewed in a few races, though I gave it all up when I left for art school.

"Wait," said Nicole. "You just sailed across the English Channel?"

I had. I'd waited two days because of bad weather, sleeping in the cramped space belowdecks while fog blanketed the harbor. I liked that time, the sound of rain falling, eating out of a can in my sleeping bag nest. When the sky cleared I charted a course that took me across the shipping lanes as quickly and efficiently as possible, keeping watch for container carriers plowing through the Straits of Dover. I'd passed between the monster ships without incident, and docked at a marina some way up the coast, where I could lose my little cruiser among other nondescript pleasure craft. I had no dealings with customs or immigration, and took a train back to London, hiding in the toilet when the ticket inspector came through.

At the appointed time, I met the witnesses at a restaurant in Soho. They actually stood up to applaud when I walked in. I said nothing about how I'd got there, but affected an air of great mystery. It seemed, as I'd intended, like a kind of old-fashioned magic trick, or a gentleman's wager from a Jules Verne novel.

People suspected I must have hidden away in a truck, or sneaked onto a train. Though it was before the time when migrants in small boats became a fixture in the popular imagination, the action was intended to evoke such clandestine crossings. Later, I had the boat hauled up from the coast and displayed in a gallery. I also produced a series of maps of my route. As an action it was provocative. I was declaring that I'd broken the law, disregarded the reality of a national border.

Marshal nodded vigorously at that. He seemed to know a lot about what I'd done. Nicole asked why she had never heard of it before, and started comparing it to work that had been shown at Documenta, made from lifejackets.

The third part of *THE DRIFTWORK* was *Fugue*. It was the most ambitious of the three, and as I began to talk about it, I realized that the problem was not to describe what I did, which was fairly simple, so much as what happened afterwards, the events that led me to fall away, not just from my plan, but from everything I was becoming, an established artist with invitations to show at museums and biennials around the world. It was not about Alice, not in any straightforward way. By that time the wounds of our relationship had begun to heal over. Like a spring, gradually winding down, I had thought about her less frequently, with less intensity. What remained—and what was probably there anyway, what would have been there even if I'd never met her— was a sense of self-disgust, a wish to outrun something, some version of myself that made me ashamed. I transformed it into an imperative to push harder, to go further, not to be satisfied with things that other people appreciated, or said were worthwhile.

Fugue began with an event at a gallery. The card that Marshal had found on the auction site was that night's invitation. There was an outside space that backed onto the canal, a kind of courtyard where an audience watched as I lit a fire in an oil drum and began to burn various official documents, bills and bank statements, along with a small box of possessions, including books, photos and artworks that friends had given me. It probably didn't seem very dramatic, but at that point I had very little left. I'd abandoned the Newham flat a few months earlier, and since then I'd been couch surfing, living with only the barest essentials. As the performance went on, the audience seemed restless, particularly when I started to burn books. A few people left. Those that remained watched me undress; they took photos as I burned my clothes in the fire. I left the space naked. The gallerist had instructions to wait for fifteen minutes, then report to the crowd that I'd gone, but that the performance was ongoing.

And that was it. Someone or other once said that art is purposeful purposelessness. I was trying to make something less defined even than that, a kind of artwork without form or function except to cross its own border, to cross out of itself and make a successful exit.

From my childhood I have a vague memory of the title sequence of an old television series, something I must have sat and watched with Nan, in which a man runs along a beach removing his clothes—office worker clothes, a suit and tie—then plunges naked into the sea. It is presented as a comedy, with lighthearted music. We see him swimming out, away from the shore. It is an escape, of course, but it is also death. The man will swim out to sea and sooner or later he will get tired and be unable to swim any further. He will sink and drown. The show was about a discontented suburban businessman. As a small child the lesson I took from it was that it would be better to die than to live a mundane life. I filed this information away and it became a seed or grain of sand around which my future personality formed. In a way this was one of the most decisive artistic experiences of my life.

"So you left," said Alice. "How long were you planning to be away?"

We were getting into more difficult territory. I had deliberately not set a time limit. I needed it to be a significant period, long enough for the action to be more than symbolic: an event, rather than just a statement. It was important to me that the work was open-ended. It would be over when it was over. I wasn't the first person to make such a gesture. Other artists had dropped out before me, or called strikes, refusing to make or show work. Usually they acted for political reasons, or to draw attention to something they disliked about the art system. I didn't think there was any political meaning to my gesture. No one was waiting for me to make more art and nothing would change if I didn't. It just seemed to me that being absent was more interesting than being present. Everyone I knew was obsessed with staying at the center of things, having attention drawn towards them, but there are objects—black holes, certain kinds of particle—that we can't see directly. We know they're there, because they bend light. We experience their effects, their traces. That's how I wanted to be, to deform the artworld by my invisibility, the knowledge that I was elsewhere.

Nicole wondered if I ever thought it was going to be permanent. I said I'd tried not to ask myself that question. If I allowed myself to think it was going to end, I would just be on vacation, a vacation from art. There had to be a risk. I had to put myself in play. I had saved up some money, and I'd seen very little of the world, so I decided to travel. I took my first ever plane and arrived in Bangkok, disoriented, but also relieved in a deep bodily way that I hadn't anticipated, almost exhilarated to be far from art and artists, from the expectation that experience had to be transformed into work if it was going to have any meaning. I realized I had been a sort of machine, ingesting life, shitting it out again as art.

I wandered around Asia for most of a year, and soon tired of the backpacker hostels, the bovine kids checking their email in internet cafés. When I ran out of money I was in Goa, and for a while I found work managing a guesthouse, refereeing disputes between the different beach tribes, shoeless German junkies, hearty British public schoolboys, the odd monolingual Japanese solo traveler, finding his lonely way via sign language. I negotiated with wary Israelis who'd just finished their military service and seemed to see the Indians as just another kind of Arab, there to be pushed around. I rescued naïve Dutch girls from predatory "guides." I tried to get everyone what they wanted. The Israelis wanted to rent high-powered motorcycles, the Dutch girls wanted better locks on their doors. Everyone wanted drugs. Hash, opium, expensive ecstasy pills smuggled in from Europe.

I saw what happened in the shadows behind the beach, under cover of the relentless thumping of the music. The shakedowns, the payoffs to police, the rapes and beatings. After a while I couldn't listen to another hammocked sage talking mystical nonsense as he passed a chillum, and the vacuity of the place began to destroy my spirit, the moronic four-to-the-floor kick drum of acid trance beating me down down down down. I'd also fallen back into using drugs—it was hard to abstain in a place so saturated with them—and I began to spend my days on a chair on my veranda, watching cosmic dramas unfold across the cracked floor tiles. I no longer understood why I'd given up my life in London to be a dreadlocked fling for tourist women. One day I woke up, cut my hair and moved on.

I thought about going home; by then I'd been away for over two years, but I hadn't found the thing I was looking for, the signal that would terminate *Fugue*. I left India as a deckhand on a yacht, cleaning and polishing metalwork on a vessel that belonged to an American who I never met. I wasn't technically qualified, but I met someone who got me the right papers. The yacht was luxurious and bland. There was a Jeff Koons balloon dog in the dining room, and over the bed in the main suite was a

Warhol screen print of a dollar bill, in case the owner ever woke up and forgot he was rich. During my time on board, the only guests were wealthy Indians who were helicoptered off in the Seychelles. After that we transited through the Red Sea into the Mediterranean, going part of the way with an armed escort and a pair of South African security contractors playing cards on the main deck. I left the boat in Venice, about nine months after I'd boarded, then hitched my way across Italy into France.

As I stared out, day after day, at the infinite blue of the Indian Ocean, I was as fulfilled as I ever expect to be. Yet during my time on the yacht I came to the conclusion that this replete solitude was a problem, a sort of failing on my part. I'd wanted to live without an artistic identity, but at the same time, to live entirely within the frame of art. Part of that was to give up being a professional artist, a person whose selfhood—or at least its products—circulated in the market. So that was what I'd done. My experiences were now just experiences. When I did something, it wasn't an action. It had no surplus meaning. The pipe was just a pipe. And yet, I was still performing *Fugue*. Whatever I happened to be doing was art. Perhaps in some way this made me free, but it was unsatisfying. People don't exist alone. We exist in relation to each other. Maybe I was free in my mind, but it was the kind of freedom that would wilt when exposed to the world. There is, or was, an artistic tendency that purported to address this—artists would cook dinner in galleries, put on events, make various rudimentary simulations of community. I had no problem with that, but it seemed remedial, as if the point of art was to do some rather half-assed social repair. I needed to find out for myself what community actually was. It was a word that got used so much, but I didn't understand it. I had no feeling for what it involved.

Through people I met on the road in Asia I'd heard of an area in the southwest of France that had become a haven for autono-

mists, people who wanted to build an alternative society from
the ground up. I liked the idea of living experimentally, of trying to make a new world instead of adapting to the given one. I
made my way there and found an isolated rural zone of woods
and marshland. Scattered across it were at least thirty collectives, perhaps a hundred and fifty people in all. There were farms
and communes, eccentric buildings made of reclaimed materials,
shacks and cabins and rickety towers. The residents were political activists, back-to-the-land farmers, radical environmentalists,
a fractious, stubborn and idealistic rabble. Some were fighting
the state. Others just wanted to be left alone. They didn't understand or care about the world I came from. I was just another
person who had turned up, who was prepared to do a shift at the
bakery or help build a shelter.

That was where I learned, or tried to learn, how to lead a collective life, to perform work for the good of all, to build a wall,
milk a cow. I made some friends. I started a relationship. Together
Gisele and I talked about having a child. We led a hard, physical
life. We washed in cold water, breaking the ice on the pail in winter, wrapping ourselves in coats and sweaters to go outside to the
composting toilet behind our cabin. The artworld began to seem
alien to me, its values and preoccupations silly and effete. My
imagination was no longer directed into making scarce collect-
ibles, but towards a future free of domination and exploitation.
The old questions—about what was art and what wasn't—ceased
to preoccupy me. When I thought of my past as an artist, the
person I saw didn't seem outrageous or bohemian. Just the opposite. I'd believed that by making art I was swimming out to sea,
like the man on the beach in the TV title sequence. Actually I'd
just been on my way to work, ready to spend another day at the
office.

One day I woke up to find that three years had passed and outside my window were bulldozers and riot police with batons and

shields. We threw stones and choked on tear gas and watched as our home was demolished. It is hard to convey the trauma of that day. Our friends and neighbors had helped us build the cabin. Every inch of it represented care and labor, and in just a few minutes it was reduced to splinters. The authorities made it impossible for us to rebuild, and so the people of the Zone were scattered to the winds. A few of us met and talked about finding somewhere else, some other unwanted patch of land, but we didn't have the heart. We were tired and demoralized. There was no way to keep our life together. Gisele and I soon found that we couldn't make it in the city, not as a couple. We were ungainly and slow. We had mud on our feet. Looking at each other, all we could see was what we'd lost, what we were struggling to do without. We broke up and she went to live in another rural collective in Normandy. Once again I was alone, drifting.

I thought about going back to London, but I couldn't imagine sitting on the tube, standing in line to buy a salad to eat at a desk. One of my friends from the Zone, a man who had no respect for the law, sent me to Spain with the address of a bar on the Costa del Sol and the name of the Moroccan who owned it. For a while I crewed for him, running drugs from the North African coast in small yachts, a line of work that seemed to me no better or worse than any other, until one night I found myself soaked and freezing, hiding behind some rocks as police with flashlights scoured the beach, looking for our cargo. Soon after that another crew member, a man suspected of informing, was found at the bottom of a cliff. Scared for my safety, I signed on to a commercial vessel going across the Atlantic, the quickest way I could think of to vanish. It wasn't a happy experience. The crew were mostly Filipino and Bangladeshi, a few Russians, men who were far from their homes and families and had little to distract them. There was a slow trickle of internet, barely fast enough for email. The only entertainment was a small selection of DVDs screened nightly in the mess, mostly porn and Bollywood films. Tempers frayed, and when a fight broke out between two engineers, one had to be locked in his cabin. As far as possible, I'd stayed out of the various conflicts, but there were men who didn't like me. I didn't trust anyone, and I was beginning to think I needed to watch my back. We docked at the Port of Miami, and though I was contracted for another two months, I jumped ship and set off into America.

"So you're an illegal."

I twisted round in my seat. I didn't know how long Rob had been there. He was in his painting overalls, carrying a beer. His expression was inscrutable.

I HAVE TRIED TO WALK lightly in these United States. I have tried to leave no trace. I have been a creature of the periphery, moving across a landscape of forgotten places, exurbs and strip developments, sites in states of feverish transformation or glacial collapse. The experience of being truly autonomous isn't given to very many, and I can say that, for passages of my life, I have been unwatched, unmonitored, reliant on no one but myself. I have also been bossed and pushed around, surveilled and harassed. To be unwatched is to be unseen, and at times I have been so lonely that I could taste it in my mouth. I have walked for miles along roaring highways, strafed by lights. I have been chased by feral strangers, who tried to throw me off a bridge. I have desperately wanted to go home yet been unable to identify where that would be.

I have had some terrible jobs, such as working the line at a chicken plant, where I only lasted a few days. I have prepped and washed dishes in kitchens, good and bad, the best one a café in New Orleans, the worst a giant facility outside Phoenix that produced airline meals. The jobs I have liked best were outdoors. For a while I worked the hurricane track along the Gulf Coast, cleaning out floodwater and fixing roofs. I worked construction during the fracking boom in New Mexico, watching the gas flares rise up over the sagebrush like portents of doom. I would be lying if I said I never thought about art.

I spent a month or two working on a crew running fences through featureless Nevada basin land. I could see no difference between one side and the other, no reason for us to be making a boundary. We hammered in posts, tightened wire, moved on. Then, for a while, we removed other stretches of identical fence. The boss on that job was a young guy from a big local family. He would sit in the shelter of his enormous gleaming truck, wearing a crisp canvas jacket and a black felt hat that he claimed had cost a thousand dollars, fancy boots up on the dash as he played games on his phone. Once, we were making repairs and I found a place where something or someone had blown straight through, the wire bent inwards to leave a large hole, wider than a man's body. In that yawning emptiness we were tiny figures wearing scarves and goggles against the wind and the bone white dust, agents of some great governing abstraction that was not visible to us, nor meant for us to understand.

I went on into the Northwest, where there was work in wildfire prevention, cutting line and igniting controlled burns, but it was dangerous and badly paid and I started to feel an unfamiliar need for people, for crowds and noisy communal life. That was how I ended up in New York. I bought a car and picked up fares and takeout food orders and watched all the people in my back seat as they led their busy city lives. I found I was interested in them; in their troubles, their arguments, the conversations they had on their phones. Then came the pandemic and all of that was swept away.

.   .   .

I'D COME TO THE END of my story and I felt physically drained, as if I'd been robbed or knocked down. The silence spun itself out into a thread that every person at the table followed, until we were each tangled in our own thoughts. Alice looked at me, her eyes wet with tears. For a moment it was as if we were the only two people there.

Marshal broke in, squeezing my shoulder. "I think this is incredible. I mean, you have seen some shit."

"Incredible," said Rob, flatly.

"You don't believe him?" Alice looked up at her husband. "I do."

"Of course you do."

Marshal was beginning to see an angle. "And this is the end. This is the moment of completion, right here, right now. A twenty-year-long performance. My God, don't you see? We are privileged to witness this!" He pulled out his phone and began to make a video, sweeping the table. "You've returned. You've made contact with the artworld. *Fugue* is finally over."

He shouldn't have been the one to say it, but as soon as he did, I knew it was true. I had come to the end. Whatever orbit I had been on, whatever dark and elliptical path, it was now complete. Still, something about his manner sat badly with me—the artworld general, graciously taking my surrender.

"Nothing's over," I said, truculently.

Rob sat, staring at his empty beer bottle, his arms crossed and his legs straight out, like a bored student sitting through a lecture. Alice had retreated somewhere far away. I could feel panic rising up, slowly, like freezing water inside the cellar of my chest. I'd revealed too much. I had made myself vulnerable. I had the familiar urge to keep moving, to flee, to hide.

"What will you do now?" asked Nicole, but just as she spoke, her phone rang. "I'm sorry," she said. "I have to take this." Her chair scraped across the deck as she pushed it back, and the table juddered. People reached out to steady glasses and bottles. I was saved from answering her question.

"Family," said Marshal, watching her walk away. "She really needs to set some boundaries." He looked around—at Alice, lost in thought, Rob picking at the label on the beer bottle, at me. Then he held up his phone again. "I am documenting an art-historical moment. Can the three of you scooch a little closer together?"

Rob put his hand up, the instinctive gesture of the celebrity. "Could you fuck off, Marshal?"

Marshal stood up, still holding up his phone. "I'll let you guys talk," he said, as if leaving were his own idea. I flashed on the muzzle of a gun pointing at my chest; I realized I was staring wildly into his lens.

"How do you feel?" he said to me. "How does it feel to be back?"

I understood dimly that to him I was a psychological curiosity. He was pointing his weapon at a holdout, a soldier emerging from the jungle, years after the end of the war.

"That's what you want to know?"

"Yes."

"What has how I feel got to do with art?"

He made the thumbs-up, as if I'd just given him some top-quality content, and went inside the house. Alice, Rob and I sat in silence. A wasp circled the table and Rob trapped it under a glass. The air was heavy and moist. "Are you hungry?" Alice asked. I shook my head.

Finally, Rob spoke. "One weird thing about this place," he said. "It's got Wi-Fi all over. Not just in the house. All over the property. You can walk around streaming a movie. Even up on the hill on the other side of the lake. But try as I might, I can never find the transmitters. Greg must have hidden them."

Alice scoffed. "You've never dragged yourself to the far side of the lake."

"He has."

Rob looked sharply at me. I held his gaze. "I think they're up in the trees," he said. "He's hidden them up there, where it's hard to see them."

Alice turned her gaze from me to him, and back again. "We probably need to talk," she said. "Me and Rob. So . . ."

Rob stood up and held out his hand. There was something timeless about his pose, like a figure in an old genre painting. "Come on, old girl. Let's go and have a cozy husband and wife chat."

I looked at the table. I didn't want to meet Alice's eye, or Rob's. Violence was swimming just under the surface. Alice didn't take her husband's hand. "I'll see you later," she said to me. "That was—what you just said was . . ." She couldn't find her way to the end of her sentence. She followed Rob into the house; after a few moments I heard raised voices from somewhere upstairs.

The argument sounded ugly and I wanted to be away from it. I walked down the sloping green lawn and found Nicole sitting on a wrought iron bench, making a video call. She didn't see me at first, preoccupied with her conversation.

"You look like you're in paradise," a quavery voice was saying. "It's so bright there."

"Grandma, what about your insurance?"

"Honey, don't rush me, I'm trying to figure it out."

"What happens if they furlough you? What does it say in the agreement?"

"Just a minute."

"Is that the paper? Can you read it out? Can you see anywhere it mentions furlough or furloughed?"

"It's just so long."

"I know. Don't you have your glasses?"

"They're all the way in the kitchen."

"Can you go get them?" There were some confused sounds, then a child's voice.

"When you coming home, Destiny?"

I made some noise so Nicole could hear me. She turned and acknowledged me with a curt wave. I walked by, and she carried on talking.

"No one calls me that. You being good for grandma?"

"I'm bored, Dezzy. We been inside for days. You said you be back."

"I know. I just need you to be good for her, OK? She's doing her very best. Uncle Ray come around?"

"No. He ain't."

"'Course he ain't. You know if he talked to grandma about her shopping?"

"No."

"Did he call her on the phone?"

"I said I don't know."

Nicole's fraught familial world faded away as I walked out onto the jetty. I pulled open the door of the boathouse. Chairs and pool floats, the smell of leaf mold and last summer. And two fiberglass kayaks. I dug around and found a paddle.

In the middle of the lake there was a little island, just a few rocks and a stunted willow tree trailing branches into the water. I paddled out to it. Under the willow was a little statue, caked in bird lime, a nymph or goddess pouring something from a jar. I jammed the nose of the kayak between two rocks, and planted the paddle in the soft mud. Easing myself out, I climbed up and sat under the tree. What was I going to do? It was as if, by telling my story, I'd broken a spell. I felt aimless, almost formless, blank as a newborn.

I hadn't appreciated the extent to which *Fugue* had animated my life. Though I'd long since ceased to be aware of it, I had been living for all those years inside its frame. When I was fixing a fence, or delivering takeout, or standing knee deep in gray water pumping out a flooded basement, it had given me an underlying purpose, a larger context for my actions. Now it had gone. Perhaps I should have experienced a sense of accomplishment, of having completed a mammoth task. Instead all I felt was lethargy.

WHEN I GOT BACK TO THE BARN, I was surprised to find Alice lying on my bed, wearing cutoffs and a tee shirt, just as I'd seen her on that first day as I staggered towards the door with her groceries. She was looking wryly at me, taking hits on a vape. Her long brown legs were stretched out; her hair radiated over the pillow like fire. Since Gisele, I'd been with women, but none like Alice, this Alice, cynical, spare, flensed of dreams.

"Well," she said, exhaling a cloud of mist. "Everyone wants you to stay, except Rob."

"Is that so?"

"Marshal's excited. He says this is a culturally significant event. You've passed the Nicole test too, which is impressive, because as far as I can see she doesn't like anyone."

I sat down beside her. "I think she's got a lot on her mind."

"Like what? Have you two been talking?"

"Not really. What about you? Do you want me to stay?"

"Of course I do. I told Rob I was coming up here. He wasn't happy about it. I told him I was coming to fuck you."

My mouth went dry. "You shouldn't make jokes like that."

"Who said it's a joke."

"Are you trying to get back at him?"

"Why do you care?"

It is hard not to be touched, to crave it like food or water, but I was a middle-aged man with blown-out knees and leathery skin crisscrossed with scars. I was no longer made for touch. What would happen if I leaned over and kissed her? What wounds would open up? Seeing me wince, she sat up and offered me the vape. "I didn't mean that. I'm not using you for anything. I don't know what I'm saying."

"You were fighting with him. Then you came straight over here."

"Well, he owes me."

"For what?"

"You have no idea. Rob can be—well, he gets himself into situations. He digs holes and he can't find his way out again. So I have to dig him out, even when I'm the one he's hurt."

"You always were a problem-solver."

"You say that like it's an insult."

We both laughed.

"It feels stupid talking about money to you." I shrugged, waiting for her to continue. "I've done my best, tried to rein in Rob's spending. We closed up the studio in New York. He didn't want to, of course, but there was just no way. We had to let everyone go."

"You just fired them?"

"And naturally I had to be the one to do it, not him. Too painful for him. I had to be the asshole."

"So now they're out of work in the middle of a pandemic."

"There was no money to pay them. At least the pandemic gave us some kind of fig leaf. Otherwise it would be all over New York that Rob was broke." She saw my sour expression. "Yes, I know it's shitty. It was a shitty thing to do, and believe me, people were angry. Mainly at me, of course, because I'm the Asian bitch who counts the money and Rob is just a cool dude skipping about like he's on the yellow submarine, opening all the doors."

I WAS SUDDENLY PULLED BACK to Fancy Goods, the way Alice got tangled up with running it, how her contribution was subtly downgraded by the artists, to whom she was just the girl who did the admin; an assistant, a helpmeet, not a curator or an intellectual. Rob and I shared the belief that art should be unworldly, opposed to routine. Rob, in particular, felt it was the mark of a true artist to be incapable of looking after yourself. Part of it was demonstrating that you were indifferent to convention. You borrowed money and didn't pay it back. You pulled your pants down at the bar. But he was also proud of not knowing how to do boring things, and was good at inducing other people to do them for him, whether that was laundry or filling in a tax form. He tried his helpless act with me once or twice, but I didn't go for it; Rob liked to be coddled, to be made to feel special, but I knew he secretly looked down on people who gave in and did things for him. I didn't think he respected Alice.

To twenty-something me, an artist was primarily someone who was trying not to get captured. The world was dominated by the interests of the rich and powerful. It was organized to lure you, to trick you into their service. An artist ought, I thought, to live like a spy, a spiritual fugitive. Art itself consisted of finding ways to say no, to become invisible to power. Only then could an artwork have any claim to authenticity. Even if you found it difficult, or it caused friction with others, it was necessary to refuse entanglements, because they were a way to force you to conform. When I wouldn't speak to anyone and locked myself in my studio, I was holding a line, taking my vocation seriously. In practical terms, it amounted to the same thing. Rob and I both expected other people to pick up after us. Of the two of us, I was probably the more self-righteous about it.

I lay down beside Alice on the narrow bed in the attic and I felt the warmth of her flank, her bare leg hooked over mine as she began ranting at me, or rather up at the ceiling; a woman cracked open by her anger, spilling out talk. She told me that it took a few years of being with Rob to realize how bad he was with money, how after he made a certain amount, he stopped paying attention, because he was rich and he thought that meant he would be rich forever. How he was like a child, and she had to manage all the practicalities of their life. How in the early days in New York she did everything, at home and in his studio—shipping, insurance, fire inspections, calling the plumber, all the things that bored him. Rob had been bustling around, setting up his new scene, when disaster struck; the big London collector who owned several of his paintings lost interest and dumped them all at auction, without even informing his gallerist. The market followed this collector; he could more or less single-handedly launch an artist—and vice versa. Suddenly Rob was damaged goods.

So they were in New York, trying to make it in a really expensive city, and they had nothing coming in, and to her surprise, Rob seemed totally sanguine. It emerged that he thought her mother was going to bail them out. When she explained that it wasn't so simple, he was shocked. Like me, he'd heard Alice talk about the family company, the way everyone competed to get their share of the money.

"Well, exactly. Family money, not mine. My mom did help us out early on, but she soon saw through Rob."

"Wait. You're telling me you never inherited? I thought you were going to get millions."

"Let's say my mother has some tricks up her sleeve. Rob wanted to hire a lawyer. He still does."

"He thinks she's cheating you?"

"I know she is. And she knows I know it, but she also knows I'm not as strong as her. I don't have the will to fight. I'd rather let it go, which is yet another thing Rob's angry with me about. He and my mom have wanted to get in the ring since the moment they met. I spared you that, at least. You never liked confrontation."

"I never met your mom. I don't think I ever even saw a picture."

"Rest assured, she'd have hated you. She'd still hate you. She's old now, and her only pleasure in life is paying forward all the humiliations her own mother inflicted on her." She made a rueful face. "It's funny, I can talk about this with you. Some buddy of

Rob's taught him the phrase 'cultural difference' and ever since he's refused to deal with any of what he calls my 'family stuff.' All he knows is there's a lot of money and he hasn't seen any of it."

"So Rob thought the family millions were going to buy him a life of ease."

"I don't think he was totally cynical. Not when we got together. He really was in love with me. I think he still loves me. You know, in his fashion."

"Do you love him?"

"It's not fair to ask me that. I don't know. I can't think about it. You remember, that's what he does. He crowds you out. He takes up all the emotional space until you can't even imagine squeezing your own feelings in there. Right now he's in trouble, and when he's in trouble he always needs someone to blame, otherwise, you know, he might have to look in the mirror, so his new thing is to accuse me of holding out on him. He's convinced I have secret bank accounts, safety deposit boxes full of share certificates and jewels."

"And do you?"

"He doesn't know everything, but there's no big box of money. One of my uncles got most of it, the one who actually runs the company. Like I say, to carve out my share I'd have to go to war with my mom. I mean real war. Blood on the carpet. Rob's eager to do it, says he'll handle all the legal side, but I know he won't. He'll get bored and go off and paint, or not paint, pretend to paint, whatever it is he does with his time. Then it'd be down to me, and I can't. I just can't. I guess I don't want money that badly."

"So what are you going to do? About money, I mean."

"For sure I'm not going to go through hell with my family and then meekly hand my inheritance over to Rob so he can give it to cocktail waitresses. Serious answer? I have no idea. I might not do anything. I think it's time for Rob to do something."

"And if he doesn't?"

"Well, then I suppose nothing will be done."

"Aren't you worried? I mean, about the future?"

She made a despairing gesture. "With all this going on? Have you looked around, Jay? You think there will even be a future? I'm not sure."

"I don't know. This seems like a safe place."

"Sometimes I think Marshal has a point. It could be about to go very bad. We just don't know."

"So what did Rob do back in the beginning, when he found out your mom wouldn't support you? How did he handle it then?"

"Oh, he took a job."

"Seriously?"

"Well, not an office job. He worked as an assistant to FDP."

I looked blank, and she explained that FDP stood for "Famous Dead Painter," a joke that was funnier when he was alive. He was one of the macho Germans who had reinvigorated painting in the eighties, after a decade when everyone wanted to do conceptualism. In New York, he was considered the incarnation of European seriousness, producing massive canvases in which ordinary consumer objects became decaying monuments. A supermarket spawned crematorium chimneys. Sublime mountain landscapes were revealed as illustrations from Swiss chocolate packaging.

Everyone on the inside knew that FDP was a slob who walked around his studio in a bathrobe with his dick hanging out and an open bottle of fifty-year-old Armagnac to help him get in the mood to paint. He'd work through eightballs of cocaine on a glass table and throw things at his assistants, then shuffle off to drop hundred-dollar tips at a cockroach-infested diner on Tenth Avenue where he was allowed to fill ribbed plastic glasses with Dom Perignon to wash down his greasy sandwiches. He was a monster whose wealth and cultural position licensed all kinds of terrible behavior. Every so often, after some particularly lurid public display he would get arrested, and have to take a town car straight from the precinct to a lecture hall or TV studio to offer his opinions on the Holocaust or the cultural divisions of the Cold War.

By the time Rob was working for him, his best creative days were gone, and he was leaning heavily on his assistants for ideas. Rob was smitten. He adored FDP and took to wearing an Italian suit splattered with paint, in imitation of the master. FDP loved him back, and for a while he was treated almost like a son. There were gifts and dinners, trips to Venice and Basel, weekends at fabulous borrowed houses. And because FDP went through wives and mistresses, Rob had to copy him in that too. He slept with a lot of women and Alice had made up her mind to leave him, to go back to London and try to be free again. Then, during a rare bout of makeup sex, she got pregnant.

FDP was excited. He insisted Rob bring her to the studio, where he put his hands on her belly and offered her a thousand dollars if she would let him "feel the little one's head." Rob was furious and there was a falling-out, a lot of shouting, and it still hadn't been completely sorted when FDP suddenly died. Despite rumors about prostitutes and drugs, some final orgy that had pushed him over the edge, it was a chaste death, an aneurysm that took him quietly in his sleep.

When Rob went to FDP's studio to collect his things, he found it sealed. The estate had moved quickly. They intended to catalogue everything inside, and were wary of theft. Despite his unofficial position as dauphin, he was treated like any other employee and denied access, which offended him mightily. Angry with the estate and distraught at FDP's death, Rob had been spat back out into the world. He and Alice wondered what to do next. She had Sophie. Her gallery, backed by one of FDP's collectors, was floundering.

"So that was when you had your gallery?"

"Yes. A little upstairs space in Chelsea."

"What did you show?"

"It was a sort of project space. Younger artists, people I'd met since I came here. It wasn't really a commercial venture. I gave it up after I had Sophie. It was too hard."

"And Rob?"

"Well, he hadn't shown for years. We were about to pack up and move to Berlin when Marshal entered the picture."

Marshal was very young, and his operation was tiny, just him and an assistant, but he courted Rob assiduously, flattering him, and not just flattering him, displaying a serious knowledge of his work. He would ask about paintings Rob had made five, ten years previously, telling him he was underrated, that someone should publish a monograph. Rob was charmed and Alice was impressed with his work ethic. Marshal went to every fair, followed every lead. He had an encyclopedic knowledge of contemporary art. He knew who owned what, who wanted what, and above all he knew how to sell. Rob did a show with him and every single painting was reserved before the opening.

After that, things moved rapidly. Rob became Marshal's biggest artist, and Marshal made it his business to learn how he liked to be treated. Though some critics were on the fence, saying Rob's stuff was too flip, too decorative, Marshal had a network of collectors who loved his brash style, and enjoyed being in his social orbit. Little by little, Alice noticed him beginning to incorporate some of FDP's tics into his own repertoire. He would host massive dinners in the gallery, standing on tables to give chaotic speeches, cajoling his guests into drunken excess. When she pointed out what he was doing, he denied it. She didn't push. She was busy with a baby, and aware that a lot of money was beginning to flow through their hands. So she broke the lease on the Chelsea space, which had been closed for almost a year, and reluctantly devoted herself to trying to manage her husband's chaotic career.

Everything got bigger. Bigger loft, bigger studio, bigger work.

For a while Rob was painting on the massive steel plates the city laid down as a temporary road surface when they were doing repairs. He took money to scribble on sneakers and credit cards and the labels of liquor bottles. They bought a house in Montauk, and for a while he decided he'd work up there, in a huge hangar where the previous owner had stored his collection of vintage cars. It didn't work out—too cold, too far away—and he came back to the city, renting an eye-poppingly expensive space in Williamsburg and filling it with equipment and assistants. Alice had to find someone who could drive a forklift, and then all the usual jobs, people to mix paint and make crates and take photos and do the computer work and the accounts, and of course Rob liked to run the place as a party, so there were always people in and out, drinking and giving him God knew what.

It wasn't sustainable. Rob's prices were going up, and there was a waiting list for his work, but the overheads were out of control. He never saw a toy he didn't need immediately, and he liked to be liked, particularly by people who were working for him, a legacy of his own years as an assistant. He found it hard to confront people, and often stepped over lines that an employer shouldn't cross. There was a studio manager who was charging all her personal expenses to their account. They lost money in an investment scam. Rob took it upon himself to buy a huge offset printing press that just sat in a crate because no one knew how to set it up. Always, Alice was the one who had to do the hard work, fire the studio manager and find another, contact lawyers, phone the manufacturer in Germany to try and hunt down a technician.

"And he's humiliated me, Jay. He's humiliated me again and again."

"With women?"

"We're paying one assistant who threatened to go public. Officially it was sexual harassment, but I think she was sleeping with him and they fell out. Thank God she agreed to sign an NDA, but you know the artworld, it runs on gossip. For a while there was a spreadsheet going round, problematic art men, something like that, and Rob's name was on it. So when his last show happened, this bitch journalist wrote a profile with a lot of horrible rumors. They ran a picture of him in a trucker cap looking, you know, inbred, alongside images of work he made literally ten years ago, these pinups with white paint spattered on them. Sure, it looked like what it was supposed to look like—I don't know. I stopped paying attention a long time ago, to be honest. I mean, Rob's whole thing is about being edgy, and these days I can barely look at him, let alone his stupid art. Why would I care if he threw white paint over porno pictures?"

She paused, as if expecting me to contradict her.

"Is that the kind of thing he makes?"

"No, not really. He's been through a lot of different phases. I didn't even know we were in trouble until one morning Marshal is freaking out on the phone, asking why I'm not 'out in front of it.' Like, Rob is cheating on me, fucking whoever he's fucking, and I'm supposed to be managing his reputation? They all start calling. The collectors, Marshal's little cabal. This old Miami property mogul who is a real piece of work, I can tell you, he addresses me as young lady, *listen here young lady*. Like I'm his daughter, or his assistant. Listen here young lady, if you and your husband don't handle this, the painting I'm consigning won't make its number. His tone made me so angry. I'm not working for this man. He's not my boss. This is just a guy who bought some pictures. I say to him why is this my problem and he says it's a problem for all of us. And I think to myself, why would he say that? I can't get a straight answer out of Rob about why he'd say such a thing. A problem for all of us. So I phone Marshal and he tells me a lot of stuff I really wish I'd known earlier. I find out he and Rob have been working with a group of collectors who own a lot of his work. They have a shared interest in maintaining Rob's prices, making sure that if anything goes to auction it doesn't sell below a certain floor."

"Because that would set a new price."

"Exactly. And everyone's investment would instantly be worth much less. So this old bastard had consigned the painting because he was getting divorced. It wasn't a good time, with the me-too stuff around Rob, and the others warned him against it, but he said he had no choice. He needed money. And if his painting didn't make its floor, a phantom phone bidder would have to take it on behalf of their little cartel. Rob and Marshal and the other collectors would each be liable for a share. Can you imagine how angry I was? We had no cash on hand. Almost nothing. At one time, it wouldn't have been a problem, his prices aren't that high, but right now? And Rob didn't even think to tell me."

"Did someone buy the painting?"

"Of course not. We bought the painting. One fifth of the painting, and we had to borrow to do it. It's sitting in storage right now, and I suppose it will stay there until Marshal can set up a private sale."

"If it's so bad, why do you stay with him?"

"Easy for you, walking the earth for twenty years. You have no idea about responsibility."

"You're going to lecture me about responsibility?"

She looked suddenly angry, confronted. "This is Rob's shit, not mine! All of it. You think I'm to blame because I clean up after him?"

"I didn't mean that."

"Yes, he's abusive. No one knows that better than me. Imagine how he's made me feel. But this public drama? I've worked hard. I've made a life for us. I don't see why Sophie or I should suffer because of Rob's bad decisions. It's not even about him, not in particular. It's just, you know, a moment. Rob just happened to be the idiot who couldn't read the room."

"I'm not judging you."

"I have to think about my daughter. If I left, she'd blame me. It would all be my fault."

"So you're trying to fix it."

"Something like that. After the auction, Rob skulked around for a while, like a dog that knows it's done something bad, then he told me he'd done a deal with Marshal. He was going to paint a series of canvases, and Marshal would advance us our share of the expected sale money to pay our expenses. This was last winter. I thought, fine. That's a good idea actually. It would give us some breathing space. I thought maybe I could restructure things, get the business back on track. But now he won't paint the pictures. It's like a bad dream. I try and go forward but I can't move my legs. He's been stalling, putting Marshal off. He says he's blocked."

"I'd find it difficult to paint if I didn't even own the work while I was making it."

"You're you, Jay. Rob can't afford to be precious. If it was going to be so tough, he shouldn't have made the fucking deal. By the end of last year, Marshal was losing his mind about the money, and when Covid happened he started losing his mind in general— I mean, you've talked to him, he spends all his time watching conspiracy videos. He begged Greg to let him use this place, and because Greg's kind of paranoid too, he said yes. Marshal's supposed to be security, can you believe it. He's trying to get Greg to build a bunker under the house. The pandemic really hasn't been good for him."

"It's not been good for a lot of people."

"I have a friend who keeps sending me pictures of rice. She has a whole closet filled with forty-pound bags of rice. If this doesn't work out, I think Marshal's going to drop Rob. I can feel he already wants to, but he's loyal. He invited us up here to give him one last chance to make the paintings. He got him out of the city, had the red barn cleared for him to use as a studio. He's been really generous, even though living with him is impossible. And I thought Rob would get so bored he'd finally start work."

"But he's not?"

"He's not doing a damn thing except chasing around Marshal's girlfriend. I don't know what he imagines is going to happen. It's like he wants to make our whole world come crashing down."

"Maybe he does."

"That's not comforting."

We lay and looked at the ceiling. I was high enough on Alice's vape that it seemed animated, labile. I squinted and moiré patterns emerged from the corners.

"So," said Alice, "now you know the whole sordid tale. Tell me, what do you think of my life? Ugly, no?" Before I could answer, she cupped my jaw with the palm of her hand and began to kiss me. "I need this," she whispered, as if I were arguing with her. She felt good against my body, like a circle closing, a keystone fitting into place atop an arch.

It was so unlooked for, so unexpected, Alice slipping off her shirt and shorts and moving naked against me, lithe and fierce, brushing me with her hair, grazing my mouth with her breasts, moving down, making all the connections, sending all the energies running round our impossible circuit. Past present and future collapsed as I pushed up hard into her, her hips bucking, then some kind of low moan came from—was that me? It sounded like banishment, the exorcism of years of grief, and her face was a mask of wonder as she ground against me and time was flattened and all noise ceased, all the world's buzzing.

I COULDN'T HAVE GONE DOWN TO DINNER with Alice. I couldn't have brought myself to sit round a table, fresh from what had just happened between us. I felt as if I was radiating light and heat, a human beacon visible to all. She got dressed and gave me a lingering kiss. I'll tell them you're tired, she said, but I've got to go.

Some time later, when I'd got used to the feeling that my crust had just been scrubbed off like some archaeological find, a coin or a rusty blade, I took a chair outside and listened to the night, burning a coil to ward away insects. I couldn't say what I thought about. My head was empty. I looked vacantly at the stars.

I slept in a kind of suspended animation, a deep and absolute sleep from which I woke up late, feeling oddly split, my mind running on two tracks at once. The strange peace of the previous night was still there, but also anxiety. I had spent so long trying not to get involved, to sever all my attachments and obligations. What would happen now? Would I go down and find Alice unable to make eye contact, full of regret? Would she have told Rob? I could no longer claim to be an outsider. I'd become part of a social game, *the* social game. I'd fled from it—I could admit this to myself, as I showered and dressed and walked the path around the lake, listening to birds rioting in the trees—it was what I'd fled from, because it frightened me and I had never really understood the rules. Nothing had changed about that.

As I reached the house, an unfamiliar vehicle was turning out of the driveway. I found Alice dressed in yoga pants and protective equipment, a mask and visor and surgical gloves. She was ferrying bags of food into the kitchen. Seeing me, she performed that eye-smile people did when we all wore masks.

"Amazing how everyone disappears when there's work to be done."

"Hey," Marshal called out from the living room, where he was apparently lying on the sofa. "I made the order!"

"Nicole made the order."

"On my card."

I helped Alice carry the bags into the kitchen and wipe down all the packaging. Following her instructions, I spritzed the fruit and vegetables with a "natural disinfectant spray" that came in a little glass bottle; I stowed everything in its correct place: ice cream in the freezer, kale in the crisper drawer, avocados in the big art pottery bowl on the counter. The code word on the bags was CASTLE.

Alice did something with her phone and Bossa Nova music filled the room, bringing with it an odd domesticity. She began to move around in time, and suddenly we were the owners of the house, a couple occupying their beautiful shared space, enjoying the cosmopolitan sounds of sixties Rio.

"Is this what you do?" I asked.

"Every day for months."

Two singers, a man and a woman, swapped lines in soft regretful voices as Alice and I made lunch, chopping and dressing big bowls of salad and arranging platters of cheese and cold cuts. I was succumbing to the fantasy that I was entitled to do inconsequential domestic things as I listened to those gentle voices. I knew she was doing the same. Our collusion felt involuntary; it was as if we were inhabited by shadows, adjacent versions of ourselves.

"You never used to be able to do that," she said, gesturing at the pile of julienned carrots on my board.

"Well, we never really ate."

We set the table on the terrace, brushing against each other as we laid out plates and cutlery. Marshal ambled out, but Rob and Nicole didn't make an appearance. The three of us ate in near silence, Alice and I stealing glances like teenagers, Marshal hunched forward at his place between us, shoveling in salad. The stillness of the scene—the sporadic birdsong, the faint buzzing of insects—belied something volatile in the atmosphere, an insta- bility, a potential for disaster. When Marshal's phone rang, we all flinched as if a gun had gone off.

"Hello? Greg! Yes, hi Greg. Good, thanks. All good." Marshal pushed back his chair, and stood up, brushing shreds of cabbage off his lap. "You saw—oh, yes, what did you think? He's inter- esting, right? He's someone who—I know, I know. Yes, we said that, but listen . . ."

He made a desperate face and pointed at the phone, as he went inside to take the call, the screen door clattering behind him. Alice and I were left alone.

"That might be it, for me," I said.

"That might be it for all of us. Greg was very clear. We weren't allowed to invite anyone to stay."

"I'm sorry."

"It's not your fault."

"Are you OK?"

"About leaving? More than OK, to be honest, but I want to know what you're thinking."

"About leaving?"

"Not just that, but sure. Where are you going to go?"

"Back to the city, I guess. Maybe not."

"But if you could go anywhere?"

The question opened up a sudden gulf between us. I could remember a time when I would have said the names of places— Zanzibar, Papeete, Patagonia; the Kyrgyz steppe, the Atacama

Desert. It was all she was asking for, some names to dream with. But I'd been traveling for years. I wanted to say, going somewhere isn't the point. The point is finding somewhere to stay.

Alice frowned. "Jay, are you about to disappear again? Are you going to run away because—" She trailed off, looking around to see if we were being overheard.

"If I did, would you come too?"

For a moment, the words lay between us on the table like a brick, something solid and irrefutable that couldn't be taken back. I smiled and held it and she smiled too and so we reduced it to a joke, a throwaway line instead of an invitation.

"Do you want to go for a walk? I don't want to be here when Marshal comes out."

"Sure."

Of course we ended back up at the barn. We knew why we were there, what we wanted to do. The second time it was like diving into a cold deep pool; a shock, a cleansing; I felt as if I'd shed another skin. We were lying naked, tangled up together, our breathing just beginning to slow in the aftermath, when we heard noise downstairs. Alice made a face at me and lay very still. We listened for a while to what sounded like shuffling feet, until I got up and cautiously peered down the stairs.

"Oh, hello."

It was Marshal. He was standing by my car, holding a big SLR camera. He took a picture through the driver's side window, then swung the lens towards me. Instinctively, I recoiled.

"Could you stop that?"

"Sorry, man. Just documenting."

"I was asleep."

He looked pale but exhilarated, a man with a purpose. "I hope you don't mind me coming up here. I wanted to get some images of the car, but I guess I'm too late. Looks like you cleaned it up, huh? That's kind of a shame."

"Why?"

"Patina, I guess. I wish I'd seen it when you first arrived. How long were you living in it for?"

"Why do you want to take pictures?"

"I'm sorry. I didn't mean to wake you."

He paused for me to say something, to tell him that it was OK and I didn't mind. When I didn't, he ran a hand through his hair. "I want to talk to you about—all this." He gestured at the car, at some laundry that was hanging from a line I'd strung between two posts. His eye drawn to the laundry, he took another picture.

"Marshal."

"Sorry."

"Can I?" He made as if to come upstairs. Involuntarily I looked back up at Alice, who widened her eyes and vigorously shook her head.

"I'll come down."

I pulled on a pair of shorts and sat on the bottom step, blocking his way.

"So?"

I was only half-listening to him as I pulled on a tee shirt, hyper-focused on small sounds upstairs as Alice crawled around, gathering her clothes. He was saying he felt bad, that "the girls had made the gun thing super clear." He didn't want to get into justifications. There was a storm coming but he wasn't there to talk about that.

"I'm sorry I made you feel, you know, uncomfortable. And I want you to know, I'm doing the work. But I also need to talk to you about something, Greg and Miranda are flying over from New Zealand."

"The owners?"

"Yes. I don't know exactly when. Very soon. In the next few days."

"So you want me to leave? Are you all going to have to leave too?"

"No, we can stay. They're just coming up for the day. But I had to say something to Greg. He was very angry about you being here, so I took the opportunity to pitch him on *Fugue*. You know, lemons, lemonade. I sent him some stuff. He's interested."

"What do you mean, interested?"

"I'd say he was more than interested. Intrigued would be a word. This surveillance camera thing could be very useful for us, actually. An opportunity. It kind of fits. You wandering in from the woods. Caught on infrared. Aesthetically that's strong."

"But I didn't wander in from the woods. I drove up from Queens."

"I just mean—at the very least the art angle has made him feel better about you being on the property. You know, I found a review from when you did *Unknown Masterpiece,* this crusty old newspaper critic who was writing about your work like it was the fall of the British Empire. Kind of cool, actually. And the wildest part is you were still a student. This guy was, like, totally out of his depth. He had no clue what you were trying to do."

"I think he understood. He just didn't like it."

"But it's incredible to me how you could put that together. The art-historical references, all of it, I mean, seriously. So I have questions. I hope that's not too forward of me. *Fugue* is such a radical piece. I mean seriously, an important piece. I can't imagine what you must feel right now. What you've learned."

"What I've learned?"

"About art. Your relationship to art. While you were doing it, for example. What did it feel like, for all those years? Did you always remember you were making art? Could you be sure you were—I mean, did you know you were still an artist? Even when you were, like, working in a kitchen?"

"I would have said no, until now."

"Why?"

Marshal's fractured charm had thrown me off balance, and though I'd intended to get rid of him as quickly as possible, I found I wanted to talk. Alice was upstairs, listening to his pitch. Alice from London, all those years ago. How was that possible? Everything was swirling around. No part of my life was in a stable relation to any other. Marshal certainly seemed unstable; he reminded me of Jago in many ways, and, like Jago, he seemed to understand the things I'd done. Though I knew it was absurd to respond, that I ought to be able to resist such crass mirroring, his enthusiasm made me feel that maybe I'd not been totally lost.

I was eager to get Marshal away from the barn, and he showed no sign of leaving of his own free will, so I suggested we walk to the mirror glade. As we made our way up the path, I fought an urge to look back, fearful that if I did, I'd draw his eye towards a fleeing Alice. He chattered on to me about—or so it seemed—several different topics at once, my art, which he'd clearly been researching, the pandemic, the other people in the house. His talk was a species of verbal skid, a linguistic glide across the smooth surface of things. He apologized again for the gun. He posited theories about the origin of Covid. Did I think it was engineered? Would it be the pretext for some kind of crackdown? He told me that he'd rented a storage unit in the city and filled it with supplies. A bike. A go bag. Water sterilization equipment. The person who really had it all nailed down, he thought, was Greg. Who wouldn't like to press a button on a watch and have a team instantly scrambled to extract you? The amazing thing was that I had no idea about my reputation. I ought to be aware that people—art people—talked about THE DRIFTWORK. How would I feel if he used the word "legend"? Did I know anything about the shelf life of MREs?

We reached the glade, and I caught sight of my louvred reflection in the mirrors. As always, the place seemed to me like a gate, a portal to another world, but instead of yearning to step through and disappear, I now felt as if someone was about to step out, my younger self, the person who'd loved Alice, who had been an artist. A loop had closed, restoring me—partially, imperfectly— to an earlier state. Nothing was ruined, though everything had been lost. I was vaguely aware that my face was wet with tears. Somewhere in the background, Marshal was still talking.

"You like the mirror piece, huh? Young German artist. The only good thing in the park, if you ask me. Don't say that to Greg. I understand why you're emotional. Look at where we are. It's paradise. You could use that word. It'd be fair. Paradise is a walled garden in I forget which language. That's what it's all about now. High security parkland. Personally I'd be happier if we had a better water source. That lake water is full of microbes. It'd go straight through you. And I'm going to talk to Greg about hardening the perimeter. You know I haven't actually left this place in two months. Crazy, right? You'd think it'd be relaxing, but it's not. I don't sleep. How about you? Do you sleep?"

"Better than I have for a long time."

"You're not anxious?"

"I had it. They say you can't get it again."

"It's not the disease. It's all the stuff around it. If it's a bio-weapon, what else are they prepared to do?"

"Who?"

"The Chinese. Unless it's a false flag. And even if it's not a weapon, the Chinese Communist Party is obviously not being straight with us. We don't know the whole story about that lab. But I suppose you're right. Nicole is always telling me I should keep it in perspective, whatever that means. And I see it. From your point of view, I see it. The virus is part of your art now. You survived and you're back."

"I guess."

"I need to know, have you been documenting? What kind of records have you kept?"

"None."

"Absolutely none? No diary, no photos?"

"Not a thing."

"Are there any objects that you've kept with you the whole time? A tool of some kind? Do you have, like, a favorite knife?"

I shook my head. "I don't have a favorite knife."

"Have you thought about what you'll do next?"

"I guess I'll need a job."

"I mean about *Fugue*."

"What is there to do? I have to think about getting back on my feet."

"But nobody knows about it. I realize this probably isn't where your head is at, but everything rests on how you play it now. What you've done for the last twenty years is art, I know that and you know that, but it will slip away into nothingness unless you make it public. You must have planned something. When you started out, how did you think you'd end it?"

"I didn't. If I'd thought about how it would end, it would have drained the whole project of meaning. I had to be open to the possibility that it would never end."

"That's incredible. An incredible answer. I wish I had that on tape. I think if people understand what you've done, you will—and I'm serious here—be hailed as one of the most significant artists of your generation. But if you don't bring it to a formal close and allow people to—you know, sit with it, really contemplate—then you're just some guy who left the artworld. One person says oh isn't he that dude who went missing and the other says I heard he came back and then they go on talking about their friend's show. You'll stay a curiosity, a footnote."

I was distracted. I'd caught myself using the past tense. *I had to be open, it would never end.* So it had ended. I understood what he was saying. In the logic of art, it made sense. I just wasn't sure I was ready to submit myself to that logic again.

"Think about it," Marshal said. "I can help you do this. Even if it's not me, then you need someone like me. Someone with my skill set. If you want to bring in someone else, then fine. But I'm here. And I would be honored to be part of it. My proposal is that I record you, debrief you. Let's get it all on tape. Then we work out a plan of action."

We headed downhill towards the barn. "How do you feel about social media?" asked Marshal. He saw my expression. "OK. Let's not run before we can walk."

As we approached, I scanned the building, half-expecting to see Alice's face at one of the upstairs windows. Marshal suddenly clapped his hands together.

"I'm convinced that's it. The car. That's the piece."

"It's just a car."

"But it's a trace, evidence of how you were living."

"It's how I'll be living again, soon enough."

"Don't be absurd. That's over. You won't have to do that again. Are you hungry? Let's go see if one of the girls has rustled up some food."

We found Alice in the living room, unconvincingly pretending to read a book. She looked flushed. She must have run back to the house. Marshal told her about Greg and Miranda, and she did a good impression of someone who was hearing about it for the first time. "They're coming here to see Jay?"

"Well, as a sort of secondary thing. They're actually coming to see a painting."

"One of Rob's? Is there anything to show?"

"You tell me. But no, not one of Rob's."

He was about to explain when we heard noise outside. Rob pulled open the sliding door to the living room, and Nicole stormed in. The two of them seemed to be in the middle of an argument. Rob was looking sheepish, Nicole furious. She walked over to Marshal and poked him in the chest.

"What did you tell him?"

"What do you mean?"

"I need to know what you told him."

Marshal looked askance at Rob, who broke out in a sloppy day-drinker's grin. Marshal turned back to Nicole.

"Maybe we could do this in private?"

"I think Alice would like to know what you told him. Did you say you gave him permission to paint me? You actually used the word permission?"

"Does he want to paint you?"

"Don't act innocent. You want me to stand up naked on this man's block? Maybe he wants to see my teeth?"

"Nicole, get a hold of yourself."

"Am I part of some transaction between you and him?"

Rob adopted a soothing tone. "I want to make images of powerful Black women. Marshal, tell her."

"Tell me what, Marshal? Did you say he could sleep with me?"

"Of course not."

Rob giggled. "Though you ought not to rule it out."

"Fuck you so hard Rob."

Rob shook his head. "They're always so sensitive."

In one fluid movement, Nicole spun round and slapped him. The force was considerable, and Rob staggered, sitting down with a bump on the rug. Alice gasped. Nicole looked as if she couldn't believe what she'd just done.

"That's great," said Marshal. "That's just great." It was as if something inside him snapped. His voice wavered, rising steadily. "I'm sick of this! I'm sick of all of you. None of you know how to take care of yourselves! I'm not sleeping! Do you know what that's like? Lying there in the darkness and making lists of all the things that could go wrong? I am running everything here and no one takes it seriously."

Alice rolled her eyes. "When did you last cook a meal, Marshal?"

"I do other things! So guess what? Greg's coming. And you are all going to cooperate because if you do not then the wheels are going to fall off and we are going to be back out there in the midst of a pandemic. Nicole and Alice, start thinking about catering. Rob, you, my friend, are going to get off your ass and help me sell a painting."

"What painting? One of mine?"

"You haven't got any fucking paintings. If you had done a painting I would fucking sell it to Greg. But no, it's another painting. Someone's going to bring—damn it. Just a moment. I need to call the gallery."

He stomped out onto the deck, sliding the door closed behind him.

"Catering?" said Nicole to Alice. "Did I just hear him say that?"

"What painting?" Rob asked.

Alice turned to Nicole. "Are you OK?"

"No," she said. "Not really."

As she looked at Rob, Alice's face was a cold, hard mask. "You selfish prick."

"I didn't touch her."

There was a period of awkward silence, then Marshal came in again. I felt myself relax slightly when I saw he wasn't armed; only then was I even aware that the thought had been in my mind. With a kind of Napoleonic grandeur, he started telling everyone how it was going to be.

"The painting is arriving in the morning. My guys are driving it up from the city. We'll stage it in the house."

"WHAT PAINTING?" asked Rob again.

"It's one of FDP's."

Rob staggered to his feet. "Which one?"

"A late one. One of the *Tourist* paintings."

"He did those when I was working for him."

"Yes."

Rob looked as if he were about to throw a punch. "What are you doing, Marshal?"

"Selling a picture. It's a bonus that you're going to be here. You can tell him about it."

"Me? Oh no."

"Oh yes. You have a personal link to the artist. You were around when the work was being made. You can help me convince Greg and Miranda that they want to be part of that story."

"I said no, Marshal. You seem to have forgotten I want nothing to do with that old cunt or what's left of his reputation."

"I need you to do this for me."

"Sorry, mate."

"Sorry mate? That's what you have to say? When you have fucked me? When you have taken me for a goddamn fool? Is that what you think? You think I'm a fool? Some kind of mark that you can string along forever? I paid you a year ago! Six paintings, Rob, and you have produced nothing! Not a fucking thing!"

"I'm not a machine."

"No you are not."

"Creativity's not like turning on a tap, Marshal."

"If I hear another word of fridge magnet horseshit out of your mouth I swear I will fucking punch you! You're going to do me this favor, Rob. If you're not going to paint me your own fucking pictures then you will do this for me. I am serious. It is what I want. It is what I need from you. I am not sleeping. I am not doing well. And you are not helping!"

"Jesus, why is everyone on my case? What is it you want me to do? "

"You are going to tell Greg and Miranda wonderful, moderately scandalous stories about FDP and his great passion and his unusual creative process and you are not going to be shitfaced or make sarcastic remarks and you are not going to embarrass me. I have done so many things for you. I am the only reason your career is not dead in a ditch. Now you're going to do one thing for me. One thing!"

"You can't ask me to help sell one of his paintings."

"Yes I can! Yes I fucking can! Yes! Yes! Yes! You are not a good person, Rob. You are not a kind person!"

"Marshal, do you know how it ended between me and him?"

"I don't care. I am going to do an hour of yoga so that maybe I will survive until forty. Tomorrow the painting will be delivered and all this drama is going to stop, you understand? From all of you! We are going to be happy team players, getting ready to welcome Greg and Miranda."

With that, he marched off upstairs. For a moment, we all sat in shell-shocked silence. Nicole looked from Rob to Alice to me. "I'm sorry," she said to Alice. "None of this is what I wanted." Then she went upstairs too.

"Don't start," muttered Rob, seeing that Alice was about to say something to him.

"What is it, two in the afternoon? And you're already drunk?"

"I said don't start."

"A couple of weeks ago I was thinking about confronting Nicole and asking if she was sleeping with my husband. Thank God I didn't! I would have made myself ridiculous. Anyone can see she doesn't want you. She doesn't like me, but you? You really disgust her."

"You take your cheap shots, but I'm the one trying to make something. I'm trying to make art. You think it's easy?"

"Being you? Yes, Rob, I think it's easy. You forget, I know exactly what you do."

From upstairs came a sudden thud of bass, Nicole exorcising her demons, or covering the sound of an argument with Marshal. Rob went in to the kitchen, filled a glass with water, drained it. He came back in to the living room and looked sourly from Alice to me, seeming to consider what he was about to say.

I stood up. "I'm going to go."

"There's always a silver lining," he drawled.

Alice shot me a quick grimace of apology. As I walked away down the path, I could hear them begin to argue with each other, over the sound of Nicole's music.

I wandered in the woods, without purpose or direction, putting one foot in front of the other as I tried to process what was happening. For the first time since I'd been swallowed up by that vast domain I felt hemmed in, aware of the fence enclosing me. My first impulse was to leave, immediately, to fall forward into whatever awaited me next. I had enough money for gas. I just needed to choose a road. But Marshal was right. If I wanted to salvage something from the years of *Fugue,* then I would have to find an ending. Was salvage the right word? What would I be saving, and from what? Did I really think time was lost if it wasn't converted into art? No, not anymore. The people I had known; the things I had built or repaired; the scars on my body—they were real. They had been my life. Those years weren't lost years.

I WENT BACK TO THE BARN, hoping to find Alice there. I waited for her, sure she would come. For a long time I sat outside, watching the evening shadows lengthen across the meadow. A red-tailed hawk circled overhead, looking for mice. Finally, as the sun fell below the treetops and the ground began to turn cold, I walked down to the house, where all the lights on the deck were burning.

I found the others at the table, sprawled out like exhausted fighters around the wreckage of a takeout dinner. A drinks cart had been wheeled out from the living room. Alice was sitting between Rob and Marshal. As I came towards them, Rob slung a possessive arm around her. I realized that he and Marshal were very drunk. Nicole was missing. I wondered if she'd left. I wouldn't have been surprised to hear she was already on a train heading back to the city.

"Hi Jay," said Marshal. "Want a cocktail? It's basically gin and lemon and this violet stuff that turns it blue. You like cherries?"

I took my drink without cherries. It was ice cold and went down like a transmutation, some CGI effect in a movie where the freeze-ray turns a human body into crystal. With the gin inside me I almost didn't care about Rob's surly stare, his caressing hand on Alice's neck.

"I don't know what's wrong with Nicole," said Marshal. "She saw something on the internet, some video."

Rob chipped in. "The cop kneeling on the guy's neck?"

Marshal nodded. "Yeah. It looks bad. I can understand why she's upset."

"It's the internet, though. You never get the whole story."

Alice gave me a dark look. Rob's hand had found its way inside her shirt. She shrugged it off.

"So, to recap," she said, "Greg and Miranda are coming the day after tomorrow, and Marshal's going to sell them a picture. The picture's coming tomorrow morning and Rob's going to be helpful and I'm going to be helpful, but the big question is are you going to be helpful? Apparently Greg would like that."

"Have you met him?" I asked.

"A few times. Just at parties. Marshal knows him pretty well."

Marshal was mixing another round of cocktails. He nodded, performatively modest. "I consider him a friend."

Rob snorted.

"What?" Marshal looked annoyed. "He's a very genuine guy."

Marshal was obviously proud of his access to Greg. He was, he said, a transformative figure. Greg was in the payments system. He was in cloud storage. He was in satellites and climate mitigation. When Marshal said the words Greg is coming, he wanted everyone around the table to feel the gravity of that advent, our imminent proximity to the great chthonic forces beneath the surface of things.

"How did you get connected with him?"

"Miranda started bringing him to shows."

"Miranda is the third wife?"

"No, second."

"How old is Greg?"

"Early sixties, I guess."

"And Miranda?"

"She's thirty-five. It's respectable."

"And she's the one who cares about art?"

Marshal named one of the bigger East Coast MFA programs, where Miranda had studied. "He was collecting before her, but he didn't know what he was doing. He had, you know, a Hirst spot painting, a bad Picasso, some random shiny sculpture he picked up at Miami Basel."

"FDP is kind of a stretch, then."

"I don't think so. She already got him to buy a bunch of messy paintings. They have a Baselitz, for example. FDP would make sense with that. It's an expensive picture, but the subject will appeal to him. Greg likes anything with a boat in it. You know, exploring, buccaneering, opening up new frontiers. He doesn't have much sense of who FDP was, but that's where you'll come in."

Rob raised his chin from his chest and frowned.

"Sixty-eight," said Alice. "Wikipedia says he's sixty-eight."

"Just tell him FDP stories. Tell him about the butter knife. That's a good one. Hey Jay, you want to hear about the butter knife?"

Marshal made more drinks, goading Rob to tell a rambling tale about being with FDP at dinner hosted by a collector, some titan of finance with a penthouse overlooking the park. As Marshal and Alice had evidently heard the story before, Rob was forced to tell it to me, or at least project it in my direction. FDP had sold the collector a work. It was in the dining room of the penthouse, and the dinner was being held so FDP could admire the hang. As dessert was served, FDP claimed to see an error, something unfinished that he needed to fix, at once, right away. Despite himself, Rob began to enjoy his anecdote, describing the fluttering and whispering around the table as FDP produced some tubes of paint from his pocket, grabbed a side plate to use as a palette, mixed a shade of blue, and, with a butter knife, made a single, imperceptible alteration.

"It was totally planned, of course," Marshal explained, handing out cocktails with an unsteady hand. "Why else would he have brought paint to dinner?" He dabbed at the spills with a wedge of paper takeout napkins. "I don't think he actually touched the canvas, but that was the genius of it. The collector and his friends loved it. They wanted to believe that the artist could see something no one else could."

"Well," I said. "They don't pay all that money just for paint."

The talk drifted on for a while, stilted and occasionally incoherent, but without particular malice. Marshal revealed that he thought of himself almost like a couples therapist. His job was to make Greg and Miranda feel the picture as a mutual pleasure, experience the decision to buy it as something they had arrived at together, an expression of their love. "I have to make them believe that if they own an FDP, they're going to have the best sex they've had in years."

He trailed off, as if contemplating the intercourse of the one percent. His face took on an ashen cast. Suddenly he stood up, knocking back his chair.

"Got to go to bed."

"You OK?"

"Sure. I just need to lie down. Maybe Nicole will let me in the room."

"Show her who's boss," advised Rob.

Alice stood up too. "Come on, Rob," she said. "Big day tomorrow." He seemed to think for a moment, then allowed himself to be led away. As they stepped through the door, he stumbled and Alice put a steadying hand on his elbow, which he shrugged off. For a moment, she hovered in the doorway, looking back as if she were about to say something to me; then she followed her husband. I was left alone at the table, surveying the wreckage of their dinner. The sound of cicadas thickened the darkness.

THE SCENE THE NEXT MORNING had a science fiction quality. Figures in masks and plastic hazmat suits were lifting a crate out of a box truck. As I walked up the slope from the lake, one was moving around the others, talking and gesturing. I could hear Marshal's voice, slightly muffled by a respirator, exhorting his movers to be careful. The atmosphere was tense, as if they were handling something dangerous and volatile, explosives or a flask of nerve gas.

Nicole was on the deck, sitting cross-legged on a yoga mat, a surgical mask pushed down under her chin. She was frowning at her laptop. The previous night's meal was still on the table nearby. Racoons had been through it; bits of food and smashed crockery were strewn across the floor. Through the window I could see the dystopian figures moving the crate into the house. The contrast was jarring, as if I were simultaneously present in two realities, one in which the pandemic was several orders of magnitude more dangerous than the other.

"Sorry about the mess," said Nicole, "but I guess it must be the maid's day off. You want a mask? I have a spare."

"I'll just keep out of their way."

"I should tell you, I'm gone. Probably today. I'm about to lose my mind if I have to be around these people anymore."

"So you and Marshal . . . ?"

"He knows it, even if he doesn't know it."

"Where will you go?"

"To the city. Someone needs to look after my grandma."

From inside the house I could hear the sound of a power tool, as the movers started unscrewing the crate.

"You saw it, right?" She was looking at me with a peculiar intensity. "The way that officer just killed him, right there on the street?"

"This is something on the internet?"

"No, it's not 'something on the internet.' It's a Black man being slowly and publicly asphyxiated by a white police officer."

"I haven't seen it."

"Well, maybe you should. Maybe you should see it."

I said nothing. She looked exasperated. "I guess you've decided to stay here."

"For now. I have things to work out."

"You and Alice?"

She shrugged off my stare and went back to her screen.

"Where are they?" I asked. "Alice and Rob."

"No idea. They went for a walk, probably so they can carry on fighting."

The screen door clattered and Marshal appeared on the deck in a hazmat suit, like an emissary from the pathogenic future. "Can you come in?" He spoke to me only, ignoring Nicole, his tone professionally brusque.

"I don't think I have the right gear."

"It doesn't matter. You've had it and they're wearing PPE.

"You see, I'm worried it looks too big," he said, as he took me through the kitchen. "It does dominate the room. What do you think? Maybe we should move the furniture out?"

The two assistants were getting ready to take the empty crate. Seeing me walk in, maskless, they stepped back.

"Don't worry," said Marshal. "He's had it."

I looked at the suits and the high-grade masks. "How did you get all this protective gear? Hospitals don't even have this stuff."

"I keep a supply in storage. I have chemical and radiological rigs too. What do you think? Should we move the furniture out?"

In the open living area that took up most of the ground floor, chairs and sofas had been pushed back to make room for a large canvas, about six feet wide and four feet high. It depicted a giant white cruise ship disgorging passengers into a semi-submerged city, in which waves lapped around ruined classical buildings. The ship and some of the buildings were depicted with a meticulous precision, tiny details brushed on, while other parts of the painting were filled in with crude, almost violent strokes. If you looked closely, among the ruins were structures that seemed out of place, columns that might have been rolls of paper towel, giant bottles, one with a peeling gin label. In the foreground, crowded into the frame, were the tourists, horrific semi-human figures, all wearing orange life vests.

"It's a late work called *Blue Ruin*. He did a series of these. You've really never seen them?"

"After my time."

"They were in the big posthumous show, the one everyone went crazy for? All of them have the tourists, though sometimes they get abstracted. Just these little black forms. They're some of his most sought-after works."

"He was a good draftsman."

"And funny too, which I think is an underrated quality in painting."

"Who does it belong to?"

He smiled discreetly and pretended to examine the rug. "A client. This is the best one in private hands. The others are mostly in museums."

As we talked, the assistants carried out the crate, and loaded it back into the truck. Marshal went to see them off and I stared for a while at *Blue Ruin,* losing myself in its imagery of disaster. It was a good painting. It had been a long time since I'd looked carefully at a picture, trying to see how it had been made.

Marshal came back in to the room. He'd taken off his respirator, which had left a red mark like a wavy brand across his forehead. As he stripped off his protective suit, my eye was drawn by a flash of color against the green of the trees outside. Rob and Alice were making their way down the hill from Rob's studio. Together, Marshal and I watched them trudge along the path.

"Moment of truth," he said, pulling open the sliding glass doors to the deck. "Hey!" he called out to them. "It's here! It arrived!"

Alice waved limply, and they carried on towards us. As they got closer, I could see how dejected they looked, their shoulders down, their gait leaden, bedraggled survivors of some emotional shipwreck. Alice had been crying. Rob was sweating and fidgety. When he caught sight of the picture, his eyes widened and for a moment I thought he was having some kind of attack, a stroke or seizure.

"Oh fuck no." He turned to Marshal. "Not that one. Of all the pictures—just not that one."

Alice rounded on him, instantly furious. "You said you'd do it. You just promised me five minutes ago."

"I meant it. I'd do it for any other picture, but not that one. I can't."

"Whatever your weird problem is," said Alice, "you need to get over it. Marshal has been incredibly generous to us, letting us stay here. You're abusing that."

"I can't."

"Why not?"

"Because I said so, OK? You need to listen for once."

"I don't understand," said Marshal. "You have some kind of issue with this picture?"

Rob didn't reply, just went back outside onto the deck and

stood for a moment, as if deciding what to do. Then, without another word, he stalked off up the hill to the red barn. We watched him slide open the door and tug it shut behind him.

Marshal turned to Alice. "You need to deal with him."

"Of course," she said, brightly. "It's my job. I'm the one who deals with Rob. But first let's have lunch."

Marshal pointed out that it was ten in the morning. Alice shrugged. "We need to clear up. The raccoons made a terrible mess on the deck. Then we can cook something nice. I have some salmon. I can poach that, or maybe do it in the pan with a soy glaze. If we were in the city I could get bok choy . . ." She seemed to be soothing herself by narrating the menu, bringing down a blanket of good living to smother her stress.

Faced with the prospect of chores, Marshal remembered that he had calls to make. Alice and I gathered cleaning supplies. As soon as we stepped out onto the deck, Nicole picked up her laptop and moved down to the bench near the water. Alice didn't try to speak to her, or ask her to help. I piled a tray as Alice swept the floor.

"Are you OK?" I asked.

"No, but let's not talk about it."

We went back inside. She put on her Bossa Nova playlist and performed a few hesitant steps. I found a knife and a cutting board. The music sounded kitsch. I wished she would switch it off.

"You seem much better," she said. I wasn't sure what she meant.

"I'm better than I have been for a long time."

"I still think you ought to see a doctor."

"I'll get on that."

"But seriously, if you died, what would you want me to do?" Her tone was light and ironic, but the lightness didn't go all the way down.

"You can bury me in the mirror glade."

"You like that place."

"I do. It feels like an exit."

"But if I buried you in the woods, would anyone miss you? Who would you want me to notify?"

A pause began to form or congeal, thickening the air between us. I was about to tell her that there was no one, that I was on my own, when her phone sounded a jaunty ringtone. "Hello darling," she said. "Is everything OK?" I had a glimpse of a teenage girl on a screen, long hair falling over her eyes. Alice moved into French, and as she went into the next room to talk, I was reminded how little I really knew about her life. She had this girl, her daughter with Rob. Together she and Rob had held a newborn, marveled at all the first things—steps and words and drawings—attended school events, dried tears. These thoughts grew like a stone in my stomach. How absurd I was, how foolish my little hopes.

My self-laceration was interrupted by Nicole, who burst breathlessly into the kitchen, a wild expression on her face. "I think you should come outside," she said.

I followed her out onto the deck. "Up there," she said. "Up on the hill." The sight was so flamboyantly surreal that I had to laugh. There was the painting, *Blue Ruin,* moving along the path that led to the studio. The building, up on a rise behind the house, was an artful fake, a modern construction in the style of an old Dutch barn, with red siding and a gambrel roof pierced by large skylights. The painting looked for all the world as if it were walking there by itself and it took me several long seconds to understand that Rob was carrying it. As we watched, he reached the barn and propped it up against the wall, like any old board, while he opened the door.

"What's that on his back?" asked Nicole.

I knew what it was. It was Marshal's rifle. We watched in

silence as Rob took the painting into the studio and closed the door.

"Jay? What's he doing?" Alice had come out onto the deck, clutching her phone. Her voice was tight, brittle. "Did he have the gun?"

"Yes."

"Sophie, I'll call you back, OK?"

Nicole began waving frantically to Marshal, who was coming up the lawn from the direction of the lake. Seeing her, he broke into a jog and bounded up the steps. "What's the commotion?"

Nicole tried to explain. "Rob took the painting."

Marshal looked baffled. "What do you mean?"

"He took the painting up to his studio."

"He did what?"

"He carried it up there."

"Oh my God. If he's damaged it—oh my God."

Marshal was actually wringing his hands. Then he ran off up the path towards the red barn. As if released from a spell, the rest of us followed. Marshal got to the door and started pulling at the handle, but Rob must have locked it from the inside.

"Rob! What are you doing? Let us in!"

Rob's voice was muffled. "Fuck off! I don't want to see any of you!"

"Open up! What are you doing with the painting?"

"I haven't decided yet."

"Marshal, he has your gun."

Marshal swung round to face Nicole. "He what? How? Which gun?"

"What do you mean, which gun?"

"I have more than one. A long gun?"

"It looked like the same one you were carrying before."

"Shit. I doubt he knows how to load it, though."

He went back to pounding on the door. "This isn't funny, Rob.

You have several million dollars in there, several million dollars that doesn't belong to you. Did you scrape it, at all? Did you put it down on the ground?"

There was no response, and suddenly Marshal lost control. He started slamming himself against the door, cursing Rob and demanding that he open up. Nicole tried to calm him, but he pushed her away with some force, so she stumbled and almost fell. Angrily, she threw up her hands and started back down to the house, calling back over her shoulder that whatever was about to happen, she wanted no part of it.

Marshal ignored her. "Open up!" he yelled, his voice strained and oddly high-pitched. "Open up, you bastard! If you won't do it I'll shoot the goddamn lock off!"

He gave Rob a chance to reply, and when he didn't, he let out a yell of exasperation and headed off downhill, cutting across towards one of the out buildings. Alice took over at the door. "Rob? Rob, honey, talk to me. What are you doing? What's the plan here? Marshal's going crazy."

"Tell him I don't want to talk to him. And tell him I know how to load the gun."

"The gun's loaded?"

"Stand back! Step away from the door!"

Alice was terrified. "Don't shoot!"

"I'm going to shoot up at the roof, not at you."

We moved away, and there was a report, then an incredibly loud crack, as a large pane of skylight glass came crashing down inside.

"Now, leave me alone! I'll come out when I know what I want to do."

"Please, Rob," said Alice. "I'm begging you. Don't fool around with the gun anymore."

From inside came the sound of laughter, which broke up into throaty coughing.

Marshal came back, shuffling towards us over the grass. Something strange and obscene had happened to him. I thought he must be hurt, that somehow his guts were spilling out, but as he got closer I could see that the smears and streaks on his clothing were paint, a fleshy pink tone, the color of medical devices or sex toys. He had paint on his hands. His shoes were soaked in it. He was, if it were possible, more furious than he had been before. Barely mastering his rage, he told us that Rob had poured paint over all the weaponry in his cache. "My Glock. The shotgun. Vests, ammo, sights, the whole damn lot. It's all unusable. I could kill him. What I don't understand is how he found it."

"We all know where the cache is," said Alice. "It's in the garage."

"I think he's taken some ammunition."

"The gun's definitely loaded. He shot out one of the skylights."

"He what? That's what the noise was?"

Marshal banged on the door again, leaving a small pink smudge against the timber. "Rob? Don't do anything. Don't hurt yourself. And stay away from my painting, you asshole."

"You think that's helpful?" Alice was agitated. "Please just try and lower the temperature."

Marshal flapped his hand at her in what I suppose was intended to be a calming gesture. Then he kicked the door and started yelling again. "Give me the damn gun, Rob!"

Rob's voice was quite close. "I'm going to shoot the painting!"

"Don't shoot the painting!"

"I want to shoot it!"

"I am begging you, Rob!"

"If you carry on fucking yelling at me I am definitely going to shoot it. Now go away and let me think."

I disengaged Marshal from the door. "Let's go back to the house. We can talk there."

Marshal nodded. As we went back downhill, I almost had to

support him. He seemed traumatized, unable to deal with what had happened. As we got to the house, he realized he was leaving pink footprints on the wooden deck, and jumped back onto the path. I watched him hop up and down, cursing as he removed his shoes.

Alice and I slid open the door to the living room, and heard an irregular thumping sound. Nicole was dragging a heavy case down the stairs. She looked past us.

"What happened to you?"

Marshal had his shoes in his hand. He looked at his girlfriend, dressed for travel, standing beside her luggage.

"Not now, Nicole. For the love of God, not now."

"Not now what?"

"I don't have time."

"I can see that."

"So let's just, I mean—the suitcase. The whole—whatever this is. You don't need to do it. You don't need to do anything dramatic."

"I'm not doing anything dramatic, Marshal. I'm calling a taxi."

He turned to Alice. "We need to bring in the police. Rob is completely out of control."

Somehow this was the last straw for Nicole. "God damn it, Marshal. You make that call, a bunch of trigger-happy morons will arrive and stand around chewing gum and waiting for him to come out and after a while they'll get bored and they'll shoot him. So then your friend will be fucking dead, OK? Is that what you want?"

"He's white, Nicole."

"I am going to pretend you never said that."

"Just stating facts. And there's the painting. They wouldn't risk it. We need someone trained here. A hostage negotiator."

"Trained?"

"Maybe the FBI."

"And you wonder why I'm leaving? You and I live in different worlds."

Alice said, almost in a whisper, "He's going to kill himself."

I'd been thinking the same thing. Something about her tone quietened the room.

Marshal shook his head. "He wouldn't do that, would he?"

"I don't know. But he's in there with a gun, and—well, we just said some hard things to each other."

"What can we do?" I asked.

"I guess I'm the one who has to sort it out. He's my husband."

I didn't like the idea at all. Rob was an angry man, with a weakness for the familiar. I could imagine him falling into a narrative, deciding to go out with his one true love beside him. I pleaded with her. "I'll go with you."

"I don't think the optics of that would be good."

"Please, Alice. Just let him cool down. Don't go up there now."

I couldn't get her to change her mind. Anxiously, I watched her walk up the path, wondering if it was the last time I'd see her alive.

Nicole sat down on the sofa. "So there we are, another white man wanting to burn down the world to salvage his fragile ego."

"That's not fair," said Marshal.

"I don't give a fuck about fair. Making it all about himself. A whole goddamn Broadway show of pain."

"Don't move. I'm going upstairs to change."

I watched out of the window as Alice reached the barn. Nicole was saying something to me, but I wasn't really listening.

"Tell me, does your car work?"

"Just a minute."

"You know what's happening in the city, right? There's a curfew. People are burning cop cars. It's an uprising."

Alice was leaning against the studio door. I prayed with all my might that Rob didn't open it. My heart sank when it slid open and she stepped inside. For a moment I caught sight of Rob, as he closed it behind her. He looked savage, deranged. How long would it take for things to flare up? An argument, tears, the locked door, picking up the rifle.

Marshal came back downstairs, dressed in fresh clothes. "Is anything happening?"

"She's gone inside."

"Well, that's good, right? Alice will know how to talk him down."

"I'm not sure."

"She better, that's all I'll say. One way or another they are going to pay for any damage to that painting."

"Jesus, Marshal. Fuck the painting."

"Whatever." He turned to Nicole. "Look," he said. "Don't go. Please. Whatever it is, we can talk about it."

"Whatever it is? My car's going to be here in a few minutes."

"I mean it. I'm begging you, hang around. Let me deal with this situation. Then you and me, we'll talk. We'll fix it."

"And you'll magically start giving a shit? Marshal, when I call my grandma she always says is that your boyfriend? Yes, I tell her, he's my boyfriend. Does he know that, she asks. And I never know how to reply."

She began explaining to him why they were never going to work, why she didn't want to fix things, and he made a half-hearted defense. I couldn't take it anymore.

"Will you two just shut up!"

I couldn't understand how they could be talking about their relationship when Alice was in there with Rob and a gun. They stared at me, open-mouthed. I left the house and walked a little way along the path, to get away from them and be nearer to her, to whatever was happening to her inside the studio. I was beginning to feel a familiar dislocation, fixating on the irregularity of the planks on the side wall, an optically grating lack of symmetry that seemed to be undoing me physically, sawing away at the threads connecting me to my body. I tried to regulate my stress. What did I propose to do? Force my way in there, break down the door and bend the barrel into a knot? I was braced in anticipation of the sound, the single shot that would destroy everything.

Then, the door juddered open and Alice emerged. She came down the path towards me; she looked unharmed. I started towards her, almost crying with relief, but she shook her head and put out her hand to ward me off. I dropped my arms to my sides and waited for her to come closer.

"He's watching," she said.

"What happened?"

"Nothing much."

"You're not hurt?"

"No. Though he wouldn't give up the gun. I tried to reason with him but he said he doesn't want to talk to me."

"What does he want?"

"He wants to talk to you."

"ROB?"

"It's open. It's just sticky."

I pulled at the door, and it slid along the rails in little fits and starts. The barn was a big building, and it felt even bigger on the inside, a cavern that Rob was inhabiting in a patchy, transitory way. North light fell softly down on the white interior walls, giving the space a dreamlike stillness. I was standing near a sort of living area, an island on the expanse of sealed gray floor. An old leather sectional sofa bordered a faded Persian rug. The surface of a coffee table was almost obscured under teetering piles of stuff; a laptop balanced on a stack of art books, a plate of half-eaten food, a mirror tile smeared with powder. It wasn't hard to see how Rob had been spending his days. A patch of the wall was covered in marks, where he'd evidently been throwing a rubber ball against it. A short amble away from the sofa was a table with a record deck, an amp and a pile of LPs, cable spilling down to a pair of old-fashioned hi-fi speakers that had been carefully arranged to point at a sweet spot roughly where someone taking a nap on the sofa would lay his head. Other tables were loaded with paint and brushes and the various other detritus of a painter's life.

You can usually walk into a studio and tell if someone's work is going well. Whether it's meticulously neat or the stable-like squalor favored by so many painters, each studio has its modalities, its qualities of rest and motion. If things have been happening, there is a sense of change and process. Otherwise the neatness is sterile, the squalor just abject. Rob had set up an easel, and on the floor around it was an arc of drips and spots. There was a stack of primed canvases against one wall. Another canvas, turned face out, bore evidence of some halfhearted mark-making. My eye was drawn to a surgical mask which had been stuck on and overpainted, like a cipher for a human figure. There were some streaks of pink and violet spreading out from it, vaguely suggestive of limbs. Nothing much. A sketch, barely the beginning of an idea. Rob was painting with oils, but there were also cans of house paint lined up in long sculptural rows, and a spray rig, the kind used for custom cars. There were rolls of what looked like metal foil, and various other crates and boxes. All of this was untouched. Towards the far end, the floor was spangled with shards of glass. Air was blowing in through the broken skylight, rippling papers on the table.

In the middle of the space, in between the living area and the shattered glass, was *Blue Ruin*. Rob had set it up on a massive H-frame, some distance away from the studio clutter. In front of it were two chairs. Rob was sitting in one, hunched over something on his lap. The rifle lay on the floor beside him. My footsteps echoed a little as I walked across the open space.

As I got closer, I saw he was rolling a joint, an album cover balanced on his knees. I realized, in the era of vapes and edibles, that it was years since I'd last watched someone do that. "Well, fuck it," he intoned, into the air. "What do you want me to say? It wasn't like you were happy."

It took me a moment. "No, we weren't."

"So then."

"That didn't make it OK. I thought we were friends. I trusted you."

He nodded towards the other chair. "Do you want a drink or something? There's beers in the fridge over in the kitchen."

"No, I'm OK."

"Suit yourself."

I sat down and he finished skinning up, putting the record cover on the floor and performatively examining his handiwork. Then he lit the joint and blew on it until he was satisfied that it was burning evenly.

"I was angry at what you were doing to her, to be honest. You'd got her on so many drugs."

"It wasn't like that."

"Yes it was. When we got here, she was a skeleton. It was like looking after an invalid. I'd walk her round the park and she'd have to hold on to my arm. She couldn't sleep. She was having nightmares, sweating. Even the smell of food made her want to throw up."

"I remember she didn't eat."

"But you didn't do anything about it, did you? We were staying in a hotel, a nice one, you know, on her card, and I was going out of my mind, thinking I'd have to call a doctor. Then one day we were in that Ukrainian diner on First Avenue and I ordered cheese dumplings, because I was hungry, and of course I didn't think she'd want anything, but she asked for one, and then she had a second. She ended up putting away two whole plates of them. After that I couldn't stop her. She ate and ate. It was like she'd been in a camp. Anyway, what I want you to know is I never felt bad about taking her away. You would have killed her."

"I wasn't forcing her to do drugs."

"Yes you were. You were running all over London with wads of her money, buying them. And she wasn't built to take it, not like you. You were a beast. She didn't have your stamina."

"So I'm the beast and you're her white knight?"

"I'm her husband. You want me to apologize for running off with your bird? I won't apologize to you. Get that into your head. I will never apologize."

"You couldn't face me, though."

"Maybe that's fair. Maybe I should have told you what I thought of you."

"Maybe you should have."

He took another hit on his joint and picked up the rifle, sitting with it on his lap.

"So which one do you want? The spliff or the gun?"

"The gun, Rob. Let's take the gun out of the equation. Everyone's afraid."

He held out the joint. "Wrong answer."

I took it, though getting stoned was the last thing I wanted to do. Rob watched me, appraisingly. My distaste must have shown on my face.

"Straight edge, eh?" He pointed the gun at my stomach. "You want this?"

"Rob."

"Get two beers out of the fridge! Go on! Do it!"

Seeing my expression, he laughed and stood up, slinging the rifle over his shoulder. "I'm just messing with you. I'll get them."

I sat and looked around, trying to control my breathing. Chances were I could have got to the door, but it was heavy and far away, and there was something else in me, something fatalistic that kept me rooted to my seat. When he first saw me, the ghost of his past, Rob had asked if I was there to kill him. A projection, maybe. A premonition. It was out of my hands. He came back and handed me a beer, sitting down and pushing back his seat so the front legs rose off the floor.

"Cheers."

We clinked bottles, and I gulped down the cold liquid, which was suddenly welcome. My throat was very dry, and something in the air was making my eyes itch.

"So, you and Marshal, eh?" Rob took a conversational tone, though his mouth was fixed in a sneer. "Sounds like you're his new project. His chosen one. I haven't heard him this enthusiastic about an artist in a long time."

"Is that so?"

"You two will do good business."

"I don't want to do any business with Marshal."

"You ought to. The artworld likes nothing better than someone who doesn't seem to want it. That's always been my problem. They can smell it on me. It's a dirty smell."

I handed him back the joint. "I haven't decided what to do yet."

"What do you mean? It's what you came here for, didn't you?"

"I didn't come here for anything. I know I can't prove it to you, but this isn't part of some plan."

He stared at me, trying to decide whether I was telling the truth. His right leg was bouncing up and down, a meaty thigh slapping restlessly against the seat. The tremor was familiar but unnerving; the muzzle of the gun on his lap was facing me, bobbing up and down in a little agitated ellipse.

"Could you put that down, Rob?"

"This? It's bothering you?"

"Yes. Or at least point it away from me."

"Fair enough." He reversed the barrel. "Better?"

I nodded, and we sat for a while in silence. He inhaled deeply on the joint. The smoke hit him the wrong way and he began to cough; he turned and spat on the floor, wiping his mouth with the back of his hand in what I read as a deliberately boorish gesture; the lord of the manor, who can do as he pleases. "You know that stupid story Marshal made me tell you last night? The one about the stunt FDP pulled at the dinner? There's another part to it. As it turned out, the collector wasn't actually happy at all. I heard that when his guests had gone home, he sat up late into the night, staring at his painting, trying to work out what FDP had changed. However long he looked, he couldn't see anything, and it began to upset him. After that, every time he looked at it, he felt irritated, so eventually he had it taken down from his dining room and hung in his beach house. Finally he couldn't see the point of owning it anymore, and put it up for auction."

"No one likes to feel they've been made a fool of."

"You think that was it? He just knew FDP had conned him?"

"What else would it be?"

"I think it gave him imposter syndrome. Fear that if he couldn't see what FDP had changed, and it was obvious to others, then he was only playing the part of a great art connoisseur, flying around on his plane to the auctions and the fairs."

"You sound like Jago."

"Jesus, Jago. Poor bastard."

"He used to talk about what part everyone was playing."

"A lot of those rich guys have it. They know they don't deserve their money, and they're always terrified someone will realize they're just wankers like the rest of us. It's why they get into ridiculous pissing competitions over things like art. None of them can ever back down."

"So you're saying you don't think you should tell that story to Greg."

He laughed. "FDP knew he'd fucked up. The collector had told one or two of his friends and of course they told other people, and by the time the painting was sold, it was kind of an in-joke— how FDP was such a dickhead that he made one of his biggest collectors unable to look at his work. He hated to be reminded of it. I was there when someone said something to his face, and there was an actual fistfight outside that French restaurant they all used to go to in Tribeca." He looked at me, judging my reaction. "Bad, right? Everything you despise about the horrible art-world." Then he swung the gun back in my direction and braced the stock against his shoulder, as if ready to fire.

"You're better off out of it, Jay."

"Come on, man."

He did a little uptight imitation of my voice. "Come on, man." Then he shook his head, violently, as if trying to work something loose. "Every day, I ask myself, how did I get here? What did I fucking do? I just wanted to be free, you know? Of course you know! That was your whole thing, never having to bend the knee." He lowered the gun. "I can't decide how much of what you told us the other night is true, but if it's even half, then, well, cheers. You won. You did it. You've been a free man. More than me, at least. What I don't understand is why you want to come back."

"To art?"

"It's all such bullshit. Running a studio, everyone waiting for you to tell them what to do. It's fucking stressful. And then they want health insurance and if you stare at someone's tits it's work-place harassment. I'd swap places with you in an instant."

"You would?"

"At least people let you alone. I'm so screwed, mate. It's cancel culture, you're walking on eggshells all the time, especially with the young ones, they're like fucking Red Guards. So you're bet-ter off out of it. It's not as if you ever even liked it that much. You always acted like you were above it, all the shit you have to do to stay in the game." He raised the gun again. "Here's what

I think. You always reckoned you were better than me, because you didn't try and sell things. But now you don't make any work, so you're—I don't know—you're nothing."

He would have done it then, if he was going to. Pulled the trigger, made me nothing. But he carried on talking. He said he wanted to live, and he didn't think there was anything wrong in that. "You always talked about who was an artist and who wasn't. That's what you were interested in, saints and sinners. It was never about actually making art."

"You mean it wasn't about craft."

"Oh, fuck off. I wanted to be free so I could paint. You wanted—well, I don't know if you wanted anything. I think you just didn't like people very much. I know you never thought I got you, but I did. All this?" He gestured around him at the studio. "You'd hate it. Or, I don't know. Maybe not. Maybe once Marshal picks you up you'll suddenly start going out to table service clubs and buying bottles of vodka with sparklers in them."

"Like you?"

"Like me."

He swung the gun towards the picture and made pew-pew noises, like a little boy playing war.

"And now what do I have to deal with? My wife thinks I should work off my debts by helping Marshal make his commission. On this! What a joke! I ought to punch it full of holes."

"Is that what you want to do? Shoot the painting?"

"I can't bullshit some collector about why this is evidence of FDP's genius."

"Why not?"

"Because it's mine. It's my picture. I painted it. He never even saw it until it was dry."

"I didn't know he worked like that."

"He didn't. I wasn't following his instructions. I painted it."

"But the style, the motifs, they're FDP's."

"No they're not. They're mine."

"Come on, Rob. Marshal told me he painted a whole series, and all that stuff with the packaging and the bottles, that's more or less his whole deal."

"The bottles are mine. He put in those toilet rolls."

"I thought you said you painted it."

"God, this is complicated. First thing you have to know, he only did the series after he saw this painting. And I wasn't even going to show it to him."

"I'm confused."

"It is confusing. I'll try to explain. FDP had a building in Tribeca, four floors, more square footage than he knew what to do with, really, so I had a studio in there for a while, my own studio, making my own work. That turned out to be a terrible idea, because what I really needed was some distance from FDP and his drama. Anyway, when he died—he died suddenly—the estate sealed the place up, and paid someone to do an inventory, and some of the work that got catalogued as his was actually mine."

"Seriously?"

"Sure."

"Why didn't you say anything?"

"It was such a mess. I'd had a fight with him. There was the situation around this picture and then he put his hands on Alice, which was a red line for me. We weren't really in contact. But it's my picture. I'll prove it to you. Look down here."

He pointed out one of the little tourists, streaming out of the ship. It was different from the others, and I could see it was like the figures he used to paint, years previously when we'd been friends, the versions of himself that he used to put into his work. This one was abstracted almost to unrecognizability, but I could decipher the paunch, the tousled hair, a single stroke of black that I knew was a cigarette dangling from the mouth.

"You see, right? It's my picture."

"Well, I can see you did that, but you said he painted some other parts."

"This is why it's impossible! It's totally fucking impossible! He took it from me. I mean literally took it from my studio and carried it over to his. I'd been his assistant for three years, so I knew his tricks. Anything you brought into his orbit belonged to him. He had absolutely no shame about stealing. You know how a toddler will just reach out and put something in its mouth? He took ideas from all his assistants, and you just kind of had to deal with it, but I knew this was a good painting and I wanted to keep it out of his way. I was actually going to move it—store it somewhere else so he didn't see it, and then one day I came in to find he'd taken it to his studio and he was sitting in front of it with a fucking sketchbook. I was angry, of course, and we had an argument, and the old cunt did what he always did when he hurt someone, he threw money at me. He said he'd buy the painting. I told him it wasn't for sale, he named some stupid figure, and then he doubled it, and eventually I gave in. I wasn't happy, but there wasn't a lot I could do, short of walking out with the thing under my arm, and at the time it was more than I'd ever made and . . ."

He trailed off. He put the rifle down so the stock was resting on the floor, then hunched over it, the barrel under his chin. I wondered if I could kick it away, prevent what he seemed to be about to do, but the horror only lasted a moment and he stood up and went up close to *Blue Ruin,* scraping a fingernail lightly over the painted surface.

"He put that on it. Fucking vandal." He was indicating a patch of blue, uncertain streaks that had been worked over, hatched with marks that looked like they'd been made in wet paint with a brush handle. "When I saw he was making—well not copies, but other versions of my work, I confronted him again. I said I was going to take the picture back and he threatened to have me arrested for stealing his property and I said he still hadn't paid me and then he wrote a check, I'm talking a really massive check, and I was so angry I tore it up. I told him it was my painting, and he had to give it back. And he said—I'll never forget this—he said, Robert, if I touch a painting, it's mine. My hand gives it life. And then he picked up a brush and started adding strokes—these stupid little daubs right here. Look, he said. Now it's my work. I just multiplied the value of your little painting fifty times. And the worst of it was, it was true. He could draw on a restaurant napkin and the owner would accept it to cover dinner. I'd seen him do it. There was no way I could win."

"And it's a good picture too."

"You mean that? You like it?"

"Yes."

"It'd be better without all those marks. And those things too." He waved the gun at a cluster of buildings which I now saw had been painted over something else. He stood back, and we both stared at it for a while. It was a dystopian scene, bleak, but also funny, the swarm of little figures coming out of the cruise ship, sloshing around in the water as they explored the inundated city.

Rob's joint had gone out. He rummaged around in his pockets for a lighter. "FDP knew he'd crossed a line. He sent me another check and when I didn't cash it, he called and kept me on the phone for hours. You're about to have a family, you aren't thinking clearly, that sort of thing. He wore me down. In the end I just wanted to forget about it, so I deposited the check and moved on. And then he died, and some of my drawings were still in his studio, and there was the work he'd been making, the other tourist pictures and—you see the problem? It's all knotted up, too complicated for anyone to understand. And no one has any incentive because even now a painting by FDP is worth ten times one of mine. So it's his picture. Except it's not. It's my picture, with his scrawls on it." He scraped the barrel of the rifle against the surface. I wondered if he was working himself up to something.

"It's all so fucked, Jay," he said. "So fucked." Then he slung it over his shoulder and walked off to busy himself in the kitchen.

I breathed out, wondering what Alice was thinking, as she waited in the house. Maybe she wasn't in the house. Maybe she was outside, listening at the door. I wondered if Marshal had called the police. I half-expected to hear sirens, but there was nothing, birdsong. Rob came back with tequila and limes.

"Let's get wasted," he said, in a sorry attempt at a roistering growl. He sounded exhausted, his throat raw. It was as if he'd forgotten the context, or buried it, and in his mind we were now just two old friends, catching up. We did shots of tequila and bit down on wedges of lime. He said things like "That's the way!" and "Now we're cooking!" and I wondered if his grip on happiness had always been so tenuous and strained. I felt the liquor working its way into my bloodstream and I tried not to think about disinhibition and guns, and I forced myself to stay present, not to count the paint cans or the remaining panes in the skylights, not to focus on the many small things around me that were misaligned.

Rob talked about money. Painting, he said, had given him a life. "It bought my mum a house, you know? She doesn't live in that council flat anymore. And of course my sister sponges off me, and Sophie's school—you have no idea what these New York schools cost. She has to wear a uniform. Dressing like the fucking nineteen-thirties but they're all little bitches, doing drugs and sending nudes to their teachers."

"She's doing that?"

"I don't know. I don't think so. I'm fucking scared, mate. I love her, but I'm an idiot. You know me. I could never hold on to anything and now I think it's all slipping away again. I can only imagine what Alice has said to you. I'm sure she's told you we're broke. The truth is Marshal fucking owns me and I can't even do the work. Why lie? I can't do what he wants. I could probably shit out some pictures, but there's no point. They'd be bad. The world doesn't need any more bad pictures, at least not from me. Then, on top of that, I have to deal with you turning up. And now"—he waved again at *Blue Ruin*—"I fucking have to deal with this."

"What do you want to happen?"

"You could fuck off, like I asked. My life would be simpler if you vanished. And if this fucking picture vanished. Obviously it'd be simplest of all if I vanished. Maybe I should do what you did. Just walk out, go on the road." His shoulders sagged. What he said next came out in a half-whisper, and at first I wasn't sure I was hearing correctly. "Don't take her away from me, Jay."

"Sorry?"

"I admit, I haven't been good to her. I've lied, I've fucked other women, from the very start. I'm an asshole and I don't deserve her, but don't take her away from me."

"You think she's going to leave you, for what? For a guy who lives in his car? I have about three hundred dollars to my name, Rob, and I've had to sweat for every single one."

For a moment I could tell he was thinking, really thinking about what I'd said, about the material differences between his life and mine. I saw him shrug it off. "I should burn it, right? That's what you'd do."

"The painting? Why do you think I would do that?"

"The big gesture. The dramatic fuck-you. Just look at it. When I see that picture, I see my work, but also millions of dollars of some other cunt's money. It's like I'm seeing double."

"You'd be in court for years. You'd spend the rest of your life in court."

"I could just wipe it all off."

"You'd still get in trouble."

"It's my painting."

"Whatever you're doing, Rob, I'm not part of it. Your relationship to that picture is none of my concern. I'm thinking of Alice. She's worried you're going to crash and burn and you'll take her down with you. Her and your daughter."

"She said that? Bullshit, of course. She's got money, family money in Switzerland, or wherever. The Cayman Islands. She's not going to starve. What do you reckon? Maybe I just mess with it a little. How much could I change without anyone noticing?"

"There must be documentation. Insurance photos, gallery records."

"Oh yeah, all that. It was in a big touring show a couple of years ago. That was a particularly low moment for me, seeing it at the Whitney."

"So you can't change anything. You alter it and sooner or later someone will notice."

I could tell he wasn't really listening to me. He was caught up in some scheme, some drama that was developing in his head. He went over to his music and started flipping through records. Finding the one he wanted, he pulled it out of its sleeve. Soon the space was filled with nineties indie rock, one of the Manchester bands he was sentimental about, the soundtrack to his teenage excesses. That's right, I thought, you won't back down. You don't need me to tell you anything. I watched him roll a metal cart of supplies up to the painting and begin rummaging around until he found a bottle of solvent and a rag. He held them up to me and grinned.

"Seriously?"

Laughing, he started collecting tubes of paint, a palette, making preparations for work. I remembered how much I used to like to watch him work.

DURING AN ARGUMENT, Alice once said to me that I mistook unhappiness for love. I pointed out that it was just as true of her. What we both craved was intensity, and ultimately it didn't matter whether the charge was positive or negative, as long as there was energy in the system. Of course that was when we were young, and just being alive felt heroic; when we blazed out into the world and I still believed that everything could be mended.

I watched Rob mix his paints, humming along to his music. He saw me pick up the rifle. He was thinking about stopping me, but I could tell he was also relieved, that by taking the weapon I was removing a temptation, lowering the stakes in a way that he was too proud to do himself. "See you later," he said, cheerily, as if I'd just popped over to the studio for a cup of tea. "See you later," I said, and stepped out into the sunshine.

I walked slowly down to the house. My senses were painfully sharp; the grass had the look of emeralds and there was a metallic taste in my mouth, but I was present—in myself, in the world. I was alive. Alice came running up the path and clung to me as if she were losing consciousness, a weight around my neck. I held out the weapon awkwardly to one side, feeling as if we were playing out the final scene of an old Western, that at any moment someone would shout cut. She whispered in my ear. Thankyou, thankyou.

Nicole had left and Marshal was distraught. He was on the phone to the police, pacing up and down in the living room, but he was having trouble making himself understood. "He's holding it hostage," he said. "Not who, *what*. It's a painting . . ." I told him what Rob was doing, and he went running back up to the barn to try and stop it. I suspected he was already too late.

Alice was hugging me tight because she knew it was time for me to go. I'd heard the stories, told on every construction site, in every restaurant kitchen; twenty people lying under foil blankets on the floor of a freezing cage; facilities with no names where they could lose you for weeks or months. The chain of events set in motion by a simple demand for ID could be catastrophic for me, and I had no wish to get involved in whatever was about to transpire between Marshal, Rob and the authorities. I handed the rifle to Alice, who held it against her chest, like a scepter or a bunch of flowers.

"You could just hide out in the barn," she said. "No one would find you."

"I don't think that's wise."

"As if anything you ever did was wise."

"I'm going to get the car."

"I'll come with you."

"No. I have to do something. I'll find you here afterwards."

She nodded, reluctantly. I could sense her behind me as I walked down to the lake, her watching eyes plucking at my back like fingers tugging at loose threads. I took the path by the waterside, then headed past the barn, up the hill towards the mirror glade. Maybe, I thought, she was right. I was being too hasty. All I had to do was lose myself in the woods. I could stand still, under the trees, camouflaged by a lattice of shadow; moss would grow over me; I would become a green man, part of the land. When I walked out into the glade, I caught sight of my splintered reflection and understood that what I was experiencing was just the stillness between two waves. I had rested; now I would move on. Quickly, I made my ending.

The first fugueur was a man called Albert, who was unable, doctors said, to stop himself from leaving his life in Bordeaux and walking across Europe, as far as Moscow and Constantinople. Albert was an ordinary man of the eighteen-eighties, who worked, when he was at home, for a gas company. He traveled without papers, and in his altered state he was often unable to recall where he came from or even who he was. He was arrested, beaten, thrown into jails and hospitals. Once he was part of a group of prisoners forcibly marched to the Russian border. I had lied to Marshal. There was one thing I'd carried, one object I'd had with me during all my days of fugue, a tiny pen portrait of Albert that I kept in a locket, like a picture of a lover. I knelt down among the pillars and buried him there in the mirror glade. Then I walked back down the hill.

Of course, the engine started first time, as if the car had been waiting for the moment of departure. I pulled open the barn doors and drove out, past the glittering water, the little island in the middle intermittently visible through the trees. A series of last things: the boathouse, the jetty, the green lawn leading up towards the deck. I pulled up at the front of the house, where I'd parked when I first arrived with the groceries.

Alice was standing under the wisteria, cuffing her wrist with her fingers, her weight on one foot, the other leg relaxed. I remembered what it was called, a word that had eluded me before. *Contrapposto,* the pose of classical sculpture.

"I can't come with you," she said.

"I know."

"I'm sorry."

"I'm sorry too. For everything."

Paradise, as Marshal said, is a walled garden, and for a while in that high security parkland, time was rescinded. The past met the present in every leaf and shaft of sunlight, and it seemed to me, at least for a while, that I could return to who I had been twenty years earlier and salvage my love for Alice from the wreckage.

I'd never really thought Alice would sit beside me in the car, which no longer smelled of air freshener and takeout food, but of the barn where it had rested, of wood and dust and settled organic life. We hugged, slightly stiffly, because it seemed too risky to allow feeling into it, and I drove away from her. The silver thread that connected us was stretched to the breaking point. The automatic gate slid open, and it snapped. In the end, after so many days and nights under the trees, it was all over in a few minutes.

The outside world was a series of confrontations: the first billboard, the first stoplight, the first cars full of strangers, a reminder that beyond the fence the crisis was still going on, and there existed a great mass of humanity, masked, unmasked, going about its business or stuck at home, careful or careless, frightened or skeptical or sick. The highway cut a furrow through the landscape and I knew I was falling forward into things that did not form part of my story with Alice. As I drove, the place I had left—the little house with the wisteria over the door, the lake, the endless green canopy of trees—began to seem insubstantial, a vision, a bubble, and the time I had spent there no more than a dream.

ACKNOWLEDGMENTS

The work of many artists has informed this novel, though none of my fictional artists and artworld people are portraits of anyone real. Thanks to everyone who talked to me or gave me somewhere to stay while writing, chiefly Taryn, Jake, Sylvia, David, Ryan and Dana.

Large parts of this book were written at the Fondation Jan Michalski in Montricher, Switzerland, and the Hermitage Artist Retreat in Sarasota County, Florida. My gratitude to both organizations for the gift of silence and time.

Writing a book is a solitary occupation, but publishing it is a team effort. My thanks to my editor Carole Baron and everyone at Knopf for the care and attention they have given to each aspect of *Blue Ruin*. Thanks also to Andrew Wylie, Tracy Bohan and everyone at the Wylie Agency, for being in my corner.

As always, my deepest love and thanks to Katie and the children, all equally, though to be fair Katie's comments were the most useful.

A NOTE ABOUT THE AUTHOR

Hari Kunzru is the author of six previous novels: *Red Pill, White Tears, The Impressionist, Transmission, My Revolutions* and *Gods Without Men*. His work has been translated into twenty-one languages, and his short stories and journalism have appeared in many publications, including *The New York Times, The Guardian* and *The New Yorker*. He is the recipient of fellowships from the Guggenheim Foundation, the New York Public Library and the American Academy in Berlin. He lives in Brooklyn, New York.

A NOTE ON THE TYPE

The text of this book was composed in Apollo, the first type-face originated specifically for film composition. Designed by Adrian Frutiger and issued by the Monotype Corporation of London in 1964, Apollo is not only a versatile typeface suitable for many uses but is also pleasant to read in all its sizes.

Composed by North Market Street Graphics,
Lancaster, Pennsylvania

Printed and bound by Berryville Graphics,
Berryville, Virginia

Designed by Maggie Hinders